DANGEROUS MASQUERADE

"What are we doing, Gabriel?"

He smiled, his dimples winking at her. "I believe it's called kissing."

Summer placed a hand over his mouth. "We shouldn't do it again."

Gabriel caught her wrist and kissed her fingers. "And why not?"

"Because it's not going to work."

"Because you say it?"

"It's because we have to work together," she argued softly.

Summer gave him a long, penetrating look. She wanted so much to be Summer and not Renegade, but found it impossible to distinguish between the two identities.

"I can't afford to get involved with you. We are worlds apart, and there is no way you can fit into mine, or I in yours."

He caressed her cheek. "I can't change who I am anymore than you can change who you are. And I happen to like who you are."

She closed her eyes. "You don't know me."

"Then don't shut me out, Summer. Allow me to get to know you."

He didn't know what he was saying. No one knew Summer Montgomery. Not even her mother and father.

RENEGADE

Rochelle Alers

BET Publications, LLC
http://www.bet.com
http://www.arabesquebooks.com

*To Mildred E. Riley—for a friendship
that has spanned decades and for the wonderful
memories of Cape Cod.*

Thy hands have made and prepared me; give me understanding, that I may learn Thy commandments.

Psalm 119:73

THE HIDEAWAY LEGACY

HIDEAWAY
Martin Cole–Parris Simmons
Regina
Tyler
Arianna

HIDDEN AGENDA
Alejandro Delgado–Eve Blackwell–Matthew Sterling
Christopher Delgado
Sara Sterling

VOWS
Joshua Kirkland–Vanessa Blanchard
Emily
Michael

HEAVEN SENT
David Cole–Serena Morris
Gabriel
Alexandra
Ana and Jason

HARVEST MOON
Oscar Spencer–Regina Cole–Aaron Spencer
Clayborne
Eden

JUST BEFORE DAWN
Salem Lassiter–Sara Sterling
Isaiah
Eve and Nona

PRIVATE PASSIONS
Christopher Delgado–Emily Kirkland
Alejandro II
Esperanza
Mateo

NO COMPROMISE
Michael Kirkland–Jolene Walker
Teresa
Joshua

HOMECOMING
Tyler Cole–Dana Nichols
Martin II
Astra

RENEGADE
Gabriel Cole–Summer Montgomery
Emmanuel

Prologue

Summer Montgomery—alias Denise Hartley—willed herself to remain calm despite the shiver snaking its way up her spine.

The all-too-familiar banked sensation reminded her that thirteen months of undercover work would end in less than sixty seconds.

The tingling was a silent alarm, signaling anticipation for what would come through the doors at the airplane hangar at a private airstrip in Houston, Texas.

She was ready—as ready as she would ever be; she'd been undercover for so many years that there were times when she'd found it difficult to distinguish her aliases from her true identity.

A slight smile parted her curvy lips as she glanced casually at the man who had boasted, with her assistance, that he had become the financial genius for the largest drug cartel in the U.S. southwest. The arrogant man returned her smile, unaware that the sweep second hand on the timepiece strapped to his left wrist counted down the final seconds of his life as a prominent businessman.

"Denise, are you certain you don't want to come with me?" Richard Robertson asked. He'd raised his normally soft voice to be heard over the roar of planes taking off and landing. His private jet was fueling in readiness for a flight to the Amazon jungle where he'd planned a two-month sojourn at his Brazilian plantation.

Summer placed her hands, palms down, on the top of a table. Her eyelids lowered slightly, concealing a pair of large, deep-set, dark-brown eyes.

"I'm quite certain, Richard. I told you before I'm *business*, and what you're proposing is *personal*."

A sensual smile softened his strong features. At forty-three years of age, the Texas bank president was in his prime and totally unaware that if convicted he would spend the rest of his life in a federal prison for laundering money for drug traffickers.

He stared at the woman who had been responsible for helping him expand his network from Texas and New Mexico to Nevada, Arizona and into portions of Southern California. She was smart and stunningly beautiful—attributes he hadn't encountered in any woman in all of his business ventures. Most were merely window-dressing, but not so with Denise. She had come to him highly recommended. What had surprised him when he'd had her checked out by a reliable source was the fact that she did not exist. There was no record of a birth certificate, driver's license, or fingerprints. He took this as a sign that Denise Hartley had the protection of someone who had made her virtually invisible.

Richard's navy-blue gaze lingered on her shoulder-length, dark-brown hair secured in a loose ponytail before moving lower to the delicate curve of a pair of high cheekbones. At five-foot eight inches with a slender, tight body Denise looked more like an aerobics instructor than a drug trafficker. He knew she jogged every morning despite the weather, and lifted weights. He'd witnessed her physical prowess when she'd rendered a man unconscious with a single kick to the side of his head moments after he'd made a grievous error in judgment by groping her breasts. The memory of her well-aimed foot had been etched in his brain once he recalled her declaration that there was never a need for her to carry a firearm, because she was a weapon—a dangerous, lethal weapon.

"What can I offer you to change your mind?"

Summer's expression changed, becoming impassive. "Nothing."

Reaching across the space, Richard covered one of her hands with his, the contrast of his pale hand on her brown fingers startling. "Can I at least bring something back for you?"

Summer smiled again. The gesture was erotic enough to cause Richard's breath to catch in his throat. Pausing for several seconds, she finally said, "An emerald."

"Bracelet, earrings or ring?"

Biting down on her lower lip, she fluttered her lashes. "Surprise me."

The two words were barely off her tongue when the doors to the hangar opened and an authoritative male voice shouted, "Don't move! DEA!"

Summer's head jerked around simultaneously with Richard's. She came to her feet in a motion too quick for the eye to follow as two other men lounging in the hangar reached under their jackets for concealed weapons. A dozen agents rushed in, badges dangling from chains around their necks, each wearing blue jackets bearing the white letters of DEA on the back while brandishing semi-automatic weapons.

"Don't be stupid, gentlemen," the man with the deep voice warned.

Summer chanced a quick glance at Richard who

looked as if he couldn't believe what was happening. The blood had drained from his face, leaving it as pale as candlewax. His expression clearly read: *Don't you know who I am?*

The senior agent in charge of the raid moved closer, his eyes narrowing. A feral grin curled his thin lips. "What do we have here?" he asked, his gaze fixed on Summer. His men handcuffed Richard Robertson and his bodyguards. Drawing back his arm he slapped Summer, splitting her lip, bloodying her nose and snapping her head back.

"I knew I would catch up with you one of these days," he snarled between clenched teeth.

He attempted to hit her again, but Summer blocked the next punch when her left arm came up. He was standing, then seconds later found himself sprawled on his back after she'd kicked him behind his knees. The right toe of her black leather boot made contact with his eye before blinding pain radiated behind her head, causing the concrete floor to come up to meet her.

There were the sounds of exploding bullets, followed by the empty casings hitting the floor next to her shoulder and the acrid smell of cordite. Darkness descended slowly and mercifully, swallowing Summer Montgomery whole.

Summer woke up hours later, not knowing where she was or the time of day. She knew she'd been heavily sedated, but the painkiller was not enough to erase the dull throbbing at the base of her skull. A face and the whisper of moist breath swept over her, and it was a full minute before she recognized him.

Closing her eyes, she inhaled sharply. "One of these

days I'm going to hurt you real bad, Lucas." The words were squeezed out between clenched teeth.

"You did when you kicked me in the head."

"That's because you hit me in the face." Her words were slurring together.

"I had to make it look good, Renegade."

She opened her eyes and glared at her boss. His left eye, a hideous shade of deep purple, was nearly swollen shut. Steri-strips covered half a dozen sutures over the eyebrow. "And you did."

Lucas Shelby stared at the swollen flesh masking what should've been a delicate jaw. He knew he'd hit Summer hard, but not hard enough to break her jaw. There were abrasions on her chin and forehead from her fall.

"You must have made quite an impression with Robertson, because when we told him you'd been killed resisting arrest he just about lost it."

Turning her head slowly, Summer averted Lucas's intense stare. She would never tell him that Richard Robertson had confessed to being in love with her. She'd done nothing to encourage his attention, but her indifference still did not discourage the married banker from attempting to come on to her.

"Where do I go next?"

Lucas shook his head, unable to believe the battered and bruised woman in the hospital bed. It would be weeks, perhaps even more than a month, before she would be medically cleared to return to duty. However, each time she accepted another undercover assignment it was as if she was playing a game wherein she challenged death.

"The Director says it's time for us to work the east coast."

"Us?" she asked, not looking at him.

Lucas smiled, attractive lines fanning out around his blue-green eyes. "We're being transferred to the Boston area. There's evidence of high volume drug sales at one of the suburban high schools. This time you'll go in as a teacher." He patted her shoulder. "Feel better. I'll be back tomorrow to fill you in."

Summer lay motionless, staring up at the ceiling. In three months she would celebrate her thirty-third birthday, and she'd spent the past five of those thirty-two years as an undercover DEA agent.

As Summer Montgomery—code name: Renegade—she'd become an integral component with a team of highly trained agents responsible for the interdiction of drug trafficking. And since becoming an agent with the Drug Enforcement Administration, she had gone undercover for two years as a member of a California youth gang with ties to other gangs in Washington and Oregon, gathering evidence of their drug dealing. Her youthful-looking appearance had also served her well once she'd enrolled as a high school student in Denver, Colorado.

Infiltrating Richard Robertson's network had become a welcome respite from interacting with adolescents, but that was going to change again with her next assignment.

She shifted her head, grimacing as pain radiated down her neck. Lucas had to hit her to make her capture look convincing, but whoever had hit her from behind had nearly fractured her skull. Closing her eyes, she made a solemn vow that no one on her team would ever catch her off guard again.

One

A slight frown furrowed Summer Montgomery's forehead as she made her way across the parking lot at Weir Memorial High School. She wasn't upset by the escalating shrieks of students greeting one another after a summer recess. What did annoy her was the crowd of media personnel positioned behind wooden barricades on the sidewalk across the street from the school. Video cameras on tripods were focused to capture the images of everyone entering or leaving the building. The press had been warned by the mayor and school officials not to trespass on school property nor to interfere with students returning for the first day of classes.

The media and police presence at Weir was because of Gabriel Cole. Having the multi award-winning musician join her and another artist-in-residence as faculty did not upset Summer, but who the musician was was certain to become a source of frustration. She'd come to Weir, a school along Boston's south shore community, to expose a drug ring, but Gabriel's tenure was certain to thrust the high school into the media spotlight, and thereby possibly jeopardizing her true identity.

It was to become the first time in her career with the U.S. Drug Enforcement Administration that she would use her real name in an undercover operation. And be-

cause she'd earned an undergraduate degree in fine
arts with a concentration in theater she did not have
to rehearse for her latest role. She was now Weir's new
drama teacher.

"Good morning, Miss Montgomery. Welcome to
Weir Memorial's first day of classes."

Her frown faded as she returned the inviting smile
of the dark-skinned, shaved head man who had chaired
the faculty orientation the week before. "Good morning, Mr. Gellis."

His eyes sparkled like polished onyx. "You may call
me Dumas when we're not around students."

Summer gave him a sidelong glance as he reached
over her head and opened the door to the faculty entrance. The distinctive odor of cigarette smoke clung
to his skin and clothes. "Wasn't it you who insisted
all teachers call one another by their surnames?"

"There are exceptions, *Summer.*"

"And those are?"

He winked at her. "When there are no students present."

She nodded. "Okay, Dumas." Summer did not want
to believe he was flirting with her when his only concern should have been identifying the person or
persons responsible for dealing drugs at his school.
Two students had died of an overdose over the past two
years, and another was comatose and on life support
after ingesting more than a dozen Vicodin pills. Rumors were that the students had purchased the drugs
from someone in the school, although no one would
come forward to name the dealer.

She had been briefed at the field office on everyone

who worked or taught at Weir, and Summer knew forty-six-year-old assistant principal Dumas Gellis had played semi-pro football, was the divorced father of two adolescent sons, and had joined the faculty eight years ago. He had taught chemistry and physics for six years until he was promoted to assistant principal.

"I'll see you around," she said in parting as she made her way down the highly polished tiled hallway to the office she was to share with two other instructors.

Dumas Gellis stared at Summer's retreating figure, admiring her lithe body in a slim skirt, mock turtleneck sweater and waist-length leather jacket. A pair of sheer stockings and low-heeled suede pumps completed her all-black attire.

Gabriel Cole strolled across the parking lot dressed in the school uniform: navy blue blazer with the school's emblem on the breast pocket, a pair of charcoal gray slacks, white button-down shirt and a maroon and white striped tie. A pair of sunglasses covered his eyes and his long hair was concealed under a Boston Red Sox baseball cap. Dressed as he was made it difficult for anyone to distinguish him from the returning male students.

The principal had called Gabriel the day before to inform him that the media had planned to camp out at the school to await his arrival. And it wasn't the first time the ultraconservative school administrator had expressed her concern that his presence at Weir would disrupt the school's well ordered day-to-day existence. Gabriel had reassured her that his commitment to participate in a federally sponsored cultural arts grants program would in no way compromise Weir's academic excellence.

Adjusting the calfskin backpack slung over his left shoulder, he pushed open the door leading to the faculty entrance, sighing in relief when the door closed behind him. A smile deepened the dimples in his sun-tanned cheeks.

He had made it into the school undetected!

His shoes made soft swishing sounds on the highly polished tile floor as he walked to the office he had been assigned to, along with two other instructors hired under the grant. Opening the door, he walked in. His eyes widened behind the lenses of his sunglasses as he stared at the woman standing with her back to the window.

His gaze moved slowly over the outline of the curvy feminine figure clad in black. There was something about Summer Montgomery that intrigued him. What it was he hadn't been able to discern. They hadn't exchanged more than ten words since being formally introduced.

He'd thought her stunningly beautiful despite her youthful-looking appearance. At first glance she appeared no older than a high school coed, but after reading the booklet distributed at the orientation describing the curriculum vitae of the faculty he discovered she had graduated college more than a decade before. Additional information listed she had appeared as a lead in a popular Broadway musical production, earning her a best actress Tony nomination.

The orientation sessions were relaxed with everyone dressed in T-shirts, tank tops, shorts, jeans, sandals and running shoes. Summer Montgomery had arrived on the first day sporting a navy blue T-shirt, body-hugging jeans, and a pair of running shoes. The casual attire, fringe of bangs framing her forehead and her long dark hair swept up in a ponytail had caused most heads to turn in her direction. Her presence had male teachers smiling, and female teachers' tongues wagging. Amused and completely stunned, Gabriel had stared mutely.

Now, Summer crossed her arms under her breasts. "If you talk to *them,* Mr. Cole, they will go away."

His curving eyebrows met in a frown. "I have no intention of talking to *them,* and they *will* go away, Miss Montgomery."

She shook her head. "You're wrong, Mr. Cole."

Gabriel lifted an eyebrow. "And you're entitled to your opinion."

In that instant Summer wanted to rap her knuckles against his forehead. She didn't know whether it was arrogance or naïveté that had Gabriel believing the reporters and photographers would disappear because he willed it.

She gave him a lingering look that said: *You and I are not going to get along.* The silent warning whispered to her and her frustration escalated.

She, Gabriel, and artist Desiree Leighton had met for the first time five days earlier at a new teacher orientation. She and Desiree, fifty-eight and a self-proclaimed hippie from the 60s, had bonded instantly, but not so with Gabriel. He had sat off by himself while the principal presented an overview of Weir's history. Even after teachers met with the heads of their respective departments, Gabriel still did not interact with anyone. At the end of the three-day session Summer had two words for him: arrogant and aloof.

What she refused to acknowledge was that he was gorgeous. She had successfully suppressed a gasp when she'd come face-to-face with him for the first time. Film footage and photographs had failed to capture the power in his tall muscular body whenever he moved, or the air of authority that demanded one's complete attention once he walked into a room.

A background check revealed he had been born Gabriel Morris Cole. A native Floridian born into what was reported to be the wealthiest black family in the United States and never married, he had celebrated his thirty-fourth birthday in March, stood six-three in bare feet, weighed around one-eighty and had earned a master's degree in music education. And despite his celebrity status, he had remained a very private person. His file also contained several entries of long-term romantic liaisons with women in film and music. Other than that, he had lived a scandal-free life.

Summer had spent more than a month going over the background reports of everyone at Weir High— faculty and staff—and had come up with nothing that hinted of a suspicion of illegal drug use and/or sales. Several had been arrested for minor traffic infractions, the head custodian had had a portion of his wages garnisheed for non-payment of child support, and one teacher had filed for bankruptcy.

She stared at Gabriel as he took off his sunglasses and baseball cap. Long, gray-streaked wavy black hair flowed over his shoulders and down his back before he secured it in a ponytail with an elastic band.

Her dark brown eyes locked with a pair the color of sun-fired gold. Without warning he smiled, flashing a pair of deep dimples in both cheeks. There was something in the crooked smile under a neatly barbered mustache that was so endearing that Summer held her breath for several seconds before she returned his smile with a sensual one of her own. The unconscious gesture seemed to melt the tension between them.

Attractive lines fanned out around Gabriel's large

penetrating eyes as his smile widened. "Have you come up with any ideas for the spring music festival?"

Moving away from the window, Summer sat down at one of the three desks she had claimed for herself, unaware that Gabriel's gaze measured her approach under lowered lids. Opening a drawer, she reached for her shoulder bag and withdrew a small spiral notebook.

"As a matter of fact, I have. I spent the weekend exploring a few possibilities."

Gabriel sat down at a desk facing Summer's, leaving Desiree to claim the remaining desk in a corner whenever she arrived. Resting his elbows on the scarred top, he gave her a direct stare. "You spent your Labor Day weekend working?" The query held a hint of disbelief.

Her head came up and she glared at him. "Yes, I did. You make it sound as if I'd committed a serious crime."

"It's not a crime to work holidays, Summer," he countered, his deep soft voice layered with a thick southern drawl, "but if I'd known you intended to start on the project, then I would've asked if I could work with you."

She blinked once. "That could have become a possibility if you hadn't acted like a stuck-up snob."

His eyes widened until she could see their dark-brown centers. "Me? A snob!"

"Yes, *you.*"

"I . . . I'm not a snob," he sputtered as blood darkened his olive skin under a rich summer tan.

"You can believe whatever you choose to believe, Gabriel. You're probably so used to people, women in particular, fawning over you because of your celebrity status that you hold back a little of yourself."

"That may be true at times, but not here."

Summer shrugged a shoulder. She did not intend to argue with him. He was aloof and a snob. Picking up the notebook, she handed it to him. "Take a look at what I've come up with."

Gabriel took the book, his fingers grazing Summer's long manicured fingers. The forefinger of his left hand caressed the hair on his upper lip in an up-and-down stroking motion. He had spent the last six months growing a beard, but had shaved it off before coming to Weir. He had become so used to facial hair that he decided to leave the mustache.

His gaze lingered on her neat slanting writing; his only visible reaction was a slight lifting of his expressive eyebrows. It appeared that not only was Summer talented and beautiful, but also quite intelligent. A most winning combination when the appeal of some of the women he had become involved with was that of eye-candy. Their only asset was that they were superficially pretty. Some he dated because that was what his publicist recommended. He'd agreed to escort them to opening night premieres, Hollywood parties, championship sporting events, but he had never slept with any of them.

"I like the titles. *A Musical History of the Americas in Song and Dance. A Journey through the Americas in Song and Dance. An American Experience in Song and Dance.*"

A flicker of excitement lit up Summer's eyes. "I personally like *An Odyssey of Music and Dance in the Americas.* I believe a production covering everything from Native American and slave chants to Negro spirituals, Irish step dancing, the waltz, Bluegrass, Jazz, Ragtime, Country, Zydeco, Blues, Big Band, R&B, Rock and Roll, Folk, Soul, Latin and up to and including Rap and Hip-Hop will offer a little something to everyone: faculty, staff, students, and their families. It will cross cultures and generations."

Gabriel stroked his mustache. "It sounds like a monumental undertaking."

Summer stared at his handsome face. "You got game, Gabriel?"

Grinning, his straight white teeth showing under the mustache, he said softly, accepting her challenge, "I got lots of game, Summer. How about you?"

"More than you'll ever know," she crooned.

Leaning back in his chair, he angled his head. "I suppose that settles it. You're the lead teacher for the spring production, and I'll take the Christmas holiday program. It looks as if Desiree is going to have her work cut out for her with all of the stage decorations."

Resting her elbows on her desk, Summer leaned forward. "I'm certain she will be up to the challenge." Desiree had lived on three continents, married and divorced Kenyan and Japanese artists, had owned an art gallery in Los Angeles, and had spent several years in Hollywood as a set designer.

He nodded. "Why don't we get together this weekend and begin planning what we're going to need to put on a first-rate production?"

"I can't. Not this weekend." This weekend she was to meet with Lucas Shelby for her bi-monthly briefing session.

"When?"

"Next weekend."

"My place or yours?" Gabriel asked.

She had rented a furnished condominium apartment in Whitman, a bedroom community south of Boston with a population of thirteen thousand residents. Although there was nothing in her apartment that would link her to her undercover role, she had made it a habit not to invite strangers to her temporary residences. The place she called home was in St. Louis, Missouri. In between assignments she returned there to stay with her maternal grandmother. She saw her parents on average once a year. Both doctors with the World Health Organization, Robert and Mildred Montgomery had lived more than two-thirds of their lives practicing medicine in foreign countries.

"Yours." Summer thought she saw a satisfied light fire Gabriel's golden gaze. "Where do you live?"

"Cotuit."

"On Cape Cod?"

He nodded. "I bought a little place there last year."

The fact that Gabriel had purchased property on the Cape was not in his report. She suspected this information had been excluded because he had been exempt from the DEA's investigation.

"You drive here from the Cape everyday?"

"It's only about sixty miles each way. And now that the tourists are gone I usually don't encounter too many traffic delays."

Summer knew she had stepped into a trap of her own making. She had just committed to driving more than an hour to meet with Gabriel for their first planning session.

She gave him a lingering look. "Okay. I'll meet you at your place."

"May I make a suggestion?"

"Sure," she said.

"Why don't I pick you up at your place next Friday morning, drive you to school, then we can ride down together at the end of the day. It will save time and gas if we use one car."

The shock of his suggestion caused the words to wedge in her throat. "I need to understand something. You're not going to drive me down to Cotuit just to turn around and bring me back later that night."

Gabriel stared at Summer, his expression one of faint amusement. He liked driving, but not enough to clock two hundred fifty miles in a single day. "Of course not. I expect you to spend the weekend."

Her delicate jaw dropped. "The weekend?"

"I'm sure there's no echo is this room," he said glibly. "Yes, Summer, the weekend. If you want something as lavish as a musical production spanning several centuries, then it's going to take weeks of planning. We have to select the music, identify the appropriate instruments, and decide on vocal arrangements. Then you're going to have to work with Desiree on the set designs. And I don't have to remind you of auditioning students for the various parts, and then the endless rehearsals. If on the other hand, you feel uncomfortable staying with me, then I can always spend the weekend with you."

"You can't spend the weekend with me."

"Why? Your boyfriend would object?"

"I don't have a boyfriend," she retorted quickly. "My place is too small. I have a one bedroom apartment."

He flashed his winning crooked smile. "I can always sleep on the couch."

"I don't have a couch. I have two love seats. And I won't be held responsible if you wake up with a misaligned spine."

"You could always give up your bed."

She gave a delicate snort. "I'd only give up my bed to a sick man."

Gabriel affected a deep cough that rattled in his throat and chest.

"Stop," she said, laughing. "Okay you win this time. I'll spend next weekend with you."

Gabriel wanted to tell Summer that he would win the next time and the time after that. After all, he was a Cole. And Coles were used to winning. He had won three Grammy awards and an Oscar before he had celebrated his thirtieth birthday.

The seven-twenty bell rang signaling the start of the first class of the day. The door opened and Desiree Leighton rushed into the office, cheeks flushed with excitement. The high color brought out the vividness of her bright blue eyes.

"I can't believe I'm late. I'm never late for anything."

Gabriel stood up, gathering his backpack. "Excuse me, ladies, but I have a class."

Desiree smiled at him, locked her handbag in the desk in the corner before she rushed out behind Gabriel's departing figure. "I'll see you later, Summer," she said over her shoulder, closing the door behind her.

Summer's first class did not begin until eight-thirty. Gabriel had been assigned to the music department, Desiree to art, and she drama. Weir had applied for and had been awarded a grant of two hundred-fifty thousand dollars to develop a cultural arts program at the high school. The grant's mission was geared toward reducing truancy, increasing student awareness of the arts, while offering two full college scholarships to qualified students for a degree in music education or fine arts.

Pulling her lower lip between her teeth, Summer replayed Gabriel's offer that she spend a weekend at his house. She was amenable to developing a musical production with him, but if he thought she was going to provide him with any other type of entertainment, then she would make him regret he'd ever taken his first breath.

Two

Summer sat across a table in a twenty-four-hour diner, watching Lucas Shelby sprinkle pepper over his eggs. Tendrils clung to her damp forehead from her three-mile jog. It was only the second week in September and cooler early morning temperatures hinted that summer was quickly coming to an end.

"Aren't you going to order something to eat?" Lucas asked before he shoveled a forkful of eggs into his mouth.

She shook her head. "I'll eat later." She usually waited an hour after jogging before eating. Once she returned to her apartment she would prepare a small cup of fresh seasonal fruit, a slice of buttered raisin toast, and a cup of decaffeinated coffee.

Waiting until Lucas had taken a swallow of coffee, she said, "What do you have for me?"

Lowering his mug, he stared at the bare face of the woman he had supervised for the past three years. Her deep gold-brown complexion was flawless, her large soulful-looking eyes entrancing.

"Nothing. How about you?"

She lifted her shoulders under the jacket of her jogging suit while shaking her head. "Nothing. It's only been three days, but all of the kids at Weir appear to be normal students doing whatever it is high school kids do. School policy is that they aren't permitted to linger in the parking lot before or after classes, thereby eliminating the risk of dealing on school property. The bathrooms are monitored every quarter of an hour, and there are random locker checks."

"What about teachers?"

"Again, I'm drawing a blank. Most drive late model cars that fall within the moderate price range. The only exception is a Porsche GT2 belonging to Gabriel Cole."

Lucas whistled softly. "That puppy fully loaded will set you back a little under two hundred thousand."

Her forehead furrowed. "How do you know the sticker price?"

"I took one for a test drive a couple of months ago. It hugged the road like a starving baby latching onto his mama's tit." He noted her scowl. "I'm sorry, Summer."

She had decided to ignore his sexist reference, because within her first two years with the Department she had filed so many grievances for sexual harassment against her male counterparts that none of them wanted her on their team. Physically she could hold her own with any man, but the isolation had taken its toll on her emotionally after she was transferred from field to desk duty. She had joined the DEA to fight the war on drugs, not become a glorified desk clerk.

"Apology accepted."

Even though Lucas, a confirmed bachelor, was only in his late fifties, she had begun to think of her field supervisor as a dinosaur. His reflexes and reaction time had slowed, and she knew he was internalizing a great deal of resentment because as one of the first employees of the Department he felt he should've headed one of the regional divisions.

"Right now I'm subbing for an English instructor. She sprained her wrist after falling down a flight of stairs in her home. I've assigned her students the short stories of Edgar Allan Poe."

He smiled, wiggling his bushy eyebrows. "He's one of my favorite authors."

"I'm putting together a schedule for student auditions for a spring concert. This will give me a chance to interact with some of them one-on-one."

"I know I don't have to tell you to keep your eyes open."

She nodded. "I want you to know that I'm not going to be around next weekend."

He sat up straighter, his blue-green gaze suddenly alert. "Where are you going?"

"Down to the Cape. Gabriel Cole and I will be working together planning the spring concert."

Lucas's expression was impassive. "Try not to get caught up with his superstar status, Renegade."

Summer went completely still. "You forget who I am and why I work for you."

"I'll say it again. Stay focused."

She offered him a false smile. "If we're finished, then I'd like to get back home and showered." She stood up. "I'll meet you here in two weeks."

She walked out of the diner, swallowing back the curses she wanted to hurl at Lucas. Despite her many successes, he still viewed her as a woman rather than an agent. Even though it was against department policy to become physically and emotionally involved with a target, she knew her superiors would look the other way if it resulted in a successful mission.

Even though Gabriel Cole wasn't a target, she consciously did not plan to become involved with him other than on a professional level.

The truth was she hadn't had a serious liaison with a man in years. The last one had been an attorney she'd met after she had returned to St. Louis for an extended vacation. He wanted marriage, a house in the country, two children, a dog and a cat, while she wanted to continue her personal war against those who had taken the life of her younger brother. Charles Montgomery had died at the hands of drug dealers feuding over turf while he stood on a corner waiting to cross the street on his way from school.

The single encounter seemed to age her parents within seconds. Grief-stricken and disillusioned with American justice when the police failed to identify their son's murderer, retired Peace Corps Drs. Robert and Mildred Montgomery applied to the World Health Organization for an overseas assignment.

Summer's rosy world also came crashing down when she abruptly left a Broadway production for which she had earned a Tony nomination to return to St. Louis. She took the test for the St. Louis Police Department and was hired within months of the list being posted because the SLPD were actively recruiting to add female officers to their rolls. Three years later she was accepted by the DEA as a basic agent trainee. She had come to them with prior law enforcement and a graduate degree in Criminal Justice.

She had distinguished herself in the sixteen-week resident training program at Quantico, Virginia, excelling in the rigorous one hundred hour physical fitness and defensive tactics regimen at the facility shared by the DEA and FBI for firearms and tactical vehicle training.

Any reference to her law enforcement experience was

withheld from the Weir faculty booklet, replaced by information fabricated by the DEA's Boston Division.

A watery sun had broken through the clouds by the time Summer jogged up the steps to the building where she lived. All she wanted to do was shower, wash her hair, and then go back to bed and sleep until hunger forced her to get up again.

She knew she was tired—deep down bone tired of the undercover assignments, aliases, the risk that her cover would be blown, and her fascination with her own violent death. If she was lucky, a bullet in the head would assure a quick dispatch, but there were times when she had nightmares that she would be tortured like several other agents she had known.

Ten minutes later, she stood under the stream of running water; she closed her eyes and turned her face upward. For the first time in her life, she longed for a husband, the house in the country, children, dog and cat. She wanted to be a PTA mom and bake cookies for the holidays.

Summer showered quickly, wrapping one towel around her body and another around her head; she walked out of the bathroom and into her bedroom, falling across her unmade bed while vowing this would be her last assignment. After she identified the drug dealer or dealers at Weir she planned to hand in her badge and firearm and walk away from a lifestyle that once had been as vital to her as breathing.

Summer glanced at her watch as she stood on the sidewalk outside her apartment building. Gabriel had promised to pick her up at six forty-five, and it was now seven. A heavy fog had blanketed the area, closing Logan Airport and reducing vehicular traffic to a thirty-five mile an hour speed limit.

She peered down the street, squinting through the haze as a low-slung silver sports car eased up along the curb. The driver-side door opened and Gabriel alighted, popping the button on an umbrella.

Smiling, he held the umbrella over her bare head. "Sorry I'm late. Good morning."

There was something so infectious about his smile that she couldn't help but return it with a friendly one of her own. "Now, that's debatable," she teased.

"You're right about that. The fog is so thick along the shore that it looks like pea soup." Gabriel moved closer, inhaling the sensual scent of a perfume surrounding Summer. Not only did she look good, but she also smelled good. Today she had pulled her hair tightly off her face and into a chignon on her long neck. "Don't you own an umbrella?"

She stared up at him, her gaze widening when she noticed two small gold hoops in each of his pierced lobes. It was the first time she had seen him wear the earrings. A black turtleneck sweater, wool crepe slacks and a pair of slip-ons flattered his tall, slender physique. "I own one, but it wouldn't help in this weather. My hair frizzes up with the slightest hint of humidity. If I hadn't put gel in it this morning it would be standing up all over my head like Don King."

Taking Summer's overnight bag from her loose grip, Gabriel held the umbrella and bag in one hand as he leaned down and opened the passenger-side door for her. The hem of her raincoat parted and her skirt inched up her thighs as she sat down, revealing an expanse of long legs in a pair of sheer black hose.

Clenching his teeth, he slammed the door harder than he had intended. There was something about Summer Montgomery that got under his skin. It was an itch he could not get to and scratch. As far as women went he did not have a *type*. He had dated tall ones, short ones, light and dark ones, but none of them had him measuring his every word like Summer. She had a beautiful face, perfect body, and a very quick tongue.

He had chided himself for inviting her to spend the weekend with him once he had rethought his offer. They could've easily met at a local Starbucks or public library. However, whatever it was about Summer that annoyed him he prayed he would identify it by the time he drove her back home Sunday.

Pressing a button on a remote device, the trunk opened silently. Gabriel placed her bag in the trunk, closed it, and then walked around the Porsche and slipped in behind the wheel. He put the key in the ignition and the engine turned over in a soft purr as automatic seat belts came down over his chest and that of Summer's. Glancing at the side mirror, he pulled away from the curb.

It was two weeks into the school year, and he had barely caught a glimpse of Summer or Desiree even though they shared the same office. He had left a note for Summer requesting her address, and she had complied, leaving a note in a sealed envelope in his mailbox in the school's general office.

"How has it been going?" he asked her.

Turning her head, she stared at his distinctive profile. "More hectic than I thought it would be. I hadn't planned on substituting for another teacher."

Gabriel gave her a quick glance. "That's not a condition of the grant."

"I know, but I only volunteered for two weeks. Today is my last day."

"If that's the case, then we won't push too hard this weekend."

A shadow of annoyance crossed her face. "I'm not going to spend the weekend with you just hanging out, Gabriel."

It was his turn to frown. "I didn't ask you to come to hang out. We'll work, but when you get tired we'll stop. The spring concert is more than six months away, and if you don't pace yourself you'll never make it to May."

She knew he was right. It had been years since she had been in a theater production wherein rehearsals began at dawn and sometime ended more than sixteen hours later. She'd return home completely exhausted with bloodshot eyes, aching feet and a sore throat.

"I want it to be good, Gabriel."

"It's going to be beyond good," he said confidently. "It will be spectacular."

I hope you're right, she mused. In that instant Summer realized she had two agendas: to take down the drug dealers and put on a successful musical production.

Her grandmother said she'd burst forth from her mother's womb singing rather than crying like most babies. It had been her Gram who had taken her to dancing school, and it was Gram who had encouraged her to pursue a career in the theater. Her parents' passions were medicine and their son.

Closing her eyes, she pressed her head against the leather headrest, remembering how it felt to be on stage in front of a live audience. The excitement of opening night, the constant flutters in her stomach until the curtain came up and she said her opening line or sang her first note.

She missed the heat of the spotlights, the gaudy costumes, and the smell of greasepaint. She missed collecting playbills and the articles written by critics either praising or panning a production. She had missed so much, but most of all she missed her brother.

"Summer. Are you all right?" Gabriel had maneuvered into his assigned space in the faculty parking lot.

She opened her eyes, unaware of a single tear that had made its way down her cheek. Brushing away the moisture with her fingertips, she nodded, smiling.

"I'm fine," she said, knowing it was a lie.

Leaning closer to his right, Gabriel pressed his mouth to her damp hair. "You're not a very good liar, Summer Montgomery."

"I know." And she wasn't. Not when it involved her private life.

His right hand curved around her neck. "Do you want to talk about it?"

She shook her head and stared out of the side window. "No. I can't," she added after a pregnant silence.

Gabriel noticed a look of tired sadness pass over her delicate features, the emotion pulling her lush mouth downward. "If you ever want to talk about it or just have a good cry I'll lend you my shoulder."

Pulling back her shoulders, Summer took a deep breath. Within seconds she'd regained control of her emotions. Renegade was back.

"Thank you, Gabriel."

"Don't move. I'll get the door for you."

She sat, waiting for him, and when he opened the door for her he was wearing a long, black lightweight raincoat and holding the umbrella. He extended his free hand. She placed her hand trustingly in his, permitting him to pull her to her feet.

Holding the umbrella over their heads, Gabriel led Summer across the parking lot to the faculty entrance. Less than ten feet from the door a flash of light blinded them.

Before Gabriel could blink Summer had seized a camera from a man, ripping out the roll of film. The camera ended up on the wet asphalt.

She struggled to control her temper. "Try that again, and I'll make certain you are arrested for trespassing on school property."

Stunned, the photographer stared at his damaged equipment. Hands rolled into tight fists, he took a step toward her at the same time Gabriel grabbed the hood on the man's jacket, savagely jerking him backward.

"If you touch her, even breathe on her, I *will hurt you.*" He had enunciated each word slowly and precisely so that the photographer would not misconstrue his intent.

The man's face lost all of its natural color. Gabriel Cole towered over him by a full head. "If . . . if you hit me I'll sue you."

Gabriel shook him like a rottweiler would an annoying Chihuahua, while searching through his pockets for some form of identification. He found the man's press badge in his jacket.

"Not if I don't sue you first, Mr. Stockwell. I don't think I have to remind you that I have the resources to hire the best law firm in the country. I'll ruin you *and* that rag you sniff around for."

"You can't threaten me." His bravado had returned.

Gabriel curbed an urge to slap the annoying man. "I

just did." He shoved the I.D. back in his pocket. "Get the hell out of here before I call school security."

"Is there a problem, Gabriel?"

Summer and Gabriel turned when they recognized the assistant principal's voice. "Yes," she said. "This man tried to take Mr. Cole's photograph without his permission."

Dumas Gellis removed a small walkie-talkie from his jacket pocket, calling for school security. A minute later, two men appeared and escorted the hapless photographer into the school building for questioning.

"Are you all right, Summer?" Dumas asked, staring intently at her.

She smiled. "I'm fine." She gave him the roll of overexposed film. "You can give this back to him."

Dumas took the film, then bent down to pick up the camera. "I'm sorry, Gabriel. I thought after two weeks the media would forget about you."

"There's no need to apologize. There are some things that are beyond our control."

"*This* I can control. It will not happen again."

Gabriel nodded. "Thanks." Curving an arm around Summer's waist, he led her into the building. He did not drop his arm as they walked the length of the hallway to their office, closing the door behind them.

Turning to face Gabriel, Summer stared up at him. "You shouldn't have threatened him with physical harm."

"What did you expect me to do? Let him hit you?"

She shook her head. "He wouldn't have hit me."

"And why not?"

"Because he wouldn't." She wanted to tell Gabriel that she had been trained to take a three hundred pound man off his feet in less than three seconds. Take him down and render him unconscious.

"You're what—five-six and weigh about a buck twenty?"

"Five-eight and a buck thirty."

"Big deal," he spat out. "So, I'm off by two inches and ten pounds."

Shrugging out of her raincoat, Summer walked over to a coat tree and hung it up. "I don't intend to argue with you, Gabriel."

"Nor I with you," he shot back. "I grew up with two sisters, and there were a few times when I was forced to protect them from other boys. That's who I am. That's how I was raised. If that guy had touched you, I would have taken him apart. And do you really believe I give a damn about him suing me?"

She didn't reply or turn around. He stared at her back, then turned on his heels and walked out of the office, slamming the door violently behind him. The itch was back. An annoying itch he couldn't scratch.

There was something about Summer he found so intriguing, yet so very irritating. He'd give himself the weekend to find the answer. And if he didn't, then he was mentally prepared to dismiss her.

Three

After her last class, Summer retrieved her handbag and raincoat, then went in search of Gabriel, hoping she would find him in the music room. Peering through the glass on the door, she spied him sitting on a chair, one leg crossed over the opposite knee, arms folded over his chest. Opening the door, she walked in. A student sat in the back of the room playing scales on an alto saxophone.

Gabriel's gaze widened as he smiled at Summer. He patted a chair beside him. Moving quietly across the room, she sat down next to him. She jumped slightly, then relaxed as his hand closed possessively over her fingers.

Summer felt the strength in his fingers, inhaled the clean fragrance of his cologne mingling with his body's natural scent. In an instant everything that was Gabriel Cole seeped into her. Without hearing him speak, she recalled the drawling cadence of his baritone voice, saw the long wavy ponytail flowing down his back, remembered the comforting feel of his arm around her waist when they'd walked the hallway earlier that morning, and recalled his blatant threat to the photographer when he thought she would be harmed.

If you touch her, even breathe on her, I will hurt you.

A slight smile tugged at the corners of her mouth. She couldn't remember the last time a man, other than those on her team whose, "I've got you covered," offered to protect her.

"What are you smiling about?" Gabriel whispered close to her ear.

"You," she said, not taking her gaze off the student fingering the keys on an alto sax.

"What about me?"

"It's what you said to that photographer when he came at me," she whispered back.

Gabriel brushed his mouth over her ear; the hair on his upper lip tickled her skin. "I wasn't issuing an idle threat, Summer."

"What happened to music soothing the savage beast?" she teased. Turning her head, she stared up at him, their mouths only inches apart.

Peering down under lowered lids, Gabriel committed everything about Summer to memory: the way she stared at him through her lashes, the straight bridge on her short nose and the poutiness of her lower lip.

"There is a side of my personality that even music can't soothe. Thankfully it doesn't surface very often."

She affected a mysterious smile. "Everyone wears two faces, Gabriel, but the trick is not letting your opponent unmask you."

He stared at her, pondering her cryptic statement. "Is that what you really believe?"

She held his gaze. "Yes."

The boy completed his scales, and Gabriel refocused his attention. "Very nice, Howard."

The pimply faced student smiled. "Am I in, Mr. Cole?"

Gabriel nodded, smiling. "Yes, you're in. I want you to practice your scales over the weekend until you feel comfortable with the fingering. Monday I'll test you to see whether I want you to play with the orchestra or the jazz band."

"Thanks, Mr. Cole." Removing the mouthpiece, he bent down and put the instrument inside its carrying case.

"You should always clean your horn before you repack it, Howard."

Howard blushed. "Sorry. I forgot."

Gabriel smiled. A few of the Weir students in the music program were quite talented, but lacked the discipline to expand their talent. He planned to identify those and work closely with them.

He stood up, gently pulling Summer to her feet. "Are you ready?"

"Yes." And she was ready for Gabriel and the time they would spend together.

He helped her into her raincoat. She anchored her handbag over her shoulder, and walked with him out of the building to the parking lot. The mist had stopped and the sun had burned away the fog, leaving a brilliant blue sky with puffy white clouds.

Gabriel held the door while she slipped into the Porsche. The car smelled new, and she thought about what Lucas had said about the sticker price. Some people would have to work ten years to save enough money to buy a car like Gabriel's. Meanwhile he thought nothing of handing a car dealer close to a quarter of a million dollars for a vehicle he probably thought of as a toy—a very, very expensive toy. He maneuvered out of Weir's parking lot, driving quickly through the early afternoon traffic toward Route 3.

Relaxing on her seat, Summer said, "Your car is very nice."

"Thank you."

"It still has a new-car smell."

"I've had it for six months. It was my birthday present to me."

She smiled at him. "You're very generous to yourself."

He gave her a quick glance. "I hadn't had a new car for more than thirteen years, so I decided to make up for it."

This disclosure surprised Summer. "But . . . but you're . . ." Her words trailed off.

"Not a pauper?"

"Yes."

"True," he said candidly. "But having money doesn't translate into buying a luxury car every year. I bought my first car when I was twenty-one. It sat in a garage for months at a time because I was on the road traveling with a band."

He and a few of his college buddies had put together a band, playing the college and club circuit. It wasn't until after they'd graduated that the sextet went into the Serenity Records studio to record their first album. Once released, it had become an instant hit.

"We'd spend one night in Cincinnati, the next two in Chicago before we were onto Dallas. After a while I felt like a vagabond, sleeping in strange beds in even stranger towns and cities."

"When did you stop touring?"

"It was six years ago that we stopped touring as a group. Every once in a while we get together to do a private gig." He had stopped to pursue a graduate degree in music education. "Right after that I was asked to write a soundtrack for *Reflections in a Mirror*. The experience was like nothing I had ever encountered before in my life. I sat in a room, watching a film where the only sounds were dialogue and special effects. I had to view it twice before I gained enough confidence and felt comfortable enough to write the main theme. After that the entire score fell into place."

"It fell into place perfectly."

Gabriel gave her a modest smile. "Thank you."

It was the last two words they exchanged until they'd left the city limits of Plymouth.

Summer looked at Gabriel. His expression was stoic, as if he had been carved out of granite. "What are you going to do after June?"

He paused, then said, "I've been asked to write another soundtrack. Filming will begin in Toronto in late spring and wrap sometime in early June." He glanced at her. "How about you, Summer? What are your plans?"

"I don't know," she said truthfully.

It was true only because she did not know where she would be in June. If she exposed the drug ring at Weir before the end of the school year she would resign her position with the DEA. Once her true identity was revealed, she knew she could not remain at the high school.

"Have you thought of returning to the stage?"

She pondered his question. "At times I have."

Gabriel gave her another sidelong glance. "What's stopping you?"

Her smile was bittersweet. "It's been a long time. I'd have to get an agent, then begin the vicious cycle of reading scripts and going to auditions and casting calls. I'm not certain whether I'm up to that again."

There was complete silence as Gabriel crossed the Sagamore Bridge. He wondered what had happened in

Summer's past for her to give up what once had been a very promising stage career. He was aware that she had garnered her Tony nomination when as an understudy to a popular actress, she had stepped into the role three days after opening night to rave reviews. The original lead actress had come down with a misdiagnosed case of strep throat, which eventually damaged the valves in her heart, abruptly ending her career.

Even though she did not win the Tony, Summer had become a star. A month later, her agent held a press conference stating his client was retiring because of personal reasons.

And there were times, since he was introduced to her, that Gabriel wondered what those personal reasons could have been: a failed love affair, family tragedy, or a health problem.

He was now thirty-four, and there was never a time in his life when he had been responsible for another human being—only himself once he reached his majority. But now he wanted to become responsible for someone other than himself. He wanted to take care of Summer Montgomery.

"I'll probably set up a dance school back home," she said. The Department had fabricated a scenario wherein she had taught musical theater at a private dance school in Washington, D.C.

"Where's home?"

"St. Louis, Missouri."

"Oh, so you're one of those mule-headed Missourians that have to be convinced of everything."

She folded a hand on her hip. "We're not mule-headed."

"Isn't Missouri known as the 'Show Me State?' "

"That's because we're not easily fooled and need a bit more convincing than most."

Gabriel sucked his teeth. "Yeah, right. What you are is headstrong and willful."

Shifting slightly on her seat, Summer stared at him. "Is that how you see me?"

"At times, yes."

"You're wrong, Gabriel."

He flashed a dimpled smile. "If that's the case, then prove me wrong this weekend."

"What?" The single word exploded from her mouth.

"We take off our masks, Summer. No pretense or charades."

"Is that what you really want?"

His smile was dazzling, attractive lines deepening around his gold-flecked eyes. "Yes."

Closing her eyes, she nodded. "Okay."

A spark of excitement warmed her blood. This weekend she would step out of her role as Renegade to become Summer.

It had been a long time since she could be herself. She had played the masquerade so long that she wasn't certain where the make-believe ended and reality began.

Gabriel's "little place" was a restored two-story, four-bedroom, five-bath farmhouse with white clapboard siding, a green asphalt shingle roof, and a generous wraparound porch set on six acres of beautifully landscaped waterfront property.

Summer gave Gabriel a narrow look when he curved an arm around her waist. "A little place, Gabriel?"

"It was little before I had it renovated. I raised the ceilings in the bedrooms on the second floor and expanded both floors by a thousand square feet on either side."

Summer followed him up a staircase to the second floor. Like his car, the house smelled new. Gleaming bleached pine floors, French doors, and pale walls projected an atmosphere of openness. They walked down a long hallway, stopping at a doorway at the end of the hall.

"You're here, and my bedroom is at the top of the staircase on the right." Cupping her chin in his hand, he leaned over and pressed a kiss to her forehead. "Take your time settling in. I'll be out on the front porch."

He was there, then he was gone, but the sensations from the feel of his silky mustache remained with Summer long after she had walked into her bedroom and closed the door.

She found the bedroom large and filled with an abundance of natural light. The gabled roof made her feel as if the room was a separate structure, an intimate retreat. Walking over to the French doors, she opened them and stepped out to a private deck that offered a view of the water. A cool breeze feathered over her face, the distinctive smell of the salt water wafting in her nostrils. The tense lines on her face relaxed as she expelled her breath. She felt as if she had been holding her breath and raw emotions in check for years.

She lost track of time as she watched the foam-flecked gray waves washing up on the beach. When she turned to reenter the bedroom a clock on the fireplace mantel was chiming the hour. It was three o'clock.

She unpacked, hanging a dress, slacks, two blouses and a jacket, and putting several pairs of shoes in a walk-in closet before storing her undergarments and T-shirts in the drawers of a massive mahogany armoire.

Kicking off her shoes, she sat down on a cushioned side chair next to a table that doubled as a desk. The bedroom's furnishings were an eclectic mix of French Country and contemporary.

Reaching for a pair of sweatpants, polo shirt, a set of underwear, and a small bag filled with her grooming aids, Summer walked into an adjoining bathroom.

Gabriel leaned against a column supporting the porch, arms folded over his chest, his gaze fixed on a field of sea oats swaying gently as if dancing to their own music. A flock of seagulls swooped down along the beach, squawking noisily as they fought over scraps of food left on the beach. His nearest neighbor's toddler twin sons had made it a habit of leaving stale bread, for the "boids" every afternoon before their nanny put them down for a nap.

He had begun vacationing on Cotuit off-season because of its solitude. After the second year, he decided to buy the farmhouse from an elderly widow who had lived her entire life on Cape Cod.

Gabriel had returned to Cotuit after spending the past Christmas holiday with his extended family in West Palm Beach, Florida, with the intent of taking up legal residence in the state of Massachusetts. His parents thought he had lost his mind to consider moving so far north where the winters were long, bitterly cold, and snowy. He had reassured them that he had made the right decision even before he had commissioned an architectural firm to draw up plans to expand and renovate the century-old structure. He moved in permanently in May, and now looked forward to living year-round on the island.

He went completely still when he heard the soft click of the screen door, opening and closing behind him. He inhaled the scent of a sensual perfume before he felt the heat from Summer's body.

Lowering his chin, Gabriel stared at Summer as if seeing her for the very first time. Her unbound hair floated around her face and over her shoulders. She had removed her makeup, and her fresh scrubbed face made her appear no older than eighteen.

His gaze moved lower. Her face may have look like an adolescent's, but that was not the case with her body. A pair of hip-hugging, drawstring sweatpants failed to disguise the womanly curves of her slim hips. A smile crinkled his eyes when he noted her bare slender feet.

Moving closer to Gabriel, Summer curved an arm around his slim waist, sighing softly under her breath. Without her heels, the top of her head was level with his shoulder. He had also changed into a pair of jeans with a black T-shirt and sandals.

Smiling up at him, she said, "Everything is so peaceful."

Lowering his arms, he hugged her. "That's why I decided to move here. Even during the summer with the influx of tourists it's still a relaxing place to live."

She stared out at the ocean with a faraway look in her eyes. "It must be an incredible experience to wake up every morning and see the ocean."

Gabriel heard the longing in her voice. "You're welcome to come and hang out here anytime you feel the need to get away from the city. I have more than enough room so we wouldn't have to fall over each other."

She forced a smile. Didn't he realize what he was offering? Did he actually believe she could sleep under his roof and remain unaffected by the sexual magnetism that made him so self-confident and secure about his rightful place in the universe?

"I don't know if I could," she said, refusing to commit.

"Will you?"

"Will I what?"

"At least think about it."

She nodded. "Yes."

"Good." The single word spoke volumes.

She felt the invisible bond pulling her closer to Gabriel at the same time a gentle peace invaded her for the first time in more than ten years. Everything about him was calming and relaxing.

"Why did you leave the theater?" he asked after a comfortable silence.

She closed her eyes, struggling to bring her tortured emotions under control. "It was because of my brother." Her voice was a trembling hush.

"What about him?"

Inhaling, she held her breath before letting it out slowly. "He was killed in a drive-by shooting."

Gabriel eased back, staring at her grief-stricken expression. "Why?"

"Why?" she repeated. "I don't know why. He just happened to be at the wrong place at the wrong time. He was on his way home from school when someone in a speeding car fired two shotgun blasts at a group of kids waiting on the corner. My brother was hit in the chest. He died instantly.

"We learned later that those in the car were members of a rival gang from the other side of town. Several gangs had declared war on one another because a few members had invaded another's drug turf.

"Charles was an honor student who planned to become a doctor like my mother and father. He was kind, gentle, and the day my mother brought him home from the hospital I had promised him that I would always protect him. I lied to him, Gabriel. How could I protect him when I lived more than a thousand miles away? How, when I was in New York night after night accepting curtain calls from an adoring public?"

Cradling her face between his large hands, Gabriel shook his head. "It wasn't your fault, Summer. You can't blame yourself for something you couldn't control even if you had been in St. Louis."

"I shouldn't have left him," she whispered.

"It's still not your fault," he repeated.

Staring over his shoulder, Summer said, "I shouldn't have left St. Louis until Charles was old enough to go away to college."

"Your brother was your parents' responsibility, not yours."

She glared at him. "Didn't you say you protected your sisters?"

He nodded. "I did because I wanted to, not because I *had* to. My father was and still is more than capable of protecting all of the women in my family." Lowering his head, he brushed a kiss over her parted lips. "Let him go."

Her lids fluttered. "I can't."

"Yes, you can, sweetheart. All you have to tell yourself is that it was beyond your control. Your brother's destiny was determined before he was born."

She went completely still, her gaze meeting and fusing with his. "Do you believe in destiny, Gabriel?"

"Yes, I do," he said softly.

Summer wanted to tell him she also believed in destiny, believed her life would end like her brother's in a hail of bullets.

She managed a half-smile. "Do you believe you can change your destiny?"

He lifted an eyebrow. "No."

Keeping her features deceptively composed, Summer pulled away from Gabriel. She moved off the porch and sat down on the first step.

Gabriel stared at her ramrod-straight back. "Is there something else you want to tell me?"

"No," she said a little too quickly.

Gabriel went to sit down next to her. He studied her profile until she turned her head and looked at him. The vulnerability she had hidden for years surfaced, her mask of fearlessness slipping. Her face had become an open book, permitting him to see what she did not want him to see. He was entranced by the silent sadness he saw.

He wound a hand in her hair, his fingers combing through the thick chemically straightened strands. His head came down, his mouth moving over hers in a slow, drugging kiss that melted any resistance. Pulling her closer, his tongue parted lips in a soul-reaching message that vowed silently: *I'm here for you.*

Summer quivered at the tenderness of Gabriel's kiss, making her aware of what she had missed, needed. She kissed him back, melding her body to his, wanting to get closer. His touch, his kiss triggered a familiar, long-forgotten throbbing between her thighs.

Lucas's warning swept over her, dousing the rising passion like a bucket of ice-cold water: *Stay focused.*

Reluctantly, she tore her mouth away. She and Gabriel stared at each other, breathing heavily, their chests rising and falling with an even measured rhythm.

"What are we doing, Gabriel?" Her voice was barely a whisper.

He smiled, his dimples winking at her. "I believe it's called kissing."

She placed her fingertips over his mouth. "I can't . . . we shouldn't do it again."

Gabriel's lids lowered at the same time he captured her hand, holding it firmly. "And why not?"

"Because it's not going to work."

"Because you say it?"

She shook her head. "No, Gabriel. Not because I say it. It's because we have to work together."

He lifted an eyebrow. "You've never been kissed by someone you've worked with?"

"No . . . I mean yes."

His expression hardened. "What is it? Yes or No."

"Yes." She had lost count of the number of times she had kissed the actors she'd performed with.

"It didn't work out?"

"It worked just fine."

Gabriel leaned closer, his lips mere inches from hers. "So?"

Summer gave him a long, penetrating look. She'd tried and failed miserably. She wanted so much to be Summer and not Renegade, but found it impossible to distinguish between the two identities.

"I can't afford to get involved with you. We are worlds apart, and there is no way you can fit into mine, or I in yours."

An incredulous expression froze his features. "What are you talking about?"

"You are a celebrity—a brilliant superstar, a multi

award-winning musician. I suppose you have your reasons for becoming an artist-in-residence at Weir, but after the school year ends, you will go back to doing whatever you've been doing. Meanwhile—"

"Don't!" he shouted, cutting her off. "Please don't say it," he continued in a softer tone. "I can't change who I am anymore than you can change who you are." He caressed her cheek. "And I happen to like who you are."

She closed her eyes and shook her head. "You don't know me, Gabriel."

"Then don't shut me out, Summer," he pleaded softly. "Allow me to get to know you."

He didn't know what he was saying. No one knew Summer Montgomery. Not even her mother and father. The actors and actresses with whom she had worked so closely only saw what she wanted them to see. They did not know that her parents were doctors or that she had had a younger brother. Lucas Shelby and those at the Department knew Renegade, but not Summer.

Her parents did not know their firstborn.

The only exception was her grandmother.

"You don't know what you're saying."

"I know exactly what I am saying. We can have fun without a declaration of love or committing to each other."

She opened her eyes, more shaken than she cared to admit. She told Gabriel she didn't want to become involved with him, yet her heart refused to believe what her mind told her. She had a mission to see to its conclusion and she couldn't afford to be distracted by romantic notions.

If she had been Summer Montgomery civilian, she would have been flattered by Gabriel Cole's interest in her, but she was a special agent working for a federal law enforcement agency.

"We won't rush into it," he crooned close to her ear. "If it doesn't work out, then it was never meant to be."

"And if it does?" she whispered.

His smile was brilliant. "Then it will be wonderful."

Vertical lines appeared between her eyes. "What an arrogant thing to say!"

His smile faded. "It has nothing to do with arrogance. I know who I am and what I want."

He knew who he was while she was living a double life. The only thing she was certain of was what she wanted at that moment. She wanted Gabriel Cole more than she wanted to identify the person or persons responsible for Weir's drug dealing.

A wave of fatigue seized her, and she felt a return of the tiredness. She was tired of fighting what she wanted and needed most—a normal life doing what most women her age did. She wanted to go out dancing, take in a movie, share a romantic dinner, and she wanted a physical liaison with a man wherein she was reminded of why she had been born female.

"All right," she conceded softly. "We'll let destiny tell our story."

Curving an arm around her waist, Gabriel pulled her close. Angling her head, she rested it on his shoulder. They sat, staring at the water as the sun shifted, taking with it the warmth of the afternoon.

Four

Summer snuggled closer to Gabriel, capturing some of his body's heat. "Were you named for the Archangel of the Annunciation?"

Gabriel chuckled softly. "No. Actually I was named after an uncle. He's my mother's brother. I believe my name means God is my strength, or God gives him strength."

"Do you believe that?"

He smiled. "What I believe is that God is giving me the gift to compose music."

She glanced up at him. "Isn't your father a musician?"

"Yes. However, he's been a producer for more than thirty years. He plans to retire next year on his seventieth birthday."

"Will you take over?"

Gabriel shook his head. "No. My younger brother and sister are being groomed to head up Serenity Records."

"How old are they?"

"Twenty-five." He smiled. "They're twins."

"Isn't that a little young to head a major record company?"

"Not for Jason and Ana. In fact, all of us have grown up in the company of wannabe heartthrobs and divas, listening to demo records and sometimes being privy to contract negotiations before we reached our teens. Ana and Jason's focus has always been the business end of Serenity, while I prefer the creative component."

"Tell me about Gabriel Cole. The real Gabriel and not the one I occasionally see on *Entertainment Tonight* or read about in *People* or the supermarket tabloids. I want to know why you've elected to live on Cotuit instead of in Hollywood or South Beach? What or who are you hiding from?"

Gabriel stared at Summer, complete surprise freezing his features until she dropped her gaze. "You think I'm hiding?"

She nodded mutely. A slight smile softened his mouth. "I'm not hiding from anyone or anything." Removing his arm from around her body, he extended his long legs and rested his hands on his denim-covered knees. "I'm a loner. I've always been a loner."

"How many siblings do you have?"

"Three, two sisters and a brother. Our house in Boca Raton was always filled with music and lots of noise, noise that never seemed to bother my parents. My father said quiet homes were for the sick and dead, so we were raised somewhat as free spirits. But that's not to say we grew up without boundaries. Even before we were teenagers my father had what he called the Cole Manifesto: no underage drinking and absolutely no drugs. He said we did not want to know the punishment for a single infraction. He had me so traumatized that I was twenty-four before I took my first drink."

"I suppose your parents didn't mind you piercing your ears?"

"I was eighteen when I got the first piercing, and eight years later I decided I wanted two more. Dad, who had had his left ear pierced when he was in his late teens, had his right ear pierced on the same day. There was quite a commotion when we showed up at my grandmother's house to celebrate my Dad's sixtieth birthday. She took one look at our ears and took to her bed for the rest of the day."

"What did everyone do?"

"Hell, we partied on without her. She came around the next day, crossing her breasts while imploring the saints to help her son and grandson see the error of their ways." Gabriel made the sign of the cross over his chest, rolled his eyes upward in supplication and began praying in Spanish in a falsetto voice.

Summer punched him softly on the shoulder. "Stop that!"

He sobered, but was unsuccessful when he attempted to hide a smile. "Well, that's how she sounded."

Summer's gaze followed a lone seagull gliding gracefully with the wind currents. "You were saying you're a loner. What about all those actresses and singers you dated?"

"It was only for publicity." Women who dated the very private Gabriel Cole were never identified or photographed.

"You're kidding?"

"Nope. I never slept with any of them. We'd show up at a party, stay an hour, then I'd take them home or drop them off to see whomever it was their studios did not want them to be seen with."

"You just shattered my impression of you being a playa'."

"Sorry about that."

She smiled at him. "There's no need to apologize."

"Becoming a party animal is the quickest way to short

circuit one's career and creativity. I've never been able to compose in chaos."

"Is that why you didn't turn on your car's radio or CD player?" His car had a state of the art sound system, yet he had driven the entire trip without music.

He flashed his sensual crooked smile. "So, you noticed?"

She wanted to tell Gabriel there weren't too many things about him she did not notice. Just glancing at him she could tell his waist and shoe size. She could tell whether he was tense or relaxed by the set of his strong jaw, and she knew when he was staring at her, even with her gaze averted. It was as if she could feel the heat from his golden-brown eyes searing her skin.

"Are you working on something new?" she said, answering his question with one of her own.

He nodded, saying, "It's a little jazz number with a syncopated riff for a horn."

"Would you mind if I hear it?" His left eyebrow lifted a fraction, and Summer held up her hands. "If you're superstitious about—"

"I'm not superstitious," he said in a quiet voice, cutting her off. Pushing to his feet, he reached down to pull her up. "Come with me."

Summer followed Gabriel into the house, through the entryway, past the family room, and a formal living room with two gleaming black concert pianos facing each other, noticing both were Steinways. Her curiosity was piqued when he opened the door to another room, the overhead recessed lights coming on automatically.

Her shock was complete when she stood in the middle of a recording studio. Turning around, she took in everything: recording booth, equipment for laying down tracks, mixers, tuners, speakers, and a computer.

"Very, very nice," she said softly. "One stop shopping for composing and recording."

Tightening his hold on her hand, he led her to a synthesizer. "Do you play?"

"Only piano."

He seated her on a bench, then sat down beside her. "I want you to listen to this."

Summer watched, transfixed, as his long, slender fingers spanned the keys. His hands were exquisite, the backs broad and covered with a sprinkling of black hair. His nails were short, even and square-cut.

The first eight chords conjured up drops of water splashing into an empty tin pail as a muted horn played out a syncopated rhythm in double time. She found herself humming counterpoint to the horn.

The sound of Summer scatting along with the work-in-progress quickened Gabriel's pulse. Her voice was the perfect accompaniment to a tune that had haunted him for more than year. Touching a key, he added the soft brushing sound of a snare drum. It was perfect. All the composition needed was a piano, flugelhorn, drum and voice. Her contralto voice was a beautiful instrument.

He stopped, his fingers resting lovingly on the keys. Excitement fired his gold eyes. "Perfect. You were perfect!"

She wrinkled her nose. "The piece is wonderful."

"No, Summer, you are fabulous."

They stared at each other for a full minute until Summer lowered her gaze and peered at him through her lashes. The smoldering fire she saw in Gabriel's eyes shocked her. It had surfaced again—the magnetism that made him who he was had captured her in a web of longing from which she did not want to escape.

"Aren't you going to give me a tour of your house?"

She had said the first thing that had come to her mind. She needed to move, get away before he saw how much he disturbed her.

Gabriel inclined his head. "We'll start upstairs then work our way down." He stood up and walked out of the studio, leaving her to follow, her gaze fixed on the profusion of graying hair swaying between his shoulder blades.

Closing her eyes, Summer inhaled deeply. As Renegade, she would've been totally immune to Gabriel Cole, but this weekend as Summer she was powerless to resist his virile appeal. And, she had to ask herself did she really want to resist him. She knew the answer even before her mind had formed the question: *No.*

Gabriel was reserved and formal as a tour guide when he showed her the bedrooms and adjoining baths on the second floor. Fireplaces, sitting rooms, and French doors, allowing for an abundance of natural light were repeated in all of the bedrooms, but that was where the similarities ended. Furnishings in each depicted a mix of contemporary and French country, Queen Anne, Mediterranean, and Spanish. Every bathroom featured a dressing room, freestanding shower stall, bidet, and sunk-in bathtub with a Jacuzzi.

"I had the second floor expanded to include private bathrooms for each of the bedrooms."

Summer walked alongside him as they descended the staircase. "What made you decorate each bedroom with a different style?"

"I wouldn't know a Queen Anne from a Louis the twentieth."

"The period ended with the sixteenth," she corrected softly.

"Whatever," Gabriel drawled, repeating the word which seemed to have become the only one in Weir's student population's lexicon.

She smiled at him. "Hey. That was very good."

He returned her smile. "I don't know anything about decorating, but what I didn't want was a farmhouse or early American look. I have an aunt who is an interior decorator who offered me several options. The second story one period, the first story another, or each room a mix. I do like contemporary, so I went along with the more eclectic styles. The only exception is the living and dining rooms."

The formal living and dining rooms were filled with exquisite mahogany pieces, reminding Summer of the elegant homes she had seen in the Caribbean. Gabriel had expanded the lower level to include a media room complete with a seventy-two inch wall-mounted plasma television screen and two smaller screens for simultaneous viewing of other channels. The elaborate audio/video and lighting system, activated by a press of a few remote-control buttons, visually concealed any evidence of equipment. A comfortable sofa, love seat, a quartet of armchairs and the walls covered with framed classic movie posters of Black films invited one to come and stay for hours.

Summer was totally enchanted by what Gabriel referred to as his entertainment room. The space, twice the size of the media room, was set up like a nightclub: recessed lights, a raised stage with a keyboard, space for dancing, bistro tables and chairs, and a colorful jukebox with hundreds of CDs. It was apparent he had spared no expense when it came to decorating his home.

She peered into the jukebox. "How many CDs do you have?"

Gabriel stood behind her, his breath whispering over an ear. "I lost count after eight hundred. I have them programmed on a changer. What do you want to hear?"

Peering at him over her shoulder, she smiled. "You pick something."

Leaning over, he pressed nine buttons in rapid succession and the familiar opening beats for Michael Jackson's "Billy Jean" came through the powerful speakers.

"Oh, no you didn't," she said, swaying and snapping her fingers.

Gabriel crossed his arms over his chest, watching Summer imitate the King of Pop's celebrated dance steps. By the time her bare feet moonwalked across the floor, he was singing along with her. "Billy Jean" segued into Tina Turner's "You Better Be Good to Me," then Wilson Pickett's "In The Midnight Hour."

He found everything about Summer uninhibited and expressive. She sang from her soul, moving as if she had been born to dance. There was no doubt she was a natural talent.

She collapsed in his arms, her breasts pressed to his heaving chest. Waiting until she'd regained her breath, Summer smiled up at Gabriel smiling down at her. "You'll have to excuse me, but it's been a long time since I've just let myself go."

He saw the excitement in her eyes. Whether she wanted to accept it or not, Summer was a consummate performer. "You're an incredible talent."

"And you're a very kind critic," she countered. Pulling away from him, she floated down to the floor, folding her legs in a yoga position.

Sobering, Gabriel sat down beside her. "It has nothing to do with kindness. You are what you are."

"Does this mean you're ready to sign me to your father's record label?"

He wanted to tell her that if he offered her a contract with Serenity Records it would be for life. Now that he had found a woman who appeared to share his passion for music, he did not want to let her go.

"Yes. That is, if you want it."

Reaching up, she twisted her hair, tucking it into a tight bun at the back of her head. "If you had offered me something like this ten or even fifteen years ago I would have accepted it without batting an eye. But times have changed and so have I." She gave him a smile that made his insides quiver like gelatin. "Thank you anyway, Gabriel."

He forced a brittle smile. "We could be the new Marvin Gaye and Tammi Terrell. Moving closer, he launched into a rendition of "If I Could Build My Whole World Around You." Gabriel sang Marvin's part, and Summer Tammi's, the words flowing from his heart to his lips. And he did want to build his whole world around her. He wanted to calm her fears, make her laugh until her sides hurt, and protect her forever. What he did not want to acknowledge was that he was beginning to like Summer more than he wanted to.

Like a small child, she crawled trustingly into his lap and rested her head on his shoulder. He held her close singing in her ear, "Like sweet morning dew I took one look at you, and it was plain to see that you were my destiny."

Summer went completely still when she recognized the words to "You're All I Need to Get By." She pressed her fingertips to his mouth. "No more. Please."

He caught her small wrist, holding it firmly. "Why not?"

"You're moving too quickly."

He shook his head. "Wrong, Summer. If I move any slower we'll both be ninety before we acknowledge this . . . this thing that's pulling us together."

She pressed her forehead to his. "I feel it, too."

"What do you plan to do about it?" he asked, his tongue tracing the fullness of her lower lip.

Renegade would have had a quick answer for him, but it wasn't her alias sitting on Gabriel Cole's lap, enjoying the touch of his mouth on hers. It was Summer Montgomery, completely unmasked and unplugged.

"Wait until the time is right to act upon it," she whispered, then parted her lips to accept the heat of his kiss. It sang through her veins like the words of the love song they'd just shared. Somehow she found the strength to pull away. Running her forefinger down the length of his nose, she gave him a demure smile. "I think it's time we close this nightclub."

He nodded, smiling. "We'll reopen it again after I prepare dinner for you."

"You cook?"

"A little."

Summer gave him a skeptical look. "Why can't I believe you whenever you say that word?"

Rising to his feet, he pulled her gently off the floor, brushing a gentle kiss across her forehead. "I thought in the eyes of the law everyone is considered innocent until proven guilty."

She wanted to tell him that she was the law, but held her tongue. Instead, she enjoyed the protection of his arm around her waist as they made their way to the kitchen.

Five

Summer sat in a dining area in the kitchen, across the table from Gabriel, her gaze fixed on the outline of his mouth under the black mustache. The facial hair was new because in all of the photographs she had seen of him he had been clean-shaven. The mustache changed his face, adding maturity and character.

She wasn't certain which of his features she liked best: his hair or eyes. The thick, wavy salt-and-pepper hair flowing down his back was masculine and *very* sexy. Then, there were his eyes—large gold-flecked and penetrating. It was as if they missed nothing, and there were times when she believed he could see what she managed to hide: a sensual longing she had never felt before. And she was mature enough to know that if she did sleep with Gabriel it would only elicit a physical dependence on him—a dependence she could not risk because of her dangerous masquerade.

She felt lethargic after eating a cup of flavorful lobster bisque, a whole grilled red snapper with grilled asparagus spears, cherry tomatoes, husked sweet corn and shiitake mushrooms in yellow bell peppers. She had barely touched a green salad of endive, watercress, romaine, and spinach leaves tossed with a balsamic vinaigrette dressing.

Gabriel hadn't permitted her to assist him when he prepared everything in half the time it would have taken her. She had sat on a high stool watching him move around the spacious kitchen with the same familiarity and ease he had exhibited when playing an instrument.

Summer took a sip of sparkling water, musing. *He doesn't need a woman, not when he can take care of himself.* Gabriel had a home built for his personal needs and professional specifications. He was a more than competent cook, and he had the resources to go anywhere he wanted and whenever he wanted. He had it all: looks, talent, and money.

Gabriel raised his head and caught Summer staring at him. His gaze dropped from her eyes to her throat, where a pulse throbbed with her increased respiration, and down to the soft outline of her breasts under the long-sleeved polo.

"Tell me about Summer," he said in a quiet voice.

She stared over his shoulder. "There's not much to tell."

Gabriel put down his fork. "Tell me what little there is."

"I was born thirty-three years ago on the first day of summer. Hence my name." She watched Gabriel's expressive eyebrows flicker with this disclosure. "My parents met in medical school and married during their third year. After their internship and residency, they decided to join the Peace Corps. They were assigned to a remote village somewhere in Peru. Once my mother discovered she was pregnant, she came back to the States, while my father stayed. Six months after my birth, my mother rejoined my father, leaving me in the care of my grandmother."

Leaning forward, Gabriel shook his head in disbelief. "Are you saying your grandmother raised you?"

An expression of hardness settled into Summer's delicate features. "She fed me, combed my hair, taught me my prayers, attended the parent-teacher conferences, and encouraged me to pursue a career in theater."

"When did you see your parents?"

"They returned twice a year for short visits. They came back to stay the year I turned five. Mother was pregnant again. I suppose the impending birth of a second child quelled her wanderlust. Mother and Father bought a large house. I didn't want to leave my grandmother, so Mother asked her to come live with us. The happiest day of my life was when Mother brought Charles home from the hospital and we all gathered around the crib to tell him how beautiful and special he was.

"My mother stayed home for four years. Once Charles was enrolled in a private nursery school, she joined my father on staff at a municipal hospital. They worked long hours and different shifts, so it was Gram who stepped in once again, becoming my surrogate mother.

"All of my friends thought it was cool that I had two parents who were doctors. What they didn't know was that I would've given anything to have a mother and father who worked a nine-to-five. At least I would've seen them more than I did."

Lowering her head, she stared down at her plate, struggling with the resentment that surfaced when she least expected it. She lifted her chin, meeting Gabriel's stunned gaze across the table. "After Charles was killed my parents contacted the World Health Organization for an overseas assignment. They're now in

South Africa working as part of a medical team hoping to stem the spread of AIDS."

Picking up the goblet, she took another sip of water. "When I have my children I will *never* abandon them—not for anything or anyone."

Gabriel stared at Summer, unable to believe she had changed in front of his eyes. Her expression was filled with a cold loathing that frightened him. He met her gaze, seeing pain, pain he was helpless to vanquish.

And if you had my children you would never have to abandon them—not for me or anything.

A band tightened around his chest when he realized his unspoken thoughts. What was wrong with him? In the past he had never considered marriage or fathering a child. It wasn't something he wanted. He was content, living day-to-day, writing and possibly teaching music. He had volunteered to participate in the cultural arts grant program after interning at a middle school during his graduate studies.

His passion with music he fully understood; his reaction to Summer he could not.

Perhaps, he thought, he shouldn't try to analyze his feelings. He would follow his own advice and enjoy their time together without a declaration of love or a commitment.

Covering one of her hands with his, he tightened his grip when she attempted to free herself. "Do you know what kind of man you'd want to marry and father your children?"

Summer's cold resentment vanished, and she couldn't keep herself from laughing. Shaking her head, she said, "No. How about you, Gabriel? Have you selected that special woman you want to spend the rest of your life with?"

"No." There was no expression on his face. He released her hand. "Do you want to begin work on planning the concert tonight, or would you prefer we start early tomorrow morning?"

Summer glanced at her watch. It was after seven-thirty and she was beginning to feel fatigued. She usually got up before five to jog her requisite three miles, and covering three classes a day for the injured instructor had tested her mental stamina.

"Tomorrow."

"How about a movie before we turn in?"

She smiled. "Sure."

"Why don't you select one while I clean up the kitchen?"

"Let me help you."

"No, Summer."

"Yes, Gabriel."

They stared at each other, neither willing to concede. In the end, it was Gabriel. "Okay."

Summer sat on the love seat next to Gabriel, his right arm resting over the back. The rhythmic cadence of drumming came through hidden speakers as the opening scene from *Last of the Mohicans* appeared on the large screen. She loved history, and because Daniel Day Lewis was one of her favorite actors, she had chosen the film. The fingers of Gabriel's left hand tapped on his thigh, keeping tempo with the magnificent soundtrack.

"We could use a tune like that one," Summer whispered to Gabriel. The scene was a group of actors dressed in Eighteenth-Century costumes dancing to the music of an Irish reel.

He nodded. "That's from "The Gael," he said softly.

She experienced a flutter in the pit of her stomach in the next scene as Hawkeye kissed Cora Munro, the character played by Madeline Stowe. Gabriel's arm had slipped down to Summer's shoulder, his fingers tightening as he pulled her closer.

Summer felt herself being drawn into the lives of the characters on the screen and that of the man holding her in his protective grasp. All of her resistance fled as she slumped lower, her head resting on his solid thigh. Reclining, she stared at the screen in the darkened room while Gabriel's fingers traced the outline of her ear and the column of her neck.

After a while, she closed her eyes with the soothing stroking motion, falling into a deep dreamless sleep.

Gabriel knew by the measured rising and falling of Summer's chest that she had fallen asleep. Staring at the serene expression on her face, he loathed having to move her. Reaching for the remote, he paused the DVD.

Gathering her gently in an embrace, he stood up, walked out of the media room and made his way up the staircase. She did not stir when he placed her on the bed and covered her with a quilt. Moving over to the French doors, he drew the pale silk drapes over the floor-to-ceiling glass.

The antique clock on the mantel softly chimed the quarter hour. It wasn't ten, much too early for him to retire for bed. It was a Friday night, the beginning of the weekend and he did not have to get up early for classes the next day. He took one last look at Summer, then walked out of her bedroom, closing the door quietly behind him.

* * *

Gabriel sat on the porch, rocking gently. He had pulled on a cotton sweater over his T-shirt to counter the cool nighttime temperature. The sound of water washing up on the beach was calming and hypnotic, and he tried not thinking about the woman sleeping in an upstairs bedroom, but failed miserably.

He had found her feisty, but then without warning, she exhibited a vulnerability that tugged at his heart. Her mother and father were alive, yet she had grown up separated from them for more than half of her life because of their humanitarian causes. Didn't they know that their only cause should have been raising and nurturing their children?

She had referred to her parents as Mother and Father instead of Mom and Dad. How different it had been for him, his brother and sisters. There had never been a day when as children they did not awaken in their own beds and not see either their mother or father. Once his mother decided to resume her nursing career, she had become a private duty nurse. Serena Morris-Cole refused to accept a case that would take her away from her young children at night, because of her ritual of talking to each one before they recited their nightly prayers.

Gabriel became suddenly alert when he heard the distinctive sound of an automobile's tires on the sand-littered road. He stood up. A car he did not recognize maneuvered into the driveway and stopped in front of the two-car garage. He waited, not moving, for the driver to alight from the mid-size vehicle. Distinctive lines fanned out around his eyes when he recognized the slender figure striding toward him.

Gabriel bounded off the porch, arms outstretched.

"Hey! What are you doing here?" He was not disappointed when he felt the warmth of his sister's embrace and her soft kiss on his cheek.

"I had to see you and give you my good news."

Cradling Alexandra's face between his palms, he smiled down her while shaking his head. "You could've used the telephone, Alex." There was a hint of laughter in his voice.

"I was already in Boston so I thought I—"

"When did you get in?" he asked, interrupting her.

"This afternoon. I had a scheduled meeting with several members who are overseeing the northeast Trust's Waterfront Historic Action League in New Bedford." She had come to support the WHALE project, whose focus was the rehabilitation of a fire-damaged commercial building in the historic whaling community. "I'm scheduled to fly out of Logan tomorrow morning at eleven. I came because I have good news for you."

As an architectural historian, Alexandra Cole had become a liaison for the National Trust for Historic Preservation's Northeast Region, which included Connecticut, Delaware, Massachusetts, Maine, New Hampshire, New York, New Jersey, Pennsylvania, Rhode Island, and Vermont.

"Come inside and we'll talk." He led Alexandra up the porch and into the house. Gabriel loved both his sisters, but Alexandra was his favorite because Ana had her twin brother, Jason. It was Alex he'd watched over and sought to protect because she was sentimental and passionately romantic. As a child she'd go into hysterics and pine endlessly whenever a family pet died or ran away, and their father finally had to issue an edict: no more pets.

Directing her into the family room, Gabriel studied his sister. At thirty, she appeared incredibly chic. Her stylishly cut short curly hair framed a doll-like face with large gold-brown eyes, a pert nose, and full mouth. A black wool crepe suit, ivory silk blouse, black leather pumps, a strand of perfectly matched pearls around her neck and studs in her pierced lobes completed her corporate look. The summer sun had darkened her olive skin. She could have easily become a model for a tanning lotion.

Easing her down to a love seat, he held one of her hands. "Do you want something to eat or drink?"

Alexandra shook her head, smiling. "No, thank you. I ate dinner at the hotel before I left." She glanced around the room. "I really like what Aunt Parris has done here. Your house looks like a home. All you need is a wife and a few kids to make it look completely lived-in." She had purchased a two-bedroom condominium in Arlington, Virginia.

Gabriel ignored his sister's reference to a wife and children. He peered closely at her. "Tell me your good news."

A mysterious smile curved her full lips. "I'm getting married."

Gabriel was momentarily speechless with shock. Whenever he spoke to Alexandra she hadn't mentioned she was dating anyone. A muscle in his jaw tensed.

"Who is he?" The three words were squeezed out between clenched teeth.

Alexandra stood up and walked over to the French doors overlooking the rear of the house. Strategically placed floodlights illuminated the backyard. "Please, Gabe."

Rising to his feet, he closed the distance between them. "Please what?"

Her hands closed into tight fists, her nails biting into the tender flesh of her palms. "Don't say it like that."

"How else can I say it, Alex?" His voice was low, soothing. "You come to me in the middle of the night with the news you're engaged to be married. I'm shocked, stunned and surprised."

Turning around, Alexandra stared up at her brother. "I thought you would be happy for me."

"I am, Alex. But . . . but it's so unexpected. You never said you were seeing anyone." Her mysterious smile was back. "Do I know him?"

Alexandra nodded. "Yes."

Gabriel's gaze narrowed. He was unaware of his heart pounding wildly in his chest. "A name, Alexandra."

He prayed she wouldn't tell him that she planned to marry the singer she had met at a party in South Beach. Alexandra had gone out with him several times before he saw footage of them together on *Access Hollywood*. It was the first and only time in his life he contemplated murder. He couldn't believe his conservative sister had decided to date a man who had become notorious for hosting parties that were rumored to be drug orgies lasting for days.

Unknown to Alexandra, Gabriel had flown to Miami to have a man-to-man and heart-to-heart talk with the former Duane Jackson. Their meeting lasted less than three minutes, and when Gabriel left the palatial beachfront property he knew his sister would never see her hip-hop boyfriend again.

"Merrick Grayslake."

He froze. "Michael's friend?"

"Do you know another Merrick Grayslake?" she spat out angrily.

Gabriel swallowed an expletive at the same time he threw up his hands. "How the hell did you hook up with him?" he shouted in Spanish.

"Don't yell at me!" Alexandra shot back in the same language.

They had grown up in a house speaking English and Spanish. Their father had learned the language from his Cuban-born mother, and Serena, who had grown up in Costa Rica, was also bilingual.

Running a hand over his face, Gabriel tried to compose himself. Merrick was their first cousin Michael Kirkland's best friend. He had met him for the first time at Michael's wedding, and had found the man mysterious and somewhat sinister-looking.

Why was it, he thought, was his sister drawn to men who were the opposite of her? If they weren't living on the wild side, then they were on the edge. He didn't know much about Merrick except that he lived somewhere in West Virginia and had at one time worked for the CIA.

Taking her hand, Gabriel led Alexandra back to the love seat, sitting and pulling her down next to him. "Talk to me, Alex."

"I met him for the first time at Michael's wedding. We shared a few dances, and he asked for my number. I gave him my cell phone number because of my chaotic traveling schedule. Whenever I returned to D.C. we would meet for dinner or drinks. I must confess that I felt uncomfortable around him for a long time, then one day it disappeared and I saw him in a whole new light. At first I was impressed with his intelligence, but once I got past that I saw him as a lonely, misunderstood man."

"You're marrying him because you feel sorry for him?"

"Of course not. I'm marrying Merrick because I love him. I also want to tell you that I'm . . ."

"You're what?" Gabriel asked when she did not complete her statement.

"I'm pregnant."

His shock and surprise fading, Gabriel's face split into a wide grin. "Hot damn! I'm going to be an uncle."

Alexandra threw her arms around his neck. "Thank you for being happy for me."

He kissed her forehead. "How can I not be happy for you? When's the wedding?"

Pulling back, her eyes sparkling like multifaceted citrines, Alexandra blinked through happy tears. "Soon."

"Does Grayslake know he's going to be a father?"

"Yes. I told him last night." She sobered. "We hadn't planned on a baby, it happened despite our taking precautions."

"How far along are you?"

"Not quite two months. You're the first one to know—other than Merrick of course."

"Why didn't you tell anyone you were dating him?"

"I didn't want to say anything until I was certain he was the *one*. Our relationship changed after he called, asking that I join him in Europe last year. Of course I'd been there many times when I was an art student, but I saw it differently because I realized then that I had fallen in love with Merrick."

Gabriel's smile was tender. His sister was in love. "You're really happy, aren't you?"

She nodded. "So much so that I'm frightened."

"Have you guys set a date?"

"No. But I don't want to wait too long. Looking like someone who swallowed a melon isn't too cool for a bride. I know you're teaching now, but when are you off?"

"We're off for Columbus Day, Veteran's Day, Thanksgiving, and of course the Winter Recess."

Alexandra shook her head. "That's too far away. It looks as if you're going to have to fly down for a weekend. You have to sing at my wedding."

"Let me know and I'll be there." He angled his head. "What about your job with the Trust?"

"If there's an opening in the Southern region, then I'll request a transfer."

"And if there isn't?"

"Then I'll sit home knitting booties and piecing quilts until the baby comes."

"What do you want? Boy? Girl?"

"I don't care as long as it's healthy."

"Will I be able to find you in the West Virginia hills?"

"We plan to use the house in West Virginia for our vacation getaway. Merrick and I have talked about buying property in a D.C. suburb. The Central Intelligence Agency has been after him for years to come back, so he's returning as an intelligence research training specialist."

"That sounds good. You, Michael and Jolene can raised your kids together."

"What's nice is that our children will get to see one another more than we saw Michael and Emily."

"You're right," Gabriel agreed. Michael and Emily Kirkland had grown up in Santa Fe, New Mexico, and they usually saw them at family gatherings once or twice a year. Emily still lived in New Mexico with her husband and three children, but her brother had moved to the D.C. area after having been assigned to the Pentagon as a captain in the U.S. Army. Michael had met his future wife, Jolene in Georgetown. She had given birth to her second child, a son, last Christmas.

"When do you plan to tell Mom and Dad?"

"Next weekend. I'm planning to fly down to Florida see them on Friday."

Gabriel glanced at his watch. It was only minutes before midnight. "I hope you know you're spending the night here."

She nodded. "I don't think I could make it back to Boston without falling asleep behind the wheel."

"Did you bring luggage?"

"I have an overnight bag in the trunk of the car."

"Go upstairs and get ready for bed. I'll bring your bag up."

Alexandra stared lovingly at her older brother. "Thank you, Gabe."

"For what?"

"For being you."

He cradled her to his chest, kissing her cheek. "Love you, Sis."

"Love you back, Bro."

The house was silent by the time Gabriel slipped into bed—alone. Two women slept under his roof: his sister and a woman who had intrigued him from the first time he saw her.

A wry smile curved his mouth as he folded his arms under his head. His sister was pregnant!

Alexandra had found love with a man she'd planned to share her life with, and he wondered if he would ever share that experience with a woman.

Turning over, he stared at the blackness of the sky through the glass on the French doors. He had thought his life complete. He had his music, a house built to his specifications, and enough money to last him several lifetimes. His life was full, yet it was empty. And after spending several hours with Summer, he had come to the realization that it was not the *things* that would make him whole, but a someone.

She unknowingly had become that someone.

Six

Summer skipped down the staircase in her jogging gear. She had awakened feeling more refreshed than she had in months. After leaving her bed, she drew back the drapes, opened the French doors, and inhaled a lungful of tangy salt-filled air. She'd stood on the deck, watching the sky brighten with the dawn of a new day before she went into the bathroom to brush her teeth and shower.

The aromatic smell of brewing coffee and the strains of soft music playing greeted her as she stepped off the last stair. Making her way to the kitchen she stopped, her jaw dropping, when she saw Gabriel sitting at the kitchen table sharing a cup of coffee with a dark-haired woman. His unbound damp hair hung down his back like satin ribbons.

Her gaze met those of the woman's and when she smiled, Summer knew she was Gabriel's sister. Both had gold-brown eyes and a dimpled smile.

Alexandra lifted an eyebrow at her brother. "Shame on you, brother," she said softly in Spanish. "You didn't tell me you had a girlfriend."

Gabriel jumped up, his chair crashing to the floor in a loud clatter. He stared at Summer, looking her over seductively as if he had never seen her before. She stood under the arched entrance dressed in a gray sweatshirt, matching pants and running shoes. Her hair, secured in a single braid, fell over one shoulder. He picked up the chair without taking his gaze off her.

"I'm not his girlfriend. We are colleagues," Summer said in a quiet voice.

Gabriel blinked once, coming out of his trance. "You understand Spanish?"

"Yes." And she had to thank her parents for that. They had perfected the language after having lived in Peru for several years. Having the facility to speak more than one language had become an asset when she had submitted her application to the DEA.

Walking into the kitchen, she extended her hand. "I'm Summer Montgomery."

Rising to her feet, Alexandra leaned over the table and shook Summer's hand. "Alexandra Cole. "Your *colleague's* sister."

Gabriel pulled out a chair at the table for Summer. "Would you like a cup of coffee?"

She sat down, taking in everything about him in one sweeping glance. He'd showered, but hadn't shaved, and the stubble on his chin and jaw made him appear dark and dangerous. The white T-shirt stretched over a broad chest failed to disguise his toned pectorals and flat abs. She stared at his black drawstring sweatpants. He was so breathtakingly virile that she found it hard to draw a breath without it catching in her throat. Her gaze lowered. His long, slender tanned feet were bare.

"No, thank you. I usually don't eat or drink anything before jogging."

He captured and held her gaze. "What would you like for breakfast?"

"Fruit, a slice of toast, and decaf coffee."

Retaking her seat, Alexandra smiled at Gabriel. "If you're taking orders, then I'll have grits, eggs, bacon or sausage, and biscuits."

He frowned at her. "If you keep eating like that, I'm going to start calling you porky."

"Bite me, Gabriel Morris Cole!"

He wrinkled his nose at her. "Sorry, Sis, but I'll leave that task for Merrick."

Alexandra stuck out her tongue at her brother. "You're gross."

Summer enjoyed the good-natured bantering between Gabriel and Alexandra, but felt like an intruder. Pushing back her chair, she stood up. "Please excuse me. I'd like to complete my jog before the sun gets too hot. I'll be back later," she said, turning and making her way out of the kitchen.

Alexandra watched Gabriel staring at Summer's retreating figure, a knowing smile curving her lips. "She's beautiful."

"That she is," he said matter-of-factly.

"You like her don't you?"

He didn't look at his sister. "Yes."

"Does working with her pose a problem for you?"

"For me, no."

"What about her?"

"She's reluctant."

"Does that matter to you?"

Shifting slightly, he stared at Alexandra. "No. I can't change how I feel about someone just like that." He snapped his fingers. "We've agreed to take it slow and see what becomes of it."

"That's the same thing Merrick said to me. And now we're planning a wedding."

Gabriel held up a hand. "Back it up, Alex. No one said anything about getting married."

"Don't you want to get married? Start your own family?"

"I don't consciously think about it."

"You didn't answer my question, *Gabriel*."

"And I don't intend to answer it, *Alexandra*."

"You don't have to," she said smugly. "And because you're being evasive tells me that you do."

"Just because your fairy godmother has sprinkled you with love dust, it doesn't mean it will happen to me."

"It's going to happen, Gabe," she predicted. The expression on his face when Summer entered the kitchen was one Alexandra had never seen before, and she had seen her brother with enough women to know this one was different.

"Next you're going to tell me that you can read palms."

Alexandra's expression changed as she sprang up at the same time she covered her mouth with a hand and raced to the half-bath near the pantry.

Gabriel stared at the space where his sister had sat. "Morning sickness," he whispered.

No, he told himself. He did not want to marry or father children. He would leave that to his siblings.

Summer ran along the two-lane road parallel to the beach, her stride even, arms pumping smoothly at her sides. She felt free, freer than she had at any other time in her life. The only exception was when she had been on stage. Once she stepped into a role, she became the character. It was the same when she went undercover.

It did not matter whether she was Keisha, Denise or Michelle, each role was played to perfection.

But now she was Summer, undercover agent and drama teacher. She was sleeping under the roof of a man who reminded her that she was a woman—one with desires and needs.

There was something about Gabriel that soothed her while also making her heart race and pulse throb. When he'd held and kissed her she had to fight her overwhelming need not to beg him to make love to her.

Stay focused. Stay focused. The two words echoed in her ears in concert with her rubber soles meeting the asphalt. "Damn you, Lucas," she whispered.

It was as if her supervisor had become her conscience, reminding her of who she was and what was expected from her. She had always given Lucas what he wanted. When was she going to give herself what she wanted? She couldn't remember the last time she had truly enjoyed herself with a man, and Gabriel Cole was offering her an opportunity to laugh without censuring herself, enjoy being alive, and more importantly, to be a woman.

Raising her left arm, she glanced at the pedometer strapped to her wrist. She had jogged a mile and a half. Crossing the road, she reversed direction, smiling. She was willing to accept what he was offering without a commitment or declaration of love.

A frown furrowed Gabriel's forehead as he watched the taillights on Alexandra's rental car fade from his line of vision. He'd tried, unsuccessfully, to convince her not to drive back to Boston alone, that he would accompany her, but she had rejected his offer. Her argument was how would he get back to Cotuit, and his response had been that he would hire a car service. Of all of David and Serena Cole's children, Alexandra was the most stubborn. A wry smile replaced his frown. There was no doubt Merrick Grayslake had his work cut out for him once he married Alexandra.

The image of the woman who had occupied most of his waking thoughts the past twenty-four hours walked toward him. Hands resting on her hips, her chest rose and fell in a deep, even rhythm. The beginning of a smile tipped the corners of his mouth as she moved closer. He wasn't disappointed when she returned his smile.

Breathing deeply, Summer inhaled a lungful of ocean air. "What are you smiling about?"

His smile widened. "You."

"What about me?"

"I think if I'd had a teacher who looked like you I would've been certain to get left back every year."

Summer gave him a sassy grin. "Are you flirting with me, Gabriel?"

"Oh, hell yeah, Summer."

Winding her arm through his, she rested her head against his shoulder. "Have you no shame? You could've at least pretended you weren't."

"Shame, Summer? Have you forgotten I'm a decadent musician? Shame is not in my vocabulary."

She smiled up at him. "But didn't you tell me you were one of the nice guys?"

He stared at her under lowered lashes. "Nice, but a bad boy."

Summer went completely still. "I like bad boys."

"You do?"

"Yes."

"Why?"

"Because they're never boring."

His crooked grin was back. "I usually don't makes promises, but I can promise you that we *will* have a good time together."

"And I can promise you that you will have the ride of your life."

"Ouch, Miss Montgomery, I'm afraid of you."

"You should be," she teased.

Gabriel covered the slender hand looped over his arm. "Alexandra won't be sharing breakfast with us. She wasn't feeling well, so she decided to return to Boston, hoping she can get an earlier flight back to D.C." His sister had reassured him she would hire a private jet for her return trip. She had also called her fiancé, asking that he meet her at the airport upon her arrival.

"Are grits still on the menu?"

He nodded. "What else do you want?"

"Salmon cakes."

Lowering his head, he pressed his mouth to her ear. "Anything else?"

"Biscuits," she whispered.

Gabriel lifted an eyebrow. "Now, that's questionable. I'm rather hit and miss with biscuits."

"Then, I'll make the biscuits."

"Can you make them with cheese and chives?"

She gave him a warning look. "Don't push it, Gabriel."

"Okay," he conceded. "I'll accept the generic brand."

Easing away from him, Summer said, "I need to shower."

Gabriel's gaze was riveted on her face before it

moved down her body, then reversed itself. "Do you need help washing your back?"

Heart pumping wildly in her chest and pulse echoing in her ears, Summer saw the smoldering flame in the large golden eyes. There was a maddening hint of arrogance about him—an arrogance she admired because it complemented rather than detracted from his image as a musical superstar.

His invitation was a passionate challenge she wanted to accept. She longed for the protectiveness of his strong embrace, communicating without words that she was safe, that she had nothing to fear. She wanted to lie in his arms, her naked body pressed to his, experiencing what it meant to be born female. And she wanted to experience the fulfillment of making love with a man who had slipped under the barrier and made her forget she was Renegade.

"Not this morning." Her voice had dropped an octave.

Gabriel hadn't moved. A rising sea breeze stirred his unbound hair around his face, but he made no effort to push it off his forehead. "When, Summer?"

"I'll let you know."

Gabriel's smile did not meet his eyes as he stared at Summer with an intensity that heated her blood. He inclined his head. "I'll be waiting."

Turning, she walked in the direction of the house, feeling the heat of his gaze following her. It wasn't until she closed the door to her bedroom that she was able to draw a normal breath.

She did it!

She had indirectly told Gabriel Cole that she would share her body, but not her life with him.

Seven

Summer kneaded shredded cheddar cheese and dried chives into a mound of dough on a floured butcher-block countertop. Gabriel stood several feet away chopping Vidalia onions and red and green bell peppers like a trained chef before folding the mixture into a bowl of canned pink salmon.

She gave him a sidelong glance. He had secured his hair on the nape of his neck with an elastic band. "You handle that knife like a pro."

"I learned to cook before I was tall enough to look over the stove. My mother would sit me on a high stool while she prepared what I thought of as the most delicious and eye-appealing dishes. I think I was transfixed by the colors of the spices she used in most of her Caribbean-style dishes. In teaching me and my brother to cook, she continued the tradition of Cole men not having to depend upon a woman to fill their bellies."

And there was no doubt Gabriel enjoyed cooking. The ultra-modern kitchen was designed for a chef. A variety of pots and pans hanging from overhead hooks, two eye-level ovens, a built-in microwave, and a massive Viking range with a stove top grill were ideal for cooking for a couple or a crowd.

Gabriel smiled at Summer. It was apparent she also knew her way around the kitchen. She had combined all of the ingredients for the biscuits without measuring any of them. "Who taught you?"

"Gram. She made all of her bread. I was in college before I ate a store-bought loaf for the first time."

"How did you like it?"

She grimaced, wrinkling her nose. "I hated it. I felt as if I was eating glue. That was the first and last time I ate it."

Gabriel filed away this information. He hadn't perfected the art of baking his own bread. However, there was a nearby bakery where he could buy fresh-baked goods.

"How old is your grandmother?"

"Eighty-two."

"She's a youngster compared to my grandmother. *Abuela* will celebrate her one hundred-third birthday in December."

"God bless her."

"He has," Gabriel confirmed. "Other than being frail, she's still very alert. The only thing I find different about her is her refusal to communicate in English. So, if you don't speak Spanish then you're what kids call 'assed-out.' By the way, where did you learn to speak Spanish?"

"Both my parents are bilingual. Remember I told you they lived in Peru for several years. My father also knows enough French to get by in any French-speaking country. Did you learn Spanish from your grandmother?"

Gabriel shook his head. "Like yours, my parents are bilingual. My Cuban-born *abuela* taught all her children the language, while my mother grew up in Costa Rica."

"Is she Costa Rican?"

"No. She was born in Ohio, but moved there when her widowed mother married a Costa Rican."

"How did your mother meet your father?"

"He'd gone to Costa Rica for a business meeting with Mom's stepfather, and was assaulted before he arrived. It became somewhat of a fairy tale when Mom nursed Dad during his convalescence. One thing led to another and before long I was conceived."

"Are you saying you were conceived in Costa Rica?" Summer asked as she filled a baking pan with a dozen biscuits, pricked the tops with a fork, then brushed them with melted butter. Opening the door to the pre-heated oven, she placed the pan on a rack and closed the door.

"I did the math. My folks were married early September, and I was born March thirty-first. A seven pound, eight ounce baby is a little large for a six-month preemie."

Summer laughed, the sound low and sensual. "Perhaps they couldn't wait."

"Dad said that he took one look at Serena Morris and fell head over heels in love with her."

"Good for him. He saw what he wanted and went after it."

Gabriel formed patties from the salmon mixture, dropping them onto the heated griddle. Everyone had remarked how much he reminded them of his father, in looks and personality. And like David Cole he had taken one look at Summer Montgomery and felt as if he had been pole axed.

He did not know if what he felt for her was love,

only because he had never been in love. But what he did feel was a combination of curiosity and desire. He was curious to know the real Summer—the one under the tailored attire when she was at Weir and the one who wore a pair of sweatpants with the same sensual aplomb of a Victoria Secret's model in a lace thong.

Her passion for music matched his, while he was intrigued by her aloofness. But there was something about her, something she'd kept hidden, that he knew instinctively she would never share with him.

It was at that moment that Gabriel knew why he had invited Summer to his home. It was not to plan a spring concert, but to get to know her. And he wanted to know everything about her, which in turn would help him to understand why he was drawn to her with an intensity he had never felt with another woman.

It did not matter whether they were three feet or three hundred feet from each other—her pull on him was as strong as the moon on the tide.

Summer washed the flour off her hands in a sink on the cooking island. "I suppose I have to change my initial opinion of you."

His hands stilled. "And that is?"

"I thought you had grown up a spoiled rich kid whose every whim was indulged."

Smiling, Gabriel shook his head. "Not so. I had my share of being grounded. I preferred Dad grounding me rather than my mother. After a few days, Dad would forget why I wasn't allowed to hang out with my friends or go to the mall. Not so with Serena Cole. What she would do is dredge up old infractions to add on to the sentence. Alex and I called her 'the warden' behind her back. It wasn't until I was a teenager that I asked Dad why he would sometimes salute Mom. He confided that he'd once called her 'the little general,' and paid for it by having to sleep in the guest wing for a week. I wasn't sexually active at the time, but I knew exactly what he was referring to. He said they eventually made up, and nine months later, Ana and Jason were born."

A wide grin crinkled the skin around Summer's eyes. "I suppose they'll never forget that reconciliation."

"You're right about that. My parents wanted four children, but hadn't planned on having twins. Alex came along four years after me, and Jason and Ana five years after Alex."

"They waited a long time in between births."

"That was my mother's decision. She said she wanted to avoid sibling jealousy whenever a new baby arrived."

"It sounds like you had a lot of fun growing up in a big family."

Gabriel shrugged a shoulder. "I know if having four children is a what you would call a big family."

"Nowadays it is."

"I'd say anything over six is big."

"That's a basketball team."

He went completely still. "You like basketball?"

"Does a cat lick its whiskers?"

Gabriel's smile was dazzling. "Will you go with me to a few games?"

"Which teams?"

"Celtics and Knicks."

"Do you have tickets?"

"I can always get tickets."

Summer glared at him under lowered eyebrows. "From scalpers?"

Gabriel stuck his tongue out at her, and she offered

him a wide grin. "I happen to have some juice in certain venues, Miss Montgomery," he teased.

"If that's the case, then count me in. But it has to be on the up-and-up." She could not afford to become involved in something that was outside the law.

Gabriel wanted to tell Summer that he did not have to resort to illegalities to get what he wanted because of his net worth. Whatever he wanted could be accomplished by a single telephone call.

They sat down to eat breakfast, and neither could remember the last time they'd shared a more pleasant dining experience. The meal was exceptional and their partner incomparable.

Summer lay on her belly on a blanket on the beach with Gabriel, enjoying the warmth of the sun on her bare shoulders. They'd cleaned the kitchen, then spread a blanket out on the beach to brainstorm their plans for the spring concert. Rolling over onto her side, she stared at him staring back at her.

"What do you think of using a timeline?"

Resting his head on a folded arm, Gabriel's gaze dropped to her mouth. "In what way?"

"We begin with the origin of music. And because we know the drum and voice were the first instruments, we can use ancient rhythms. Then we can simulate string instruments like a lute or lyre, tambourine, horns, and bells until we get to the forerunner of the piano."

Reaching over with his left hand, Gabriel brushed several strands of hair that had escaped the single braid away from her cheek. Summer's hand moved quicker than his eye could follow, grasping his wrist in a strong grip. His gaze widened. Her reflexes were incredibly fast, and her fingers much stronger than they appeared.

"Don't," she said quietly, pulling his hand away from her face. "You're distracting me." She released his hand.

It was Gabriel's turn to move quickly as he shifted, straddling her. "That's because you're distracting me."

Summer knew it was useless to try and push him off her without inflicting pain, so she suffered the crush of his body pressing down on hers. She felt every muscle in his body as her softer curves melded against his length.

She studied the lean dark-skinned face inches from her own. The warmth of him swept over her like a protective blanket. "What do you want?"

Long, thick black lashes lowered, concealing the golden orbs as he stared at her parted lips. "It's not what, Summer."

"Then who?" she whispered.

He smiled the lopsided smile she found so attractive. "I'm surprised you have to ask."

Despite her reluctance, she returned his smile. "But, I have to ask, Gabriel."

"Do you really want to know the answer?"

"Yes, I do," she said, continuing to play his game.

He lifted an eyebrow. "You, Summer Montgomery."

His admission made her insides throb with an excitement she had never felt before. "How? Why?"

Gabriel increased the pressure of his groin against her middle, permitting her to feel his swollen flesh. "This is how. Why—I don't know."

Anchoring the heel of her hand under his chin, she pushed up, snapping his head back. Seconds later, he lay on the blanket staring up at her. Summer knew she hadn't hurt him as much as she had stunned him. "I'll accept the how, but whenever you find out the why, let me know. Until that time, don't touch me."

Gabriel sprang up, eyes flashing fire as he wrestled her down to the blanket. Her knees were sandwiched in between his, her wrists imprisoned in his stronger grip.

Burying his face between her neck and shoulder, he pressed his mouth to her ear. "I like you, Summer. A lot," he growled.

Everything about Gabriel was a turn-on: his body, voice, smell, and his sensuality that she felt seeping into her veins like a blood transfusion. She could not deny the excitement of him wanting to sleep with her. But there was no way she would make it easy for him, because it had never been easy for any man to get her into his bed.

"I'm not one of your groupies."

"I don't do groupies," he countered.

"And I don't do one-night stands."

"Neither do I," he said, breathing heavily in her ear.

Gabriel knew if he did not get off Summer he would embarrass himself. The hardness pulsing between his thighs threatened to explode, and what he wanted was to take the woman under him to another dimension with him once he released his passions inside her fragrant body.

Closing her eyes, Summer shook her head. "No, Gabriel."

"No, what?"

"I can't. Not now. It's too soon."

He released her wrists and rolled off her body. Lying on his back, he threw an arm over his eyes and waited for his traitorous body to return to a flaccid state. He cursed himself. He had practically forced himself on Summer.

"I'm sorry." The apology had come from deep within him.

Summer saw his tortured expression, and her heart turned over. She resisted the urge to touch him. "There's nothing to be sorry about."

His arm came down and he stared at her with a dumbfounded expression on his handsome face. "You're not angry with me?"

She shook her head, smiling "Pissed, yes. Angry, no."

"Is there a difference?"

"For me, yes. And you really don't want to see me get angry."

Gabriel managed a half-smile. "I'll try and remember that."

Extending her hand, Summer smiled. "Let's walk and talk. I think that's a lot safer right now than sharing a blanket."

He took her hand, stood up, then pulled her gently to her feet. Holding hands, they walked the beach, each lost in their private thoughts.

Eight

It was during the return walk that they talked about the concert. "What about costumes?" Gabriel asked. "How authentic do you want them to be?"

"As authentic as possible. We can always rent them from a store in Boston that specializes in costuming. But first I have to check and see how much money is left in the grant. The head of the business office told me that replacing old and broken instruments has used up more than half the grant's funding."

"Don't worry about the money, Summer."

She gave him a sidelong glance. "Don't worry?"

"I'll take care of the overruns."

She stopped. "Are you saying you're going to pay for it out of your own pocket?"

"It's only money, Summer. It's not much use to me unless I spend it."

"That's easy for you to say."

His jaw hardened when he registered her sarcasm. "It's easy because I have it. What have I done with my money? I've purchased property for the first time in my life," he said, answering his own question. "And I've bought a car for the second time in more than a decade. I don't pay for trips because I use my family's private jet. I'm not into jewelry, so I don't own any bling-bling. The same goes for designer clothes. Give me a pair of jeans, a T-shirt, and an old pair of running shoes and I'm as happy as a pig in slop.

"I don't have a wife or children to support or educate, so I don't have to share what I've earned or inherited with them. Despite what you may have heard or read about me, I'm just an ordinary guy who by accident of birth was born into a wealthy family."

Gabriel noticed a momentary look of discomfort cross her face, knowing he had hit a sore spot with Summer because she had accused him of being a snob. He decided to press his attack. "Do you need some money for a personal cause? It's quite easy for me to go into the house and sign a check for you. All you have to do is fill in the payee and the amount."

Summer felt as if she had been backhanded. "You've this arrogant thing going on that you need to address."

"I don't know how you define arrogance."

Rising on tiptoe, she thrust her face close enough for her to feel his breath feather over her mouth. "Haughty, supercilious and condescending. I'm willing to bet there's not one iota of humility in you."

Crossing his arms over his chest, Gabriel smiled. "Oh, now you want to make a wager?"

Affecting a similar pose, she angled her head. "Yes."

"What are you willing to wager? But, let me warn you that if you run with the big dogs, then you'll have play by big dog rules."

"Get real," she drawled, rolling her head on her neck. "You a big dog?"

Gabriel emitted a low growl, then barked loudly in her face, forcing her to take a step back. "Ye-ahh! And I'm the biggest of the *dawgs!*"

Recovering quickly, she retorted, "Then, let's rock and roll, big *dawg*. What do you intend to wager?"

"If you lose, then you'll have to spend a weekend with me. And I get to pick where."

Her gaze narrowed. "To do what?"

"Anything I want to do."

Summer threw up a hand. "Oh, hell no! Do I have STUPID written across my forehead?"

Leaning in closer, Gabriel squinted at her forehead. "No," he teased, biting back a smile. "But I thought you told me you could hang."

"I can."

"Then accept my wager."

"Not before you hear mine."

He nodded. "Let's hear it."

"The grant has set aside monies for two full college scholarships. I want you to match that."

"Okay," he said without hesitating.

Summer knew she had walked into a trap of her own making the moment he'd agreed to underwrite the cost of the scholarships. She had set the trap, but Gabriel had sprung it.

She offered him her hand. "You're on."

He shook her hand, then began dancing, his shoulders and hips moving to a silent sensual beat. Summer stared at his gyrations, admiring the fluidity in his hips. He pulled her to his chest and swung her around and around. She followed his strong lead as he hummed a song with a distinctive Latin beat. Curving her left arm around his neck, Summer laid her head on his shoulder as their bodies swayed to a sensual beat with no words.

"How would you like to go dancing tonight?" he said close to her ear.

"I'd like that very much." And she wanted to go, because it had been a long time—too long since she had danced with a man as Summer Montgomery.

Summer spent the remainder of the morning and early afternoon on the deck outside her bedroom, writing in a small notebook. When tiring, she lay on her side, and fell asleep.

She wasn't certain how long she had slept, but when she opened her eyes she found Gabriel sitting on a matching lounger less than three feet away, writing. He had exchanged his white T-shirt for a black tank top. A profusion of thick black chest hair spilled over the neckline of the tank top. And it wasn't until after she had swallowed to relieve the dryness in her mouth that she realized not only had she been staring at him, but gaping as well. A slight breeze stirred tendrils of hair around his sun-browned face, but it appeared that he hadn't noticed. He was thoroughly engrossed in his task. He completed the page, ripped it off the pad, and tucked it under his thigh with a stack of others.

Observing him through lowered lids, Summer saw things about Gabriel she hadn't noticed: the length of his eyelashes, the sexy sweep of his raven-black eyebrows, the arrogant slant of high cheekbones under brown skin that called to mind an Inca or Mayan warrior. It was in that instant she realized that he had a right to be arrogant because he truly was beautiful—beautiful and talented.

"Are you getting up, or are you going to lie there and glare at me."

Summer sprang up. "I wasn't glaring at you."

Gabriel's head came up. "Then what were you doing?"

She met his shimmering golden gaze. "Staring."

He lifted an eyebrow. "Do you like what you see?"

Her jaw dropped. "Why, you—"

"Arrogant pig," Gabriel said, completing her statement. Putting aside the pad, he swung his legs over the lounger. "Give it a rest, beautiful."

Closing the distance between them, he sat down and pulled her effortlessly up and over to sit between his legs. His chest was pressed against her back. Leaning forward, he pressed a kiss on the nape of her neck.

"Stop that, Gabriel." Her voice was a breathless whisper.

He chuckled. "You don't sound too convincing, Summer. Are you sure you want me to stop?"

Closing her eyes, she swallowed back a moan. "Yes."

Curving an arm around her waist, he held her. "You're still not a very good liar."

"How can you tell?"

He smiled, the index and middle finger of his right hand pressed against the side of her neck. "Your pulse is accelerated."

It was her turn to smile. "Thanks for the diagnosis Dr. Cole."

"You've got the wrong Cole. My cousin Tyler is Dr. Cole."

Relaxing against his chest, Summer smiled at Gabriel over her shoulder. "What's his specialty?"

"Obstetrics and gynecology. And your parents?"

"Father is an OB-GYN and Mother is a pediatrician."

"We have a lot more in common than music."

"What's that?"

"I have another cousin who plans to become a pediatrician like his father."

"But aren't the Coles known for their business ventures?"

Gabriel nodded. "It started with my grandfather. He set up a corporation he called ColeDiz International Ltd., and began growing soybeans. Grandpa expanded his produce enterprise when he set up coffee and bananas in Mexico, Costa Rica, Jamaica, Belize and Puerto Rico. He took the profits from these ventures, bought large tracts of land throughout the Caribbean and Central America and built private villas and vacation resorts."

Summer digested this information. Because ColeDiz was privately owned, the extent of their wealth was known to only a few. "Are you involved in the family business?"

"No. Aunt Nancy's oldest son, Timothy Cole-Thomas has taken over as president. My father and uncles are involved as board members. They are not involved in the day-to-day operation of ColeDiz, but have retained voting privileges." Lowering his head, he inhaled the fragrance of coconut clinging to her hair.

It sounds like you had a lot of fun growing up in a big family. Gabriel recalled Summer's words as clearly as she had just spoken them. And he had grown up with sisters, a brother and several generations of cousins that were too numerous to count. Now, with Alexandra's pregnancy, he would become an uncle for the first time, while Summer would never be able to claim the privilege of being an aunt. She was estranged from her parents, and was now an only child.

"How would like to meet my family?" The question was out before he could censure himself.

She stiffened, then relaxed. "When?"

"My sister is getting married, and I'd like for you to attend the wedding with me."

"When?" she repeated.

"Probably sometime next month."

"She hasn't set a date?"

Gabriel shook his head. "No."

"How long as she been engaged?" Summer asked, continuing her questioning.

"A couple of days."

Shifting, Summer draped her legs over Gabriel's, and stared at him as if she had never seen him before. "A couple of days?"

"I think the Coles hold the record for short engagements. We've been known to plan a wedding in a weekend." He successfully curbed his urge to laugh when he saw an expression of astonishment freeze her features. "Please come with me, Summer."

"I'll think about it."

He pulled the braid resting on her shoulder. "I thought you told me you could hang?"

"I can."

He shook his head slowly. "No, you can't. If you're not careful, you're going to lose our little wager."

"If I go with you will it fulfill my spending the weekend with you?"

"Oh, *hell* no," Gabriel drawled. "Our weekend is just you and me, one-on-one."

Summer rolled her eyes at him. "Not only are you arrogant, but also manipulative."

Throwing back his head, he laughed. "What do you expect, beautiful? After all, I'm a Cole."

Summer scrambled off the lounger, berating herself for being drawn into a game she really did not want to play. Why, she asked herself, was she so adept at being

Renegade, but found herself inept when it came to dealing with the brilliant musician.

There was no doubt that not only had she fallen into his trap, but also under his sensual spell that reminded her that she was still a woman—a woman with needs. His presence had awakened a hunger in her she did not know she had. A hunger she had refused to acknowledge.

Hands on her hips, she stared down at him. "What time are we going dancing?"

He gave her a direct stare. "That all depends on you."

"Why me?"

Gabriel moved off the lounge chair. The shifting sun was behind Summer, bathing her in a halo of gold. "Would like to go to a place with dining and dancing, or eat at one place and dance at another?"

Wrinkling her pert nose, Summer smiled up at him through her lashes, causing him to hold his breath. "You're giving me a choice?"

His expression was impassive. "With me, you will always have a choice. It will not be my way or no way."

"You're right about that, Gabriel," she said in a quiet voice, "because it would never be all *your* way. And to answer your question, I prefer dining and dancing at separate venues."

He measured her with a cool appraising look before he glanced at the watch strapped to his left wrist. "Can you be ready in two hours?"

"Yes. Where are we going?"

"Boston."

That said, Gabriel turned and walked into her bedroom, leaving Summer to stare at the space where he'd been. She was standing in the same spot when he returned without warning and picked up the many sheets of music he had been working on.

"Two hours, Summer," he warned softly as he turned and retraced his steps.

"I'll be ready," she called out to his departing figure.

And she could get ready within two hours. However, she had to decide on what she would wear. When she packed her weekender she hadn't planned on going anywhere fancy with Gabriel. She'd brought one dress, just in case they would eat at a restaurant on the Cape.

Shrugging her shoulders, she decided to wear the dress.

Nine

Summer was sitting on a cushioned rocker when Gabriel stepped out onto the porch, dressed completely in black. She smiled. It was apparent they were partial to the color.

Gabriel caught the scent of Summer's perfume and turned to find her sitting on the rocking chair. Waning light from the setting sun provided enough illumination for him to see the outline of her long shapely legs in a pair of sheer black hose and high heel suede pumps.

Moving closer, he extended his hand. She grasped his fingers and he eased her up. Releasing her hand, he opened her raincoat to survey what lay beneath. His mouth curved into an approving smile when he saw what would've been a simple black dress on another woman, but on Summer it was sexy and provocative. The off-the-shoulder knit garment hugged her curvy body, accentuating the fullness of her breasts, narrow waist, and flat belly. It clung to slim, tight thighs before ending at her knees.

"Do I pass inspection?"

Gabriel ignored her sarcasm. "You are exquisite, perfect. I'm honored to have you at my side tonight."

Heat rose in her cheeks with the compliment. And because she did not want to spoil the moment or the evening, she decided not to remind him that she wasn't someone who sought to enhance his superstar image by becoming an accessory or a trophy for him to show off.

Her admiring gaze swept over his banded collar shirt, silk brocade vest, and wool crepe jacket and slacks. "I hope I don't have to kick some butt tonight if a hoochie mama decides to rub up on my man," she quipped lightly.

He lifted his sweeping eyebrows. "Am I really your man, Summer?"

She winked at him. "You are tonight."

Chuckling softly, he pulled her hand into the crook of his elbow and led her off the porch and around the house to the garage. Gabriel helped her into the low-slung car, then rounded it and took his seat behind the wheel. He started it up and backed out of the driveway. Pushing a button on the dashboard, the car's interior was filled with the sound of Jon Secada's voice singing the dance version of "Too Late, Too Soon." Relaxing on the leather seat, Summer listened as Gabriel sang along. She found herself tapping her foot in tempo with the upbeat tune.

She found Gabriel's voice low and drawling with Southern inflections, but when he sang, his range shifted flawlessly from baritone to tenor. Listening intently, she realized he had perfect pitch.

Gabriel gave Summer a sidelong glance, smiling. "Would you like to hear it from the beginning?"

She returned his smile. "Yes." He pressed a button to repeat the disc.

"You like Secada, don't you?"

"I think he's an incredible talent. He writes and sings all the vocals on most of his recordings. His work, unlike a lot of recording artists, is eclectic. He can sing in English with the same passion as he does in Spanish. He's also versatile enough to sing ballads and dance music. However, I'm partial to this CD because of his collaboration with Terry Lewis and Jimmy Jam."

"What's the name of this CD?"

"Secada."

"That's it?"

"Yes."

Summer closed her eyes listening as Gabriel harmonized with the talented singer. She jumped and then froze, when she felt Gabriel's fingers graze her left thigh. She opened her eyes, staring at him when he stopped at a traffic light. It was then she understood why he had touched her. He sang "Ready for Love" with so much conviction that she actually believed him.

It had gone beyond him singing along with the compact disc. The passion radiating from Gabriel was so tangible, Summer could feel it. Their gazes met and fused when he crooned softly, "I don't wanna stop. I don't really wanna stop this. I feel fine—ready for love."

"No," she whispered. The word had just slipped out.

His hold on her thigh tightened. "Yes, Summer."

She shook her head. "No!"

He leaned closer. "Yes!"

The debate ended when the driver in a car behind them leaned on the horn. Gabriel removed his hand, shifted into gear, and the Porsche took off with a powerful burst of speed.

"Why are you fighting what is so obvious?" he asked after several minutes.

Turning her head, Summer stared out the passenger side window. "What's obvious to you isn't obvious to me."

"¡Mentirosa!"

Summer turned and glared at him, unblinking. "This is the first and last time I'm going to permit you to call me a liar." Her voice was low, threatening, and those familiar with Renegade knew she was close to losing control.

Turning the wheel sharply to the right, Gabriel pulled up alongside a curb and put the car in PARK. His fingers tightened in a deathlike grip on the leather-wrapped steering wheel. This was the second time within twenty-four hours wherein he had lost control, and both times it was with Summer.

He'd grown up hearing family members calling him reclusive and moody. Even the members in his band had learned to gauge his moods by his body language. Whenever he was in a funk they avoided him. However, they tolerated his irritability because of the music. And for Gabriel it had always been the music. He had sacrificed love and permanent companionship because of his music.

But within the past two years, he had changed. The music was still important, but it was no longer a priority. Interning at a Miami middle school had permitted him to open up to others as Gabriel Cole the person rather than Gabriel Cole the award-winning musician. He would linger beyond the dismissal bell to tutor struggling students, had paid to replace another student's stolen trumpet, and genuinely enjoyed talking to parents about their children's musical talent. He had waited more than thirty years to give of himself, and since meeting Summer, he wanted to give her what he had never given another woman—his love. And like the Secada song, he was ready for love.

He'd laughed at his sister because Alexandra had fallen in love, while it had taken him a little more than two weeks to find himself in a similar situation.

Feathering the back of his hand over the hair she had pulled into a chignon on the nape of her neck, Gabriel leaned to his right and pressed his mouth to her ear. "Will you forgive me?"

Crossing her arms under her breasts, Summer stared straight ahead. "I told you before, Gabriel, it's not going to work. We're too different in temperament to get along for more than an hour without being at each other's throat."

He pulled back. "You're right, Summer. It's not going to work."

Surprised that he had conceded so easily, she looked at him. "What do you want to do?"

Gabriel could not tell her what he actually wanted to do with her. That he wanted to lie in her scented embrace just once to assuage what he had come to recognize as a craving for her.

"I did promise you dinner and dancing. After that, we'll go back to Cotuit. Tomorrow morning, I'll take you back home."

She nodded numbly before averting her gaze. His voice was absolutely emotionless and it chilled her. The muscles in her stomach tightened. It was over even before it had begun.

Why, she mused, was she so adept at pushing away men who'd expressed an interest in her? Why, she thought, when it would be so easy to become involved with Gabriel. It wasn't as if she wasn't attracted to him because she was. There was nothing about him she found repulsive. It was true that he was arrogant, but then that was part and parcel of his superstar persona.

Don't be a fool and lose him, an inner voice told her, followed by Lucas's taunt of *stay focused.* Why, she thought, couldn't she have both? Why couldn't she have a relationship with Gabriel *and* bring down the dealers at Weir? It didn't have to be mission or love when it could be mission *and* love.

Within seconds she made a decision she knew would change her and her life forever.

Gabriel placed his hand in the small of Summer's back as they followed the maître d' to the table in a secluded corner of a carriage house turned restaurant near Boston's fashionable Beacon Hill.

The maître d' seated her, smiling. "Your server will be with you momentarily." He nodded to Gabriel. *"Bon appetit,* Monsieur Cole. Mademoiselle."

"Merci," Gabriel replied in French.

The flickering candle on the table cast long and short shadows across Gabriel's lean face as Summer stared at him. "You speak French, too?"

He smiled, flashing the deep dimples in his cheeks. His teeth were a startling white in contrast to the mustache framing his upper lip. "Only enough to order a room or food."

"Have you done a lot of traveling?"

His lids lowered as he stared at the candle. "Unfortunately, yes."

"You didn't enjoy it?"

He glanced up, his gaze meeting and fusing with hers. "No. I prefer being stateside." He lifted an eyebrow when he noticed a slight smile soften Summer's lush mouth. "What's so amusing?"

She flashed a demure smile. "Us."

Gabriel's expression did not change. "What about us?"

"We're like oil and water."

"Are you saying we don't mix?"

"Not unless we're blended."

Leaning forward, Gabriel reached across the table to capture her hands. "That's not possible because you keep throwing up roadblocks. It has nothing to do with vanity or arrogance when I say I know that we are attracted to each other. And that's more than enough for me to want to see you outside of Weir."

"You want a relationship." The question had come out like a statement.

"I want whatever it is you are willing to give me." Gabriel chuckled when her mouth formed a perfect O. "Are you shocked by my candor?"

"A little."

"Well, Summer? What's it going to be? Are we going to become a couple?"

It was her turn to laugh. "Now we're a couple?"

He nodded. "You did say that I was your man tonight."

"Yes, I did."

"If I'm your man, then it goes without say that you must be my woman."

A full minute elapsed before Summer spoke again. "Yes, Gabriel," she said softly, "you can say that I'm your woman."

"You can't be my woman for one night, because I don't do one-night stands."

He had given her back her statement. "Touché, Gabriel."

A powerful relief filled Summer as she concentrated on the menu in front of her. It was printed in French. Even with her head lowered she still could feel the heat of the golden orbs studying her.

Her commitment to date Gabriel had nothing to do with her mission to expose the high school drug ring. And she had no doubt that she would identify those responsible for dealing at Weir. She would give Lucas Shelby his drug dealers, while attempting to grasp her own happiness.

Her head came up and she stared at Gabriel. She did not know where her involvement with him would lead, but she was certain when her tenure at Weir ended neither would be the same.

A white-jacketed waiter approached the table. His gaze darted from Summer to Gabriel. "Monsieur Cole, may I impose upon you to grant a small favor?"

A frown furrowed Gabriel's smooth forehead. "What is it?"

"Monsieur, a lady recognized you when you came in. She asked me if I would ask you to give her an autograph for her children."

Gabriel's frown vanished quickly. "Please tell her that I'm dining, and that I'm willing to give her an autograph if she's willing to wait until I'm finished."

"*Merci,* Monsieur. I will inform her. Meanwhile, would you like to see our wine list?"

Gabriel winked at Summer. "Will you share a bottle with me?"

"Yes."

"Please bring the list," he said to the waiter.

Waiting until the waiter was out of earshot, Summer said, "How often does this happen?"

"Not as often now as in the past."

"You could've signed the autograph now. Why make her wait?"

"She's imposing on my time with you. That is not acceptable. If she wants an autograph, then she *will* wait."

His tone though soft held a thread of steel. It was the second time Summer heard the drawling voice take on a cold edge. The other time was when he had confronted the photographer.

How, she asked herself, had she missed it? Gabriel Cole was more than the image he had cultivated as a laid-back musician. Instinctively, she knew he could become a formidable opponent when crossed.

Summer still felt the effects from two glasses of champagne as Gabriel escorted her into a dance club amid the glares from those lining up behind roped-off stanchions.

The adage that fame has its privileges was apparent when he approached the man standing at the door to the popular club. Within seconds they were led into a large space pulsing with ear-shattering music and flashing lights. Taking off the jacket Gabriel had placed over her shoulders, she handed it to him. During the drive from the restaurant to the club, she had decided to leave her raincoat in the car.

Gabriel slipped into his jacket, then reached for Summer's hand and led her toward the dance floor. Pulling her to his chest, he twirled her around in an intricate dance step.

She melted into his strength, her body pliant and yielding as they were molded as one from chest to thigh. She gloried in the silkiness of the hair on his upper lip grazing her ear, the scent of his woodsy cologne in her nose, the power in the solid muscles in his back as her arms curved under his shoulders. Tightening her hold, she pressed closer. She felt safe; she was safe.

Gabriel was shocked by the sensations shaking him as he held Summer to his heart. He had always protected his sisters, but this was the first time he had felt the need to protect a female with whom he did not share blood.

He wanted Summer! Not only to share her bed or her future, but to assume total responsibility for her.

He had laughed and scoffed at his cousins when they'd professed to falling in love with their future wives on sight; however the laugh was now on him because what he felt for Summer was nothing like what he had ever felt for any other woman.

It was the first time he'd eaten dinner and drank champagne with a woman without exchanging a word with her. Neither had felt the need to initiate conversation because it was unnecessary. They'd found a way to communicate silently. They had come from a quiet, relaxing venue to one pulsing with music and energy, and suddenly Gabriel wanted to be anywhere but at the club.

He longed to retreat to Cotuit and the solitude of his beachfront home. He wanted to sit on the porch with Summer and listen to the sound of the waves washing up on the beach. The song ended and they eased back slightly, staring at each other.

Rising on tiptoe, Summer pressed her cheek to Gabriel's clean-shaven one. "Let's get out of here."

He stared at her, complete surprise on his face. She had read his thoughts. "Come."

Elbowing his way through a crowd standing three-deep at a massive bar, Gabriel came face to face with a woman who had once dated several members of his band—at the same time. He tried to step around her, but she looped an arm through his free one, holding him fast.

"Gabe Cole," she crooned seductively. She swayed unsteadily. "Hey, baby. What are you doing in Bean Town?"

He stared down at her. "Hello, Stacy."

Her mouth turned down in a seductive pout. "You didn't answer my question, handsome."

"I'm visiting."

Stacy pointed at Summer. "Visiting *that?*"

Summer glared at the petite, redheaded woman, then looked up at a scowling Gabriel. "Can we please leave now, darling?"

Gabriel winked at her. "Of course, sweetheart." He offered Stacy a plastic smile. "Please let go of my arm."

Stacy dropped his arm as if it were a venomous reptile. "You ain't that hot, Gabriel Cole!" she shouted to his back as he steered Summer toward an exit door. Several people turned to stare at them before they disappeared through the door and into the night.

Stepping out into the cool autumn night, Summer shivered noticeably. Gabriel removed his jacket and laid it over her shoulders.

"If she hadn't been so drunk, I would've kicked her butt for mauling my man," Summer said deadpan.

A smile crinkled the skin around Gabriel's eyes as he dropped an arm over her shoulders. "Let's go home, tiger."

Summer wound her arm around his waist, her body pressed against his length, as they walked the three blocks to the garage where Gabriel had parked his car. It wasn't until she was seated and belted-in that a feeling of total relaxation settled over her. Champagne always had that effect on her. She managed to conceal a yawn behind her hand. A minute later, she was asleep.

Gabriel stopped at a traffic light, glancing at his passenger. Her head hung at an odd angle. Pressing a button, he lowered her seat to a reclining position. She moaned softly but did not wake up.

A secret smile curved his mouth when he recalled Summer talking about fighting for him. He did not need a woman to protect him, however, it was reassuring to know she was willing to take care of what belonged to her.

What she did not know was that he would do the same for her.

Summer Montgomery did not know that Gabriel Morris Cole had claimed her—she belonged to him.

Ten

A ripple of excitement had swept over Weir Memorial High with the announcement of the spring musical pageant. Students stood around in small groups in front of the bulletin board where Summer had posted an open audition for actors, actresses, singers and dancers. The lists had filled up quickly, and after two days, there were eighty-four names.

She knew realistically half would be rejected because of an inability to carry a tune, follow choreography, or remember cues. Those who did not make the first cut would be offered the opportunity to work behind the scenes in lighting, wardrobe, and stage handling.

Summer had given herself a week for the auditions. She had reserved the auditorium from the hours of two to five, Monday through Thursday of the following week. A sharp rap on the door garnered her attention. Her head came up and she smiled at the man whose broad shoulders filled out the doorway.

"Is it too late sign up to audition for the spring pageant?"

A sensual smile curved her mouth. "I'm afraid it is."

Gabriel's dimples winked at her. "Can't you make an exception, Miss Montgomery?"

"I'm sorry, Mr. Cole, but the rules state once the sheets are filled, auditions are closed."

Strolling into the office with a pronounced swagger, Gabriel pulled out the chair at his desk and straddled it. Resting his elbows over the back, he angled his head and stared at Summer. It was the first time he'd seen her with her hair loose. It flowed around her shoulders, moving sensuously whenever she moved or tilted her head.

"How many signed up?"

"Eighty-four."

He winced. "Ouch! I didn't know Weir had that much talent."

She wrinkled her nose, charming Gabriel with the gesture. "Only time will tell who has talent."

"Surprisingly, there's a lot of raw talent in this school. Selecting the candidates for the scholarships is not going to be easy."

"Drawing from a pool of seniors narrows the prospects significantly."

Gabriel could not take his gaze off Summer. During the drive from Cotuit to Whitman Sunday afternoon he'd apologized to her for his aggression in coming onto her. He had endured several anxious minutes when he encountered silence from her. Summer finally belied his apprehension saying she would accept the apology, although she did not believe his sincerity. It was only when he noticed a smile playing at the corners of her mouth that he felt that he had been vindicated.

Summer stared at Gabriel through her lashes. She knew she was staring at him like a dumbfounded fan, but it wasn't the first time she had to ask herself why was she drawn to him because he was a musician. Once she realized she was going to pursue a career in theatre she had made it a practice not to date actors, singers, dancers, or musicians. She had wanted to compete on stage, not in a relationship. But that pattern was shattered the first time she shared an offstage kiss with Gabriel.

She had spent most of her life as an actress, playing her part to perfection. It had begun with her parents. There was never a time when she would let them see her cry when they left for their medical missions, and she refused to let anyone see her joy whenever they returned.

The only time anyone saw the real Summer Montgomery was when she held her infant brother for the first time. The love she'd yearned to show her parents she showered on Charles. And the most difficult decision she had ever made in her life was leaving St. Louis for New York to further her career.

She'd arrived in The Big Apple with stars in her eyes and enough enthusiasm to light up Broadway. It had taken her two weeks to land a job with the chorus of an off Broadway musical, and a year later she sang two solos in a limited-run Broadway revival of a montage of Rodgers and Hammerstein's musical productions. Her singing ability caught the eye of a well-known producer who selected her as understudy for his next play without auditioning her.

But her rosy world shattered like the pellets that had ripped open her brother's chest. A little part of her died and was buried the moment Charles's casket was lowered into the earth. It was later, after she had joined the DEA, that she thought she had found a way to resurrect her spirit. The moment she stepped into her role as Renegade she felt alive, pulsing with the energy that went along with the dangerous masquerade.

But on the other hand, what had taken her five years

to perfect was shattered in the three weeks since she had come face-to-face with Gabriel Cole. She believed there was a mysterious, hypnotic force in the large golden eyes that had the ability to see beyond her perfect performance to see the real Summer Montgomery. Not the Summer who had become Weir's drama teacher, but the Summer who wanted to fall in love, marry and have children, the Summer who lived in fear that she would be exposed as a federal drug agent, the one who had recurring nightmares that her life would end in a hail of bullets.

Spending the weekend with Gabriel had offered her a glimpse of normalcy for the first time in her life. The mundane tasks, like sharing in the preparation of breakfast with him had become a special event. Even sitting in the tiny French restaurant for several hours and not having to open her mouth to communicate with him was an experience she would cherish forever.

And what she had shared with Gabriel this past weekend she wanted again and again—for a long time, if not forever.

Her lashes swept up, and she smiled at him. "Are you doing anything tonight?"

Gabriel was shocked at the query, but recovered quickly. "No. Why?"

"I thought I'd cook for you tonight. Is there anything you don't eat?"

His eyes roamed over her face and upper body. "No. I eat everything."

Summer felt the heat in her face when she registered his double meaning. "So do I," she said softly.

Gabriel's smile was dazzling. "Good. What time is dinner?"

"Is five too early?"

"No. I'll make certain not to eat too much for lunch." The bell rang, and he stood up. "Is there anything you'd like for me to bring?"

She shook her head. "No. Just yourself."

He winked at her. "I'll see you later."

"Okay," she whispered.

Summer watched Gabriel walk out of the office, knowing she had just turned a corner in her life. Her role as Renegade would end in less than ten months and what she was now preparing for was the role that had evaded her for most of her adult life: a woman who had found herself falling in love for the first time.

Loud voices, laughter, and a shrill feminine voice telling someone to leave her alone greeted Gabriel as he walked into the music room. Two boys had trapped a girl in a corner. He slammed the door, rattling windows, and within seconds there was complete silence.

All eyes were trained on the tall man with the long ponytail. Only a few of the students knew who Gabriel Cole the musician was, but it had only taken one day for them to become familiar with his teaching methods.

"What's going on here?" Lakeisha Hudson scooted to her chair in the violin section, while the boys who had been teasing her sat down with the others who played trombones and saxophones.

Walking to the front of the room, Gabriel gave each student a measured, penetrating stare. "I want you to understand right here, right now that this is not the schoolyard or the gym. What I just witnessed will not be tolerated."

"Oh, lighten up, Mr. Cole," a trumpet player hissed.

"Light your butt outta here, Glenn," Gabriel countered quickly. "Go sit in Mr. Gellis's office for the period."

Walking over to a wall phone, he punched in the extension for the assistant principal's office. When the secretary answered, he said, "This is Mr. Cole. I'm sending Glenn Peterson to see you for the period." He turned back to Glenn, who hadn't moved. Crossing his arms over his chest, he said quietly, "Out."

The single word got Glenn's attention immediately, along with the others in the room. The students liked their new music teacher because he had inspired them to reach beyond what they'd been taught. Most of them had learned to play an instrument while still in grade school, and although only a few were serious music students, they enjoyed performing together. Once Gabriel had announced he wanted to form a jazz band from those students in the orchestra the enthusiasm to excel was apparent.

Of all the students in the orchestra, six foot, six-inch Glenn "Tree" Peterson had exhibited the most talent. Gabriel had concluded the straight A student's musical aptitude was comparable to legendary trumpeters Louis Armstrong and Miles Davis. Tree, as most students referred to him, was point guard for Weir's basketball team, averaging twenty points each game. As a senior, Tree had to decide whether he wanted a career as a musician or one in the NBA.

The door closed behind the gangling student. Gabriel rested his elbows on the wooden podium and smiled. The tension in the room dissipated with his expression.

"Before we begin practicing this morning, I'd like to talk to you about the musical pageant scheduled for the spring. How many of you signed up to audition?" Four hands went up. "Forget it!" The students laughed. "I need you here creating music, not singing and dancing.

"The drama teacher, Miss Montgomery, is in the process of putting together a production depicting the evolution of song and dance in the Americas. I say Americas because it will cover not only the United States, but also South and Central Americas. And as musicians, it's up to us to provide the music."

A cellist raised her hand. "What kind of music, Mr. Cole?"

"Everything from Native American drumming to Ragtime, jazz, rock and roll, Country and up to and including hip-hop." A loud cheer went up in the room. Gabriel didn't think he would ever get used to their enthusiasm. "This means we're going to have to work very hard to make it a rousing success. There's going to be something for everyone: your grandparents, parents and your peers."

Howard Slavin raised his hand. Gabriel had been working with the sax player after classes ended, and the extra tutoring had paid off. Howard was now confident to perform enough in front of the others.

"When do we start practicing for the spring pageant?"

"After the Christmas recess. Remember, we still have the Christmas musical to do first."

"If that's the case, then let's kick it, Mr. Cole."

Gabriel cut his eyes at Lakeisha, successfully hiding a grin. Petite, and very cute, Lakeisha had perfected flirting until it had become an art with her. It hadn't surprised him that the boys were teasing her, because he suspected she had been teasing them. Teasing among young children was usually harmless, but in the hands of adolescent boys and girls, it was dangerous and volatile.

Picking up a baton on the podium, he tapped it rhythmically against a corner. Glancing to his right, he nodded to the violinists. "Key of A minor." Closing his eyes, he listened intently as they went through their scales.

The doorbell from downstairs chimed throughout the apartment, and Summer took a sweeping glance at everything in the living/dining area, then walked over to the door.

Picking up the receiver on the wall, she said, "Yes?"

"Gabriel," came the drawling reply.

She replaced the receiver and pushed a button, disengaging the lock on the door leading to the street. She unlocked her apartment door, leaving it ajar as she returned to the small utility kitchen.

Two minutes later she felt the warmth of a body behind her. Glancing up over her shoulder, she met Gabriel's intense stare.

"It's not safe to leave your door open."

"Why's that?"

"You never know who might just walk in."

"Like you?"

He lifted his eyebrows, smiling. "Yes. Like me."

She tried turning around, but couldn't. Gabriel was too close. "Let me go." Her voice was barely a whisper.

Gabriel stared at the hair she had swept up in a ponytail. Reaching up, he removed the elastic band,

and a wealth of thick raven strands floated down around her neck and over her shoulders.

"I like it down," he said against the nape of her neck.

She smiled. "You like lots of hair."

"No, Summer. I like you. I'd like you even if you shaved your head."

She wanted to tell Gabriel the long hair had become a part of her undercover role whenever she had pretended to be younger than she actually was. But the long hair would soon become a part of her past when she resigned from the DEA. Her plans included changing her appearance and taking her grandmother with her on a month-long cruise around the world.

"How long has it been since you've had short hair?"

Gabriel moved back, and Summer turned to face him. "Almost four years."

"It must grow quickly."

"It does," he confirmed. "Both my parents have a lot of hair."

Summer stared at him staring down at her. He was so still, only the rising and falling of his chest indicating he was alive. Her gaze caressed the high cheekbones, the sweep of lashes brushing those cheekbones, the straight nose with the narrow bridge, and the sensual mouth that she yearned to taste and caress with her own. She lowered her gaze, certain Gabriel would be able to read the hunger radiating in the dark pools.

"Are you hungry?"

Gabriel smiled. "Starved."

Her smile matched his. "Good."

"I brought something. I left it in the living room."

"You didn't have to bring anything, Gabriel."

He ran his forefinger down her cheek. Lowering his

head, he said, "Yes, I did, because I was raised never to go to a person's home empty-handed."

"Well, I was raised the same way. But I didn't bring you anything when I went to your house last weekend."

"Yes, you did, Summer. You brought yourself." Cupping the back of her head in his hand, he brushed his mouth over hers, leaving it burning.

Placing a hand on the middle of his chest, she eased him back. "Let's go eat, Gabriel."

Bright sunlight coming through patio doors bathed the dining area in a warm glow. Summer had set the table with colorfully patterned dinnerware she had purchased from Pier I. Most of the furnishings were compliments of the store. The check she had received from the government was just enough for her to purchase accessories for the furnished apartment to make it looked lived-in. If she had wanted to purchase Waterford stemware or Lenox china, then those would come from her own resources.

The furniture, purchased before she had moved in, was serviceable with oak finishes; twin love seats were covered with white Haitian cotton, and the colors of white and yellow with green accents predominated.

Her apartment was on the second floor of a two-story building, and she had to thank the Department for not having her live in a place where there was the possibility of someone stomping over her head at odd hours.

Walking into the living room, Gabriel picked up a shopping bag and handed it to Summer. She peered into it, smiling. He had brought a bottle of wine, a loaf of Italian bread, and a plastic container filled with cannoli.

"Oh, Gabriel," she crooned, "I think I'm going to keep you around for a long, long time. You brought my favorite dessert."

"I'm glad I'm able to please you."

Rising on tiptoe, she kissed him. "You please me a lot."

Gabriel knew if he didn't put some distance between himself and Summer she would become his dessert. He wanted to sweep the table of the dishes, place Summer on her back and feast on her like a starving man who had been deprived of food for a week.

And it had been a while since he had taken a woman to his bed because of a promise he'd made to himself after he'd ended his last liaison—one that had become based solely on sex. He wanted not only Summer's body, but her heart. He would not accept one without the other.

"Where can I wash my hands?"

She pointed to the short hallway outside her bedroom. "It's to your left."

"I think we're stuck with each other, " Gabriel remarked after he'd swallow a portion of the baked chicken with mustard, tarragon, carrots and leek. "You're an incredible cook."

Summer had warmed the Italian bread and served it with garlic butter and a cup of yellow split pea soup she had flavored with a pinch of toasted cumin seeds.

She took a sip of wine, staring at Gabriel over the rim of her glass. She hadn't lingered in school after the dismissal bell, and had gone to the store to shop for the items she needed for dinner. By four, she had put the chicken in the oven, which left her plenty of time to shower and ready herself for Gabriel's five o'clock arrival.

Putting down his fork, Gabriel listened intently to the music coming from the speakers of a mini-stereo system on a shelf with books, magazines and several plants.

"Nice." The single word was pregnant with emotion. Closing his eyes, he said, "Piano, cello, flute, penny whistle, Healy Irish flute, fretless bass and oboe."

Summer's jaw dropped. "How can you do that?"

Gabriel opened his eyes. "Do what?"

"Hear all those instruments."

He tapped the side of his head. "It's all up here. I've trained myself to listen with my head rather than my ears."

"You're a genius."

"No," he said laughing. "I have studied very hard."

"Modesty doesn't become you, Gabriel."

"Why?" He looked genuinely surprised at her assessment of him.

"It doesn't go along with the image."

"Who created the image, Summer?"

"The media," she said after a noticeable pause.

"Exactly. They make up what they want to believe about a person, not caring whether anyone approves of the myth they've created. My father had his share of the spotlight, and before he was thirty, he was out of it. He enjoyed performing with his band Night Mood, but what he didn't like was working nights and sleeping during the day. The guys in the band nicknamed him Dracula because he refused to go to sleep until he saw the sun come up.

"He never got involved with drugs or slept with women when touring with the band. He had become an enigma, yet the media created their own image of how they saw David Cole."

"And that was?"

"A rich playboy musician who lived hard and loved even harder."

"Is that the reason you're so reclusive?"

He shrugged a shoulder. "Maybe."

Silence descended on them once again, with only the sound of music filling the space, drawing them closer together. It was after seven when Summer brewed cups of espresso to accompany the delicate cannoli.

Gabriel had remained in the living room, examining her small collection of compact discs. Most of them were selections featuring saxophones. He slipped two on the carousel. They were John Tesh's *Sax on the Beach* and *Sax by the Fire*.

Summer returned from the kitchen carrying the cups of espresso. Gabriel closed the distance between them, took the tiny cups from her, and pulled her into the living room.

He eased her to his chest, arms curving around her waist. "You owe me a few more dances."

She knew he was talking about their quick departure from the dance club. Leaning back in his embrace, Summer curved her arms under his shoulders. "I'm sure we'll be given other opportunities to dance together."

"When?" he whispered in her hair.

"When we go away for that weekend."

Gabriel stopped suddenly, causing her to stumble, but he caught her, tightening his hold on her body.

"What happened to our wager? Are you giving up that easily?"

She turned her face into his shoulder, inhaling the seductive scent of the cologne on his shirt. "No. You want to spend a weekend with me, and I want the scholarships. As far as I'm concerned, I'm getting the better of the wager."

Gabriel wanted to tell Summer she was wrong. Both would be winners, because he knew if he spent a weekend with her, then he would want more. And the more would become every weekend of her life.

He kissed her fragrant hair. "If that's the case then I concede defeat."

Her head came up, her gaze narrowing. "What's up, big *dawg?* You gave in too quickly."

He whinnied softly, eliciting a smile from her. "Didn't anyone ever tell you not to look a gift horse in the mouth?"

"Yes," she crooned, "but they never told me I couldn't kiss one."

One moment she was standing, then she found herself lifted off her feet as Gabriel fastened his mouth to hers. She held his head and returned his kiss with reckless abandon.

Her lips parted, inviting his tongue to come and linger a while. She wasn't disappointed when their tongues met and mated. The kiss was like the meeting of two lava beds, smoking and smoldering with a passion that threatened a second eruption.

It was Gabriel, and not Summer, who ended the kiss. He wanted to wait, wait until he took her away with him. He noted her dreamy expression and her slightly swollen mouth. It was an expression he would never forget. If possible, she had become more beautiful, sensual. She was a woman who had been created to be loved.

His fingers tightened around her wrists, bringing her hands down to her sides. "I think I'd better leave while I still can."

"What about dessert?"

Angling his head, he ran the tip of his tongue over her lower lip. "I just sampled it."

Summer stood with her mouth gaping as he picked up his jacket off the love seat and walked to the door. Glancing over his shoulder, he offered her his lopsided grin. "Make certain you lock your door."

She returned his smile. "I will."

The door opened and closed, and he was gone. Summer waited a full minute before walking over to the door to slide the dead bolt into place. She returned to the dining area, picked up the lukewarm cup of espresso and sipped it.

I like him. Her inner voice was talking to her again. *"¡Mentirosa!"* she whispered aloud. And she was a liar, because she knew she didn't like Gabriel. She loved him! The two CDs had finished playing when Summer finally left the table and went to clean up the kitchen.

It was almost eleven when she brushed her teeth and slipped into bed. She was asleep as soon as her head touched the pillow.

Eleven

"Do you know how uncomfortable you make me, Renegade?"

Summer glared at Lucas. "Please, don't call me that."

"All right, Summer. Please order something to eat. I'm stuffing my face while you sit there like someone on a fast."

"You're eating because you can't cook."

Lucas Shelby's blue-green eyes paled. "Order something!"

"Is that a direct order?"

He closed his eyes, while shaking his head. "No, Summer, it's not."

The tense moment ended when she signaled a waitress. "I'd like to have a slice of raisin toast, a cup of decaffeinated coffee, and a small fruit cup." The raisin bread was the only concession she made for the store-bought variety.

"Sorry, miss. I don't know if we have raisin bread."

Summer smiled at the buxom woman who had dyed her hair a bright pumpkin-orange shade. "If you don't have any, then just bring me the fruit and coffee."

Lucas, waiting until the waitress had walked away, said, "Is that all you're going to eat?"

"What's going on, Lucas? Why this sudden interest in my eating habits?" He picked up his mug, sloshing coffee over the rim and spilling some of it on the table. It was then that she noticed his hands were shaking. "Are you all right?"

Nodding, he took a swallow of the steaming black brew. He replaced the cup on a napkin, then ran his right hand over his face. "I'm tired, Renegade. I'm thinking about getting out."

"What!"

He leaned over the table. "I'm retiring next July. I've given my government more than thirty years of my life, and now I want to live my life my way."

"But . . . but you're too young to retire, Lucas."

"*You're* too young, Summer. I'll be sixty in July, and I want out. I've sacrificed getting married and having children because I've been married to my job. Every three years I find myself mentoring more young cocky snot-nosed bastards who think they know everything because they have advanced degrees and computer knowledge. In less than ten years I'll be calling them boss. I've had enough of this bureaucratic bull . . ." His words trailed off when he saw Summer's expression. He flashed a quick smile. "I'm all right. Really."

She reaching out and placed her hand over his. "Why don't you take a thirty-day leave? Just go somewhere and chill out."

"I've seriously considered it."

She let go of his hand. "Do it, Lucas." Her voice was soft, soothing. She stared at the faint scar over his left eyebrow where she had kicked him. Her gaze moved up to his hair. Flecks of gray shimmered in the sandy-brown strands cut into a modified crew cut hairstyle.

"I can't. Not until this one is over."

"Nothing's going to happen over the Christmas recess."

"That's true with Weir. But I'm also supervising a few agents who have managed to infiltrate a group dealing drugs in a housing development near a school and senior citizen complex."

She whistled softly. "No wonder you're tired. Don't you know how to say no?"

He shook his head. "No more than you know how to say no."

She smiled. "Touché, Lucas."

What she wanted to tell her supervisor was that she also planned to retire. She wouldn't remain in long enough to collect a government pension, but she no longer cared. She had options. She could open a dance school, or teach criminal justice.

Perhaps Lucas was right. He had been caught in a time warp. He was good enough to train recruits, yet not savvy enough to understand that wars were not only fought with manpower, but also with sophisticated equipment that required special skills.

Lucas's gaze narrowed as he stared at Summer. He found it odd that he'd always thought of her as a girl. But looking closely at her he realized she was a woman. Somehow she had changed, seemingly grown up in a matter of weeks.

"How's Gabriel Cole?" he asked, taking a wild guess as to who could be responsible for the change in her.

"He's okay." Summer's expression was impassive. None of what she was feeling showed on her face when Lucas had mentioned Gabriel's name.

"Just okay?"

Tilting her chin, she regarded Lucas through lowered lids. "Have you come up with something on him?"

"No."

"Then, why bring up his name?"

"I just want to know if he's responsible for putting the glow in your eyes."

"Is it that obvious?" She'd decided to be direct with Lucas. She knew it was only a matter of time when she would have to tell him that she was going away with Gabriel.

Lucas smiled a warm smile for the first time since their meeting. "Yes, it is. Is it serious?"

Summer shook her head. "No. We're friends."

He wanted to tell her that women who looked like her did not become a friend to a healthy, normal male. But then, he thought, maybe Gabriel Cole wasn't normal. After all, he was a musician, and they were known to lead rather jaded lives.

"What's happening at Weir?" He had changed the topic.

"Not much. I'll be auditioning students in two weeks. Eighty-four have signed up for the spring musical. I'm going to spend this weekend going over their profiles."

"That should take you into early October." His forehead furrowed in concentration. "Why don't we get together again the last weekend in October. If you come up with something before that time, then call me on my cell phone."

Summer nodded, smiling. "What are you doing, Lucas?" What had happened to their bi-weekly meetings?

"I'm trying to give you what I missed."

"And that is?"

"An alternative to spending your life chasing bad guys."

The waitress returned with her order. Meeting Lucas's gaze, Summer smiled and mouthed, "Thank you."

Winking, he mouthed back, "You're welcome."

Summer climbed the steps to the sleek jet sitting on the tarmac at Logan International Airport, its engines revving in preparation for takeoff. She was going to Florida with Gabriel for his sister's wedding. And he was right about the Coles and short engagements. Alexandra Cole had officially announced her engagement one weekend and planned to marry the following weekend at her parents' home in Boca Raton.

When Gabriel asked her to accompany him, she'd encountered a momentary anxiety attack. The fact that she would meet Gabriel's family did not unnerve her as much as the fact that she had nothing to wear to the wedding. He solved her dilemma, offering to take her shopping at Copley Place where he was certain she would find an outfit in one of the many specialty boutiques.

It had taken her less than two hours to select a pair of Oscar De La Renta multicolored, silk-covered, sling backs, an exquisite beaded Judith Leiber evening purse in the muted colors of oranges, pinks, reds, black and green. The colorful shoes and bag were offset by a square-neck sleeveless raw silk black sheath that skimmed her body and ended mid calf. A matching long-sleeved jacket with side slits pulled her winning look together.

Once they'd returned to his car with her purchases,

Gabriel had kissed her passionately while thanking her for not subjecting him to spending all night in the shops while she made her selections. She returned the kiss, thanking him for paying for her purchases. The price tag on the shoes would have cost her more than half her weekly take home pay.

The ceremony was scheduled to take place Saturday at 4:00 P.M., but Gabriel had informed her that family members had been gathering in Florida all week since David and Serena Cole had announced their daughter's upcoming nuptials.

Summer felt the protective warmth of Gabriel's hand on her back as she stepped into the luxurious aircraft and was met by a man in a pilot's uniform.

"Welcome aboard, Miss Montgomery." He introduced himself as the copilot, then shook hands with Gabriel. "Good seeing you again, Mr. Cole." He took Summer's weekender and garment bag from Gabriel.

"Same here, Captain Gonzalez."

"We should be lifting off in about fifteen minutes."

Gabriel nodded. "What time do you anticipate touching down?"

"Clear weather, no wind—no later than six."

"Good." Gabriel seated Summer, then sat down beside her. He placed a call to Florida on his cell phone, completed it, then took her hand in his, squeezing her fingers gently.

Turning away from the large oval window, she met his gaze. "Do you think your folks are going to be surprised to see me?"

"Very."

"Very?" she repeated. Peering closely at Gabriel, Summer saw the hint of a smile lift the corners of his mouth. "Didn't you tell them you were bringing a guest?"

"Nope."

"Ga-bri-el," she wailed, stretching out his name into three syllables.

"Don't sweat it, sweetheart."

"That's easy for you to say. I don't want to feel like an intruder."

His eyebrows lowered in a frown. "How can you be an intruder? You are *my* guest."

It was her turn to frown. "How many times have you brought a surprise guest to your parents' home?"

"Never."

"Never?"

He kissed the end of her nose. "You're the first woman I've brought home to meet my folks."

"Why me?"

Gabriel stared at Summer. Everything about her turned him on—from her brown velvet skin, black hair that flowed over her shoulders like a cloud whenever she did not pin it up, and her eyes—dark eyes like a deep well he wanted to drown in.

Leaning to his left, he caught her lower lip between his teeth and nipped it gently. "Why not you, Summer? Didn't I tell you before that I don't want to stop this thing we have going on? I'm ready to fall in love." He smiled as her eyes widened. "How about you, darling? Are you ready for me? For us?" he whispered against her lush mouth.

She laid her left hand along his cheek, feeling stubble on his lean jaw even though he'd shaved earlier that morning. "Yes, Gabriel. I am," she whispered, meeting his hot gaze.

Gabriel closed his eyes at the same time a mysterious smile curved his mouth.

It was about to begin.

The jet touched down at the Fort Lauderdale–Hollywood International Airport on time. The evening temperature was a balmy eighty degrees. Summer felt her pulse quicken when she spied the fronds of towering palm trees swaying gently in a warm breeze. She rested her hand on Gabriel's arm as they deplaned, walked through a tunnel, and made their way to a private parking lot.

Gabriel saw his brother leaning against a late model Lexus sedan, feet crossed at the ankles, and arms over his chest. Pursing his lips, he whistled loudly.

Jason Cole glanced up, surprise apparent on his face when he saw his older brother with a woman. Taking long strides, he closed the distance between them. Arms extended, he hugged Gabriel then kissed him on each cheek.

"Welcome back, Bro."

Gabriel patted Jason's broad back. His younger brother had bulked up since the last time he saw him. "Thanks. I want you meet my guest for the weekend. Jason, this is Summer Montgomery. Summer, my brother, Jason Cole."

Summer stared tongue-tied. Gabriel and Jason looked enough alike to be twins. The only differences were hair and earrings. Wherein Gabriel's hair was long and salt and pepper, Jason's was black and close-cropped. Gabriel wore two small gold hoops in each of his pierced lobes, while Jason had elected not to pierce his ears.

She extended her right hand. "My pleasure, Jason."

Ignoring her hand, Jason leaned over and kissed her cheek. "Welcome to the family."

Summer glanced at Gabriel, but he had bent down to pick up her weekender. Jason took the garment bag from his grasp. She pondered Jason's greeting of "welcome to the family" when Gabriel had informed her no one knew she was accompanying him. How, she wondered, would David and Serena Cole view her: as an interloper or a potential daughter-in-law?

"Who's here?" Gabriel asked Jason as he wound an arm around Summer's waist.

"Everyone," Jason said over his shoulder. "Michael, Jolene and their kids came in early this morning. The New Mexico clan arrived yesterday along with Tyler and Dana. Regina and Aaron were already in Florida visiting *abuela*."

"What about Clay and Eden?"

"They came in last night."

"Where's everyone staying?"

"The women are in Palm Beach with Uncle Martin and Aunt Parris, and the guys are hanging out here."

"What's with the male bonding?"

"Michael wants to subject Merrick to a little Cole intimidation."

Gabriel shook his head, laughing. "I doubt very much if anyone can intimidate our future brother-in-law. And that includes Uncle Joshua."

Jason opened the rear door for Summer, offering her a warm smile as she settled herself on the leather seat. He stored her garment bag in the trunk, along with her weekender.

She stared out the window as Jason maneuvered out of the parking lot, heading in a northerly direction, listening as he updated Gabriel on what was going on with family members.

Summer knew she would never remember everyone's name even if she would spend a week in Florida with the Coles. There were just too many of them.

Twelve

Summer stared out the side window as Jason maneuvered onto an ascending, curvilinear driveway, through a series of gardens, past a guest house and tennis court, parking alongside half a dozen luxury vehicles under a porte cochere.

Gabriel got out and held the door open for Summer. Golden light flowed from every window in the three-story house configured in three sections. The light and the setting sun reflected off pale pink bricks on the courtyard laid out in a herringbone pattern.

He tightened his hold on her hand. "Jason will bring your bags in," he said, leading her toward a door that would take them directly into the kitchen where he knew he would find his mother.

Serena Morris-Cole sat on a high stool, her forehead resting on her husband's chest. David Cole patted her back as he whispered in her ear.

"I don't care how much he begs, don't give him any, Mom." Serena and David sprang apart guiltily, as if they had been caught doing something they weren't supposed to do. Gabriel pointed at his parents, grinning. "Gotcha!"

David helped Serena off the stool, and she went into the open arms of her firstborn, kissing him on the mouth. "You should be ashamed of yourself, spying on your folks like that."

Gabriel winked at his father over Serena's head. But David did not see it because he was staring at Summer. Turning, Gabriel followed the direction of his father's gaze.

Holding out a hand to Summer, he was not disappointed when she placed her hand in his. "Mom, Dad, I want you to meet someone who is very special to me. This is Summer Montgomery. Summer, my parents, Serena and David Cole."

Angling his head, David Cole winked at Summer. "Hello and welcome."

She returned his dimpled smile. She knew what Gabriel would look like in another thirty-five years, and it would be breathtakingly handsome. Even their voices were similar—deep and drawling. David's gleaming silver hair was close-cropped, matching the sparkle of the diamonds in his ears. She remembered Gabriel telling her about his grandmother's reaction to seeing her son and grandson wearing earrings. David turned his head, and Summer noticed a faint scar running along his left cheek.

Her attention to the scar was distracted when Alexandra swept into the kitchen, her golden eyes glittering with excitement. She went completely still when she saw Summer with her brother.

"Hello, again."

The elder Coles stared at each other, wondering how many more shocks were they going encounter before the weekend concluded.

Summer smiled at Alexandra. "Congratulations."

"Thank you, Summer. I'm glad you're here, because now I'll have another female to talk to beside Kim and my sister. Right now I'm being bombarded with testosterone overload." She turned to her mother. "The caterers just pulled up."

"Have them set everything up around the pool." Waiting until Alexandra walked out of the kitchen, Serena walked over to Summer. She offered her hand and a smile. "Welcome to Florida and to the family."

Summer smiled at the petite woman with large golden eyes and graying reddish curls, taking the proffered hand. "I'm honored to be here."

Maybe, she thought, she was making too much of the Coles welcoming her to the family.

"Nonsense," Serena countered, "we are honored to have you. I'll show you where you can wash up before we sit down to eat." She looked at Gabriel, who hadn't moved. "Don't worry, I'll bring her back."

David, making certain his wife wasn't in earshot, motioned to Gabriel to come closer. When Gabriel closed the distance between them, David rested an arm over his shoulder.

"Is there something you *need* to tell me?"

Gabriel stared into his father's near-black eyes. "No, Dad. Why?"

"Your sister waltzes in last weekend with the news that we're going to become grandparents, and that she's getting married. Your mother and I still haven't recovered. So, if you're going the same route, then please let me know *now.*"

"No, Dad. Summer and I are friends."

David removed his arm, giving his son an incredulous look. "Friends?"

"Yeah. Friends. In fact, we're colleagues."

Covering his face with his hands, David shook his head. "Damn!"

"What's the matter?"

"If you don't know, then I'm not going to tell you. I think Jason is more of a Cole than you are."

"What's up about me being a Cole?" Jason had walked into the kitchen.

David gave his younger son a direct stare. "Gabe and Summer are *friends.*"

Jason peered closely at his older brother, frowning. *"Friends* like in platonic?"

David nodded, biting back laughter. "Yes-s-s!"

"What the hell is so funny?" Gabriel roared.

Jason slapped his father's back, and they laughed so hard that tears rolled down their cheeks.

"Let me get out of here before I hurt somebody on the eve of my sister's wedding," Gabriel grumbled as he stalked out of the kitchen.

He found his sisters and cousins sitting on chairs around the pool. In-the-ground lights lit up the area like daylight. Some of his annoyance eased when he spied Summer and his mother. She was casually dressed in a pair of taupe slacks and an ivory-hued silk shirt, yet she looked elegant, tailored. Her hair was pulled off her face in a loose knot at the back of her head. A hint of makeup accentuated her large eyes.

Moving to her side, he caught her hand and led over to the small crowd gathered near the heated pool. All of the men rose at their approach.

Gabriel stared at his male relatives. "We can pick our friends, but that's not case when it comes to relatives. So, let me introduce you to the most unruly bunch of men to invade the great state of Florida.

"This hooligan, who just happens to be the former governor of New Mexico and is currently a federal district judge is married to my first cousin Emily. Christopher Delgado. Chris, Summer Montgomery."

Summer smiled at Judge Delgado. Tall, slender and elegant, his graying hair was an attractive contrast to his khaki coloring. Her gaze found his dark gaze, and they shared a smile. She inclined her head.

"Your Honor." Everyone dissolved into spasms of laughter.

"He's been trying to get my sister to call him that ever since he took the bench," Michael Kirkland drawled, pointing a finger at his brother-in-law. Christopher sat down, mouthing obscenities at Michael.

"Now, this elegant old man is Dr. Tyler Cole. Tyler, Summer Montgomery."

Leaning down from his impressive height, Tyler kissed Summer's cheek. "Gabe's jealous because although I'm eight years older than he is, he still has more gray hair than I do."

Summer smiled at Tyler. There was no doubt he was a Cole. He was tall, dark, and incredibly handsome. He had inherited the Cole's dark eyes, nose, and dimples.

"Hi, Tyler."

Gabriel moved down the line. "This next thug is my *much* older cousin, Michael Kirkland."

Summer found herself mesmerized by Michael's glittering green eyes as he took her free hand and kissed the back of it. His coal-black hair lay against his scalp, reminding her of a crow's feathers.

"Older by exactly two weeks."

She wrinkled her nose. "Thanks for clearing that up."

"Let go of the hand, Michael," Gabriel warned softly.

Michael dropped Summer's hand and retook his seat. "Yo, *primo,* there's no need to get possessive. After all, we are family."

"That's what frightens me," Gabriel countered, smiling. He moved down the line. "This gentleman is Silah Kadir. He's married to my cousin Arianna."

"Hey, Gabe. Why is it that Silah's a gentleman, while I'm an old man and Michael's a thug?" Tyler called out.

Turning around, Gabriel stared at Tyler. "It's because he speaks French."

"Oh, hell no!" Michael argued. "I speak French, *too.*"

Gabriel waved at him. "What-ever, Michael. Silah, Summer."

Silah took Summer's hand, kissed it and rattled off something in French. Although she did not understand a word, it left her cheeks burning.

She stared at Michael. "What did he say?"

"I'm not telling, because I won't be responsible for Tyler giving his brother-in-law a serious beat-down."

"I said you're a stunning woman, and that Gabriel is very lucky to claim you as his woman," Silah translated in accented-English.

Gabriel patted Silah's shoulder. "See, that's why I like you, my brother."

Summer noticed that only two of the men were still standing. The next one was no doubt a Cole.

"This young pup is Clayborne Spencer. In a few years we all will be calling him Dr. Spencer. Clay is my cousin Regina's son. Clay, Summer."

Clay reached for Summer's free hand, kissed it and rattled off his greeting in Portuguese. By this time she was laughing as hard as the others.

"Damn show-off," Gabriel said, laughingly.

Summer recovered enough to ask, "Who only speaks one language?" Not one hand went up. "Oh-kay," she drawled.

"Last, but certainly not least is the prospective groom. My soon-to-be brother-in-law, Merrick Grayslake."

Summer froze, unable to believe she knew the man standing in front of her. Tall, lean and deeply tanned with close-cropped dark brown hair—he hadn't changed much in four years; she would know him anywhere—especially his eyes, and she hadn't imagined a flicker of recognition in those silver-gray orbs.

She had just completed her training at the FBI facilities in Quantico, and had applied to take an additional course in intelligence training. Merrick Grayslake, on loan from the CIA to the FBI and DEA had facilitated the four-week training. There was nothing in her expression indicating she knew him.

Summer inclined her head. "Merrick. Best wishes on your upcoming nuptials."

Merrick smiled, if a parting of his lips could be called a smile. He leaned over and kissed her cheek. "Thank you, Renegade." He'd whispered her code name.

Gabriel did not notice stiffness in Summer's body as he turned to the two women sitting together at a table. He leaned down and kissed his sister. "Hey, baby sis."

Ana Cole flashed her dimpled smile. "Hey, yourself, big brother."

"Summer this is Ana, my sister and Jason's twin. And this lovely lady belongs to Clay. Ana, Kim Cheung, Summer Montgomery."

Summer greeted the women with a warm smile, noting the prisms of light reflecting from the diamond on Kim's left hand. There was no doubt the Coles would gather again for another wedding in the near future.

Ana stood up and hugged Summer. "You're beautiful. My brother is very lucky."

The uneasiness she felt when Merrick Grayslake recognized her lessened. "Thank you. Ana. I'm very lucky to have met your brother."

"Does this mean we're going to have another wedding, big brother?"

Gabriel ruffled her curly hair. "Zip it, kid."

Summer sat at the table with Ana and Kim. Now she knew what Alexandra was talking about when she'd mentioned testosterone overload. It was so potent it literally shimmered in the air.

She made small talk with Kim, Clay's fiancée. Tiny and delicate, she reminded Summer of a fragile orchid. A curtain of straight raven hair flowed to her waist.

"When are you and Gabriel getting married?"

Summer offered Kim a half-smile. "We're not. When are you and Clay marrying?" she asked, deftly changing the focus from her and Gabriel.

"We haven't set a date. I'd like to wait until we graduate medical school."

"How many more years do you have?"

"Two. But, we probably won't wait that long. I have a lot of elderly relatives in China who want to see me married. So, Clay and I plan to travel to China and marry in a traditional Chinese ceremony first, then have an American wedding once we return."

"That is so cool," Ana drawled.

Summer smiled at Ana. She looked so much younger than twenty-five, and Summer could not imagine her running a major record company with her twin. Jason and Ana were definitely the free spirits in the family. She thought of Alexandra as pragmatic, and Gabriel reflective.

She had come to look for and value the comfortable silence between them whenever they shared a meal. It was as if they could concentrate on each other without invading the other's privacy.

The catering staff had unloaded their van, setting candles out on each table. Within twenty minutes dozens of candles flickered like stars while a long table groaned under the platters of food set up buffet-style.

Alexandra sat down at the table, sighing audibly. "If Merrick doesn't hurry and bring me some food I'm going to pass out."

Summer half-rose to her feet. "I'll get you something."

"Sit down!" chorused Alexandra, Ana, and Kim in unison.

Alexandra placed a hand on Summer's arm. "If you're going to become a part of this family, you'll learn that the women rule and the men serve."

As if on cue, Merrick set a plate down on the table in front of Alexandra. Resting both hands on her shoulders, he massaged the muscles in her neck and upper back.

"What do you want to drink?"

Smiling up at him over her shoulder, Alexandra crooned, "A fruit juice, darling."

Ana covered her mouth with her fingers. "Michael's right," she whispered as Merrick walked away to do Alexandra's bidding, "He's *whipped!*"

"Who's whipped?"

Gabriel had come up silently. He looked at each woman, knowing within seconds that he wasn't going to get an answer. He placed a plate in front of Summer. "I didn't know what you wanted, so I took a little of everything."

"Thank you, sweetheart." The endearment had slipped out, and there was no way she could retract it as three pairs of eyes pinned her to her chair.

Hunkering down, Gabriel cradled her chin and pressed a kiss to her parted lips. "You're welcome, love."

"Ah-hhh," Ana groaned. "This is too much for me. You guys are going to have to put a lid on this love *thang* until I find a boyfriend."

"You had a boyfriend," Kim said.

Gabriel stared at Ana. "Who?"

"No one you would know," she retorted.

He stood up. "It better not be that Randy Mann, or whatever the hell his name is."

Ana stuck her tongue out at Gabriel. "You don't have to worry about him, because Jason ran him away."

Gabriel nodded. "Good."

"What's not good is having two brothers who are determined to keep me on lockdown in the love department," she said, scowling. Whenever she was annoyed Ana reminded Gabriel of their mother.

"That wouldn't be a problem if you honed your skills in the judgment department. What I can't understand is that you can negotiate a contract with the best entertainment attorney in the business, yet you lose it whenever you're attracted to the flavor of the month."

"Bite me, Gabriel Morris Cole," Ana drawled, rolling her head on her neck.

"Not!" he shot back. "I don't bite my sisters, thank you very much."

Everyone turned to look at Summer. "Don't look at me," she said, holding up her hands.

The table erupted in laughter. It ended suddenly once Clayborne gave Kim her plate and Jason served his twin.

Summer felt as if she had been adopted into a small segment of the Cole's extended family. Despite their wealth, she found them to be down-to-earth and unpretentious.

Having assuaged her temporary pangs of hunger, Alexandra dabbed her mouth with a napkin. "Summer, you can share my room tonight, because Kim will be in Ana's. Let me know if you need a massage, manicure, pedicure, or if you want your hair styled. Mom has contracted a group of beauty consultants to hook us up tomorrow morning."

Summer flashed a wide grin. "Count me in for the massage and hair." She had gotten a manicure and pedicure the day before.

"Good." Alexandra stood up. "I don't know about the rest of you, but I must get some sleep."

Pushing herself into a standing position, Summer said, "I think I'm going to join you." She smiled at Ana and Kim. "I'll see you tomorrow. Good night."

Ana and Kim also stood up and followed Summer and Alexandra.

It was near midnight by the time the seven men sitting around the table lifted glasses filled with brandy and toasted Merrick Grayslake.

Jason offered the first toast. "To Merrick, my soon-to-be brother-in-law. May your days be sunny and your nights warmer than my esteemed older brother's."

"Here, here," came a chorus of deep male voices.

"What's the matter, Gabe? You got a drought going on?" Christopher Delgado asked after he'd taken a sip of the quality liqueur.

Jason stared intently at Gabriel's brooding expression. "He and Summer are just *friends*."

"No!" they all chorused.

Leaning forward, Michael Kirkland rested his elbows on the table. *"Primo,* please don't tell me that Summer hasn't given you any. I don't know about anyone else, but I think she looks as hot as her name."

Dr. Tyler Cole nodded. "I've go to agree with you there, Michael. She is gorgeous."

Gorgeous and dangerous, Merrick wanted to tell them, but he didn't say anything. All he could do was smile.

"How long have you known each other?" Silah asked Gabriel.

"We met at a teacher orientation in late August."

"That is not too long," Silah said.

"That's too long for me," Tyler added. "I'd met, bedded, wedded, and gotten Dana pregnant in about six weeks."

"That's because you were over forty, and afraid that you would be shooting dummy sperm if you had waited any longer," Gabriel said, his expression completely deadpan.

Tyler's large dark eyes narrowed. "I don't intend to get into a pissing contest with you, cousin, but you have no right to speak about anybody's sperm because I definitely don't see any little Gabriel juniors running around here."

"Here! Here!" Michael, Chris and Silah chanted,

slapping their palms on the table. Merrick hadn't joined in because he was laughing too hard.

"Hold up, *primos*," Jason said, waving his hand above his head. "Perhaps my big brother needs a little incentive before he can do the nasty. Now, you know he moved up to New England where it's winter for at least ten months of the year, and I believe the cold weather has turned his family jewels into a Popsicle. What this man needs is sun, palm trees and tropical breezes to thaw him out."

Michael rested an arm over Gabriel's shoulder. "Your brother's right, *primo*. And I'm going to help you out. Why don't you take Summer down to Ocho Rios for a long weekend? That's where Jolene gave me some for the first time."

Christopher raised his glass. "I'll second that. It was at the stroke of midnight on New Year's that Emily gave me her virginity."

Michael glared at his brother-in-law. "Hey, you're talking about my sister."

"Give it a rest, Michael," Christopher drawled. "After pushing out three babies your sister is far from being the virgin you want her to be."

"I have to agree with Jason," Tyler said. "I remember my father telling me that he got my mother pregnant for the first time at that house in Ocho Rios."

"Think about it, *primo*," Michael said in a quiet tone. "Anytime you want to use the house just call me, and I'll make certain it's aired out and made ready for you." He had inherited the house from his parents as a wedding gift after he'd married his social worker girlfriend, Jolene Walker.

Gabriel thought about Summer's promise to spend a weekend with him anywhere he wanted. Perhaps, just perhaps he would take Michael's offer to take her to Ocho Rios.

"I will think about it," he promised.

The mock bachelor party continued well into the night as everyone toasted Merrick over and over for having the good sense to marry into the family. Sometime around three in the morning, Gabriel crawled onto one of the loungers set up around the pool and fell asleep.

It was Serena Cole who found Christopher, Gabriel, and Silah asleep by the pool. Michael, Jason, Merrick, and Tyler had managed to make it into the house, falling asleep where they lay. None had made it to their designated bedrooms.

Thirteen

The Coles, Spencers, Lassiters, Delgados, and Sterlings had begun arriving early Saturday afternoon, and by the time of the judge's anticipated four o'clock arrival, David and Serena Cole's property was crowded with five generations of family.

The ages ranged from more than a hundred to a mere six weeks. Marguerite Josefina Diaz-Cole, the family matriarch, looked forward to celebrating her 104th birthday on Christmas, while Timothy Cole-Thomas, CEO of ColeDiz International, Ltd. had become a grandfather for the first time.

Summer's presence had become the source of talk and much speculation as Gabriel introduced her to his grandmother, aunts, uncles and many cousins. The whispers of *Gabriel brought a girl* on everyone's lips was tantamount to the announcement of another engagement.

She sat next to Dana Cole, Tyler's wife, holding a nine-month-old little girl Dana and Tyler had adopted the month before. Dana told Summer that the baby's mother, a foster child herself, had died in childbirth. Her son, Martin II, had just celebrated his first birthday earlier that spring. Everyone sat on tufted chairs under a large white tent to escape the blistering rays of the sun, waiting for the ceremony to begin.

David Cole, his brothers, sons, Matthew Sterling, and Merrick Grayslake, who were summoned to meet in David's study, were all in formal attire.

Merrick had been the last one to enter the masculine, air-cooled room. He met David's fathomless black gaze without flinching. All of the men staring at him radiated power and danger, and if he hadn't been who he was he would have been sorely intimidated. But he had experienced too much in thirty-seven years to be intimidated by anything *or* anyone.

He had been abandoned at birth, having grown up being shuttled between dozens of foster homes. He knew he was of mixed blood, but had chosen to be African American despite the texture of his hair, features, and eye color. After graduating high school, Merrick enlisted in the Marine Corps where his life changed dramatically. He was recruited by the Central Intelligence Agency once they were made aware of his superior I.Q. and his ability for total recall. His overall physical appearance also proved to be an asset because of his ability to blend in well with many other ethnic groups. Within seconds, he could become a Spaniard, Italian, Turk, or a Jordanian.

His career ended after he was mugged and left on a street corner in Washington, D.C., to die. Michael Kirkland had found him, taken him to a hospital where doctors repaired his spleen but could not save his left kidney. The gunshot had mangled the kidney. After recovering, he returned to the Agency, and was transferred from the field to desk duty. Three days later, he walked into the director's office and resigned.

"Merrick, I've asked you to come in here because there is something I must say to you," David said, speaking for the first time. "I've asked my brothers, sons and a lifelong friend to be here because I want them to be aware of what's in my heart at this moment. In fifteen minutes I will place my daughter's hand in yours. And when that happens I will relinquish all claim and responsibility for Alexandra. My wife and my children are my most precious gifts, and I'm generously offering you the gift of my eldest daughter.

"I will say this only once, Merrick Grayslake. Love her, and protect her with your life. But, if you fail to do this, then look for me to come after you."

The nostrils on Merrick's aquiline nose flared slightly as he let out his breath. "Warning heeded, David." His eyes widened. "You've had your say, so let me have mine. At four o'clock Alexandra will become *my* wife, and therefore it will become *my* responsibility to protect her.

"I love her and the child she carries in her womb. And because I love her, I've broken a vow I made three years ago when I said I'd never go back to the CIA. I'm going back because I have a wife and a child to support. So that should put your mind at ease as to whether I have a job."

Everyone turned and stared at David, who managed to look sheepish.

"No, you didn't, Dad," Gabriel said softly.

"Damn, brother, that's cold," Joshua Kirkland whispered, shaking his head.

Martin Cole and Matthew Sterling dissolved into a

paroxysm of laughter that left them with tears in their eyes.

A sly smile played at the corners of Merrick's mouth. "I don't have as much money as Alexandra, but I can assure you that I can support her and the children we plan to have." He had made a small fortune in the stock market. He glanced at the watch under the cuff of his dress shirt. "I don't know about you guys, but I have a wedding to go to in three minutes."

Turning on the heel of his patent leather dress slipper, Merrick walked out of the study, leaving his bride's family members staring at his broad back.

Martin Cole's silver hair was a startling contrast to his deeply tanned olive-brown skin. Shaking his head, he stared at his younger brother. "David, you never cease to amaze me. Why the hell did you have to ask the man if he had a job?"

Crossing his arms over his chest, Joshua Kirkland continued to stare at his half brother, green eyes twinkling in amusement. "If you had wanted to know about Merrick you could've asked Michael."

"Dad would never do that," Jason said. "Whenever it concerns Alex or Ana he goes straight for the jugular. He wasn't even diplomatic about it. He could've said: by the way, my man, are you a scrub?"

Matthew Sterling stared at Jason. "Scrub?"

"Pimp, gigolo, deadbeat . . ."

"I get the picture, Jason," Matt countered.

Martin patted David's back. "I know all of this is new for you, but you'll get through it." All of Martin's children were married and had made him a grandfather of five.

Joshua took David's arm. "Come on, brother. After the first time it gets easier."

David glared at his brothers. They had teased him for years about his children not wanting to marry and have children. But all of the teasing would come to an end in a few minutes.

He shook off his brothers' arms and walked out of the study to give his daughter away in marriage to man whom he now respected enough to think of him as a son.

Summer closed her eyes, holding Astra Cole to her breasts, and mouthed the words along with Gabriel singing the Whitney Houston hit "I Will Always Love You." Alexandra had requested he sing it for her wedding, but she clung to her father's arm sobbing against his chest while Merrick waited for her at the opposite end of a red carpet with Michael Kirkland and Ana Cole.

The last note flowing from the powerful sound system faded in the still afternoon air, and still Alexandra hadn't moved when Gabriel began to play the familiar chords to the *Wedding March* on his keyboard.

There came soft gasp as Merrick strolled down the carpet and placed a hand on Alex's back. Her head came up and she smiled through her tears at the man with whom she had fallen in love.

David took Alexandra's hand and placed it in Merrick's outstretched one. "Take her."

Reaching into the pocket of his dress slacks for a handkerchief, Merrick blotted the tears on his bride's face, then led her to where the judge waited to begin the ceremony that would make them husband and wife.

David sat down next to Serena, smiling broadly. His eyes caressed her face, remembering a time when they had taken a vow to love each other until death parted them.

Curving her arm through her husband's, Serena lay her head on his shoulder. "Who do you think is next?"

"It has to be Gabriel."

Serena nodded. "One down and three to go," she whispered. "I have a good feeling about Gabriel and Summer. But, what are we going to do with the twins?"

David kissed her forehead. "Give them eviction notices. We've made it too comfortable for them. We should've set them up with their own apartments once they graduated college instead of telling them they could move back. The longer they stay, the harder it will be to get rid of them."

"Don't say it like that, David. You make it sound as if they were kittens we're trying to give away."

"I want my house back, darling. I want to be able to make love to my wife on the dining room table if I want to, and not have our son or daughter walk in on us."

Serena gasped softly. "We've never made love on the dining room table. "

David wiggled his eyebrows. "See what I'm talking about? We'll try it Sunday night. Gabriel and Summer are leaving Sunday morning, and Ana and Jason plan to drive up to West Palm tonight and spend time with Eden before she returns to Brazil with Regina and Aaron next week."

"Are you sure your heart is up to the task, darling?"

"I'll ask you the same thing after I have my dessert before the entrée."

Serena giggled like a little girl. "I like it when you talk dirty."

David pulled her closer. "That's because I've become a dirty, old man."

Tilting her chin, Serena kissed her husband at the same time Merrick lowered his head to kiss Alexandra. Flashbulbs popped as everyone stood and applauded another generation of Coles who dared risk everything for love.

The partying began in earnest as taped music blared from speakers set up throughout the expansive property. Alexandra looked ravishing in an off-the-shoulder platinum gown with a sunburst-pleated silk-chiffon bodice topping a silk-satin skirt. The garment was perfect for her petite figure. Tiny white rosebuds, pinned into her black curly hair, took the place of a veil. Three inches of jeweled Manolo Blahnik wedding sling-backs put the top of her head at six foot, three-inch Merrick's shoulder.

Summer felt the press of a hard body against her back. Smiling, she rested the back of her head against Gabriel's shoulder. "You made your sister cry."

"She was the one who requested the song, sweet-heart."

"It was you who sang it with so much passion that Alexandra wasn't the only one in tears."

Wrapping an arm around her waist, Gabriel pressed his groin against Summer's hips, permitting her to feel the swelling he found hard to control.

His mother woke up him earlier that morning to tell him to go into the house and sleep in a bed. He woke up at noon, looking for Summer, and was told she was at a salon. When he saw her again, she was sitting with Tyler's wife holding their daughter. He'd stared, stunned by her beauty and the image of the child in her arms. The sight stirred paternal instincts for the first time in his life.

A smile curved his mouth as he stared at her hair styled in a French braid entwined with white flowers. In that instant, he knew that Summer would make a beautiful bride.

Summer closed her eyes, her breasts rising and falling heavily. "No, Gabriel," she whispered.

He pressed his mouth to her ear. "I can't help it. Don't move!" His breath was heavy against the side of her neck. "Please, don't move until it goes down."

She disobeyed and moved, turning around and pressing her breasts to his chest. "Dance with me."

He held her, staring down into her dark eyes and seeing his unborn children in their satin depths. "I love you, Summer Montgomery."

Summer lowered her gaze, staring at his brown throat over the black and gray striped silk bowtie. His declaration of love was so simple and unadorned that she wanted to weep.

Pressing her forehead to his shoulder, she smiled. "I love you, too, Gabriel Cole."

He swung her around and around until someone tapped his arm. Holding Summer to his chest, he smiled at his brother-in-law. "I take it you want to cut in?"

Merrick smiled, nodding. "I promised myself I would dance with all of the women tonight, and Summer is next on my dance card."

Merrick bowed from the waist, then reached for Summer's hand. His lids were lowered, making it impossible for her to see his gaze. A minute elapsed before he said, "Do you know you've become a legend?"

She lifted an arched eyebrow. "No."

"I have friends in Washington who still talk about

you. The way you took down Richard Robertson's operation was a brilliant piece of undercover work." Attractive lines fanned out around Merrick's eyes once he smiled.

Sighing audibly, Summer glanced up to find Merrick staring down at her. "I don't want to talk about that."

Lowering his head, he pressed his mouth close to her ear. "Are you on the job?"

Summer stared out over his shoulder, her lips compressed tightly. "Not today."

"When?"

"Monday through Friday. I work at a high school in Massachusetts."

"Is that where you met Gabriel?" Merrick had asked her a question to which he knew the answer.

"Yes."

"There's high volume dealing at the high school?"

"That's what I've been told."

"It's not going to get any easier, Renegade."

A shudder shook her. "I know."

"When are you getting out?"

"Soon."

"Soon?"

"After this one."

"Does someone named Gabriel have anything to do with your decision?"

"Yes and no. I wanted out before I met Gabriel. And . . ." Her words trailed off.

Merrick dipped his head lower. "And what?"

"I'm in love with him. I want what you and Alexandra have. I'm tired of the aliases and living a double life. I live in fear that someone will recognize me and blow my cover."

"That won't happen if you get out now."

Her eyes grew large. "I can't."

"Why not?"

"Because . . . because I can't, Merrick. You of all people should know why."

Swinging her around, he dipped her. "Get out before you lose everything." He eased her until she was upright, affecting a smile for those who were watching them. "If you want what Alex and I have, then leave now. You can be replaced."

Their conversation ended when Salem Lassiter tapped Merrick on the shoulder. "May I have the next dance?"

Merrick relinquished his claim to Summer, bowing slightly. "Thank you for the dance." He gave her a penetrating stare before walking away.

Summer looked up at Salem, holding her breath for several seconds before she exhaled. She had found herself staring at him each time their paths crossed. After a while, she realized it was the long hair qued at the nape of his neck that had attracted her. Navajo and African American, Salem had inherited the best of both races: black silky hair, dark skin and cheekbones sharp enough to cut glass.

She offered him a friendly smile. "Let's see if I can remember what Gabriel told me about you. You're married to Sara, and you have twin girls."

Salem nodded. "Sara's brother is Chris's sister, who in turn is married to Emily. I have twin daughters and a son."

Summer searched her memory for his name. "Alejandro?"

"No. He's Chris and Emily's son."

Summer moaned, shaking her head. "I'm not doing very well remembering the names of the children."

"That's because there are so many children. Sara and I have three; Chris and Emily also have three children; Michael and Jolene, Tyler and Dana have two each. Arianna and Silah have one, Regina and Aaron two. You can't even begin to count the ones from the prior generation. Martin's sisters share nine children between them. Everyone stopped counting their grand and great-grandchildren once they numbered twenty."

She stared up into the dark slanting eyes fixed on her face. "How long did it take for you to remember everyone's name?"

"It was after my third annual family reunion."

"That long?"

"I'm sure it won't take that long for you."

Vertical lines appeared between her eyes. "Why would you say that?"

"You and Gabriel live along the east coast, which means you'll get to see his family much more often than the rest of us who live in New Mexico."

You and Gabriel. Salem made it sound as if she and Gabriel were truly a couple. Even though they had confessed their love to each other, they still hadn't made a commitment as to where their relationship would or could go.

The selection ended. Summer thanked Salem for the dance, and made her way over to an area where she could get a drink.

Alexandra had decided she wanted a buffet rather than a sit-down dinner. The caterer had delivered dozens of tables, each with seating for six earlier that morning. Vases of pale-colored roses lined the court-yard and patio. The large white tent was erected for the wedding ceremony in order to ward off the sun, or, if the sunny weather hadn't held, rain.

David Cole had hired a disc jockey to spin tunes, and a portable dance floor was set up between the pool and tennis court. Serena had ordered the pool covered, much to the disappointment of most of the younger children. They had established a tradition of jumping into the water fully clothed.

Feathery streaks of orange and blue crisscrossed the sky as the reveling continued while Summer waited in line for her drink.

"What is it you want to drink?" asked a familiar voice in her ear.

"Club soda."

She smiled as Gabriel went to the front and requested her beverage. No one seemed to mind that he had cut the line. He returned, carrying two glasses filled with a clear carbonated liquid.

Gabriel motioned with his head. "Let's go sit in the garden where we can talk without shouting." She nodded. The music was loud and piercing.

She followed him into a lush garden redolent with the fragrance of blooming flowers. They sat down on a cushioned rattan love seat.

Gabriel stared at Summer's profile, his gaze lingering on her bare arms. She had removed her jacket before she'd begun dancing. The day had been perfect for his sister's wedding, and he knew he would remember it always because for the first time in his life he had admitted to a woman that he loved her.

And what he felt for her wasn't frightening, but peaceful, calming, and soothing. He'd run from love for a long time only to find his heart captured by a woman who had admitted it was not going to work, that they were worlds apart, that she could not fit in his world, or he hers.

He had brought her to meet his family, and they had accepted her without question. Alex had confessed that she and Summer had spent more time talking than they had sleeping the night before.

The men were awed by her beauty and poise, while the women found her friendly and unpretentious.

He watched her take furtive sips of her drink. "What's going to happen with us once we return to Massachusetts?"

Summer shifted on the love seat and stared at Gabriel's brooding expression. "We're going to do what people in love do, Gabriel. We are going to make plans to spend that special weekend together, and then enjoy whatever comes after that."

He smiled. "When do you want to go?"

"Why don't we wait for a long holiday weekend."

"How does Columbus Day sound to you?"

Staring up into his eyes, she said, "It sounds wonderful."

Fourteen

Summer stood outside the vacation retreat belonging to Michael and Jolene Kirkland, feeling the blistering heat from the Jamaican sun on her bare shoulders. When she'd agreed to go away with Gabriel she hadn't though it would be to a foreign country. He had only hinted that she bring along her passport.

They had returned to Massachusetts after Alex and Merrick's wedding and settled back into a routine wherein they saw each other before classes began, and once or twice a week when they either dined out in a Boston restaurant or she prepared dinner at her apartment.

She had posted the names and time for auditions for all of the students who had signed up to participate in the spring concert. Once the eighty-four, three minute auditions began she knew it would also begin her undercover work. Aside from subbing for the English instructor, she had had very little one-on-one contact with students.

She and Gabriel had boarded the ColeDiz Gulfstream jet at Logan's International Airport at seven that morning. They were delayed on the ground because of strong winds, but after being cleared for take-off, the flight was smooth and turbulence-free. They finally touched down in Kingston at one in the afternoon to a blistering sun and temperatures in the low nineties.

A driver had awaited their arrival, and once their luggage was stored in the trunk of his car, Summer found herself wrapped in Gabriel's protective embrace as she sat back to enjoy the passing landscape.

The verdant beauty of the island was overwhelming: the mountain ranges, waterfalls, and beautiful beaches with pristine white sand and crystal clear turquoise waters.

The two-storied white stucco structure was completely West Indian in character: red-tiled Spanish roof, white-tiled floors surrounding the house, and Creole jalousie shutters. The cloying scent of blooming flowers and fruit was redolent in the warm air.

Gabriel had carried their bags into the house, but Summer continued to walk around, surveying her surroundings. She gasped when she realized the beach was only a few hundred feet away.

She retraced her steps, rushing into the house and bumping into Gabriel. His hands went to her shoulders to steady her. "Hold up, darling. Where are you rushing to?"

"I need to unpack my swimsuit. I can't believe the ocean is so close."

Grasping her hand, he pulled her toward the bedroom where he had put her luggage. The rooms he had selected for their stay faced the rear of the house and the Caribbean. The sound of the water was certain to lull them to sleep.

Summer slowed her steps as she walked into a room furnished with an antique mahogany four-poster bed draped in mosquito netting, a matching armoire, and rocker. A slow-moving ceiling fan stirred the air com-

ing in through the jalousie windows. Her gaze shifted
from her bags, to the bed, and then to Gabriel.

"Where's your luggage?"

His expression had become impassive. "It's in another room."

"I thought that we would . . ." Her statement died on
her lips. Heat stung her cheeks.

Taking two steps, Gabriel pulled her to his chest. "I
didn't want you to think I'd asked you to go away with
me only to sleep with you. We could've done that back
in the States."

Reaching up, she curved her arms around his neck,
pulling his head down. "I know that, silly. I could've
slept with you the day we came back from Florida, but
I wanted to wait for our special weekend." She brushed
her mouth over his, her tongue darting out and grazing
the hair on his upper lip.

Tightening his hold on her waist, Gabriel picked her
up until her head was level with his. He kissed her, his
mouth moving over hers as he literally caressed her
lips.

Her arms went around his head, holding him fast as
she parted her lips to his probing tongue. She opened
her mouth wider, inhaling and swallowing his breath.
A soft moan escaped her when his large hand cupped
her hips.

"I want you. I need you. I ache for you," he whispered hoarsely against her mouth.

Summer could not tell Gabriel how much she
wanted him because the words were locked in her
throat with the rising passion coiling between her legs.
She couldn't verbalize her need, but she could show
him.

Her right hand touched his belly before moving

under his T-shirt. Her fingers tangled in a thick mat of hair as another moan escaped her. She had become a sculptor, her hand and fingers moving over muscle and sinew. Moving sensuously against his body, she wanted to get closer until they were one.

Gabriel inhaled the scent of her skin, hair, and her rising feminine heat. A single layer of cotton separated their bodies, yet he felt his skin burning as if he had been set afire.

Holding her effortlessly, he carried out her out of the bedroom and into the one where he had left his luggage. He wanted to make love to Summer, but not without protecting her. Parting the mosquito netting surrounding his bed, he lowered her to heirloom linens. He slipped off his loafers and lay down, facing her.

His left hand gathered the hem of her dress, moving upward until his fingers were splayed over her thighs. She moaned softly, closing her eyes as her lips parted. Gabriel stared at her erotic expression, his own passion rising more quickly than he wanted it to as he moved over her. Lowering his head, he staked his claim not only on her body, but also on her heart.

Waves of heat merged with shivers of cold, leaving Summer gasping as Gabriel's tongue moved in and out of her mouth in a rhythm that sent her pulses racing and her senses spinning out of control. She opened her eyes, reached up and pulled the elastic band from his hair. Unbound, wayward waves fell over his forehead and over his shoulders. Her hands cradled his face, moving up and tunneling through the long hair. Her mouth and tongue were as busy as his when she caught his upper lip and suckled it before giving the fuller lower one equal attention.

Her nails bit into his scalp, fingertips traced the outline of his ears, pads on her thumbs sculpting the elegant ridge of high cheekbones, and her palms cradled the lean, dark face of the man with whom she had fallen in love.

Her breasts trembled above her rib cage as a swath of heat ignited a pulsing desire between her legs, bringing with it a gush of liquid.

"Gabriel." His name was a hoarse whisper filled with a desperate need that was communicated to the man straddling her throbbing body. "Love me," she murmured. "Please."

Gabriel heard the impassioned plea, Summer repeating it over and over until it became a litany. He wanted to take her quickly, mate with her as the raw passion that hardened his flesh like tempered steel throbbed against the fabric of his jeans, but hesitated because he did not know how much experience Summer had had with men.

Forcing himself to go slowly, he undid the many buttons on the front of her dress, exposing silken flesh in his journey to view what had been concealed from him since he'd watched Summer Montgomery enter the room where they were scheduled for a new teacher orientation.

It was her walk that he'd noticed initially, then her face. She had a long, graceful stride, her hips swaying fluidly with each step she took. The way her jeans had hugged her hips and tight thighs had annoyed him because he hadn't been able to control the stirring between his own thighs. It had been the first time in his life wherein just staring at a woman had turned him on.

Summer had accused him of being a stuck-up snob because he hadn't approached or talked to her. What she did not know was that he hadn't been able to come within five feet of her or she would've seen the effect she'd had on him. All she had to do was look below his waist to know that he'd been lusting after her.

It had taken hours of meditation, long vigorous swims in the cold waters of the ocean, and a grueling workout of push-ups and sit-ups to rid his body of the pent-up lust. And that was what it had been—lust. But now he was being offered the opportunity to pour his love, not lust, into a woman he loved.

His cousins had ribbed him about not making love to Summer, but it hadn't bothered him. What they hadn't known was that she wasn't someone he could bed, and then walk away from. They hadn't known that he had fallen in love with her, and that she had become the *one*—the one woman who could lift his dark moods, offer him a gentle peace that had eluded him for years, and the one with whom he wanted to spend the rest of his life.

Summer closed her eyes as Gabriel undressed her. What seemed like long agonizing minutes in fact were only seconds. The dress parted and he gasped. She opened her eyes to find him staring at an ecru-colored lace demi-bra and matching thong.

Sitting back on his heels, Gabriel smiled. "Cute, but not too practical."

Peering up at him through her lashes, she smiled. "What's not practical about them?"

He trailed his fingertips over the swell of breasts above the lace cups of her bra. "It doesn't cover enough." His fingers feathered down her flat belly and lingered on the moist heat between her thighs. "Especially here."

"It covers what needs to be concealed."

Supporting his weight on his elbows, he lowered his chest to hers. "If I can undress you with my teeth, then what you're wearing isn't practical, darling."

"You must have a very talented mouth,"

He lifted his eyebrows. "I do."

Staring up into his golden eyes, she said, "Then do it."

He shook his head slowly, his unbound hair moving sensuously around his face. "Perhaps another time." Reaching around her back, he unhooked her bra and dropped it on the floor beside the bed. Seconds later, he eased her panties down her hips, legs, and feet, and it joined the bra on the floor.

His fiery gaze made love to her naked body. Their gazes met and fused. There was no fear in her eyes, but a naked, unabashed love she did not attempt to conceal.

"This is how I love to see you."

He did not look away as he reached for the hem of his T-shirt and pulled it up and over his head. He unsnapped the waistband of his jeans and pushed them down with his boxers.

Summer lay motionless, her heart pounding in her chest as she watched Gabriel undress. He was so different from the other two men whose beds she had shared: his height, body, and temperament.

His clothes had concealed a lean, hard body. Without them he was much larger than she had originally thought. Firm muscle rippled under his pectorals and biceps as he slipped off the bed to step out of his jeans. Her mouth went suddenly dry when she saw the thick mat of black hair on his chest taper into a thin line over his flat belly and disappear into an inverted triangle of curls cradling his heavy sex.

It wasn't until he turned his back and reached down into a carry-on bag that she saw the tattoo spanning his lower back. It was a musical staff with tiny notes, but she could not make them out.

She forgot about the tattoo, her mission, and her double life as she opened her arms to receive the man she loved, one who was to become her lover. His latex-covered organ brushed her inner thigh as he settled himself between her legs.

Smiling, Summer trailed her fingertips up and down Gabriel's back, eliciting the response she wanted. Burying his face between her neck and shoulder, he moaned deep in his throat. She grazed his hips, outer thighs, up his ribs as his breathing deepened and his body quivered under her sensual assault.

It was her turn to moan when she felt his tumescence throbbing rhythmically against her mound. Eyes closed, hands falling limply to her sides, she gave herself up to the exhilarating sensation of the mustache on her bare flesh as Gabriel kissed her breasts. His tongue circled the areola, her nipples hardening quickly. He alternated rolling them between his teeth with suckling her until she arched off the mattress.

His rapacious mouth charted a path from her lips to her belly. Her soft moans of pleasure escalated into long, surrendering groans, with a rising heat simmering under her skin. Her whole body was being flooded with a desire that sucked her into an abyss of abandoned ecstasy.

Rising off the bed, Summer reached for Gabriel, hoping to capture the one thing which would end her erotic torment. She wanted and needed his hardness inside her. She needed him to relieve the burning, throbbing ache that threatened to shatter her into so many pieces that she would never be whole again.

Lifting his hips, Gabriel guided his swollen flesh

into Summer's body. If possible, the scent of her rising desire made him harder, and he resisted the urge to ram into her. He closed his eyes, gritting his teeth, as her flesh stretched to welcome him home.

It was only when he was buried up to the root, he began moving. Slowly, deliberately until he established a rhythm she followed easily. Her well-toned body moving in concert with his became a piano establishing the theme, then the soulful wail of a soprano sax taking him higher and higher. Then it changed, and the melody blended with the haunting sound of an oboe, sensual moan of a cello, and changed again with the soaring strains of violins and violas when her legs curved around his waist.

He was lost, drowning in the music they'd created with their joining. They had become one. They were one.

Summer felt like a budding flower, opening and yielding the nectar her lover could taste, savor, and possess. Gabriel made her feel things she never knew existed. Each moan, groan, thrust of his powerful hips increased the coil of pleasure building up in her womb.

It came upon her so quickly she did not have time to react. The fireball exploded at the same time she threw back her head and screamed his name. It had erupted from the back of her throat before it faded to a whisper of wonderment.

Gabriel did not want to concentrate on the flesh squeezing his in long measured convulsions, but he failed. Summer's soft whimpers in his ear took him higher and higher until he, too, exploded, the force hurtling him beyond reality.

Broad shoulders convulsed and shuddered violently as he collapsed heavily on her slender frame, the crescendo in his head fading with the ebbing passion softening his flesh nestled in her moist, feminine heat.

He did not want to move, but was forced to. He weighed too much to lie on her. He reversed their position, cradling her legs between his. They lay without moving, until their respiration resumed to a normal rate.

Summer listened to the strong pumping of Gabriel's heart against her cheek. "I thought we were going swimming."

He chuckled softly, staring up at her through a fringe of long lashes. "We just did, darling. Didn't you feel the undertow?"

She laughed softly. "No, I didn't because I was drowning in the sweetest ecstasy I have ever experienced in my life."

Gabriel dropped a kiss on her hair. What he wanted to tell her was that it was only the beginning of their life together, because he had so many places to explore, so many things he wanted to share with her.

His hand played with her hair, undoing the single plait. When her hair floated over her shoulders, he reversed their position, staring down at her as her hair flowed over the pillow.

One of his fantasies had been fulfilled: to have her in his bed with her hair flowing on the pillow. He combed his fingers through the strands. "You have beautiful hair."

"You won't say that when you see it frizz up. That's why I have it relaxed at least three to four times a year."

Rubbing several strands between his fingers, he shook his head. "It feels so soft."

"That's why it frizzes. Coarse hair will hold a set longer than what I have been blessed with."

Gabriel kissed her mouth. "You are blessed, Summer. Blessed with beauty, brains and an incredible musical talent." He flashed a lopsided smile. "You're not the only one who has been blessed." He paused, staring at her mouth. "I'm blessed to have found you."

"Were you looking, Gabriel?"

"I didn't know I was until I saw you."

They stared at each other, basking in the warm glow of love. Gabriel shifted until he lay beside Summer. He threaded his fingers through hers and closed his eyes. A comfortable silence descended on them once again.

There was no need for words. Their bodies and hearts had communicated silently everything that needed to be said.

Fifteen

Summer lay on a blanket on the beach, her face pressed to Gabriel's bare chest. The sun had set, taking with it the intense heat and leaving a warm tropical breeze. Millions of stars and a slip of a moon lit up the navy-blue sky.

It was Saturday night, and she and Gabriel would spend one more night in Ocho Rios before they prepared to return to the States Monday morning.

"Why Aaron Copland and not Duke Ellington?" she said softly.

"I suppose you're talking about my tattoo."

"Yes."

Gabriel told her he'd had the opening notes of Copland's "Fanfare for the Common Man" tattooed on his lower back a week after he'd enrolled in graduate school. The music from the Fourth Movement of Copland's Symphony no. 3 had haunted him for years. It crept into his head when he least expected or wanted it to. He copied the music for a tattoo artist, who made a stencil of the notes. The moment he'd felt the bite of the needle, he'd changed his mind. But he'd endured the pain and avoided strong sunlight for two weeks. Once the tattoo healed, the melody was exorcised from his mind.

"You're really a rebel, aren't you? Tattoos and earrings."

"I'm no more a rebel than my father or Michael. Dad has both and Michael has an elaborate red and black dragon tattooed on his golden triangle."

She smiled at his reference to the area on the lower back. "Is he really a thug?"

"Michael?"

"Yes."

"No. But he can be quite dangerous when crossed. He graduated from West Point like his father, and was involved with military intelligence before he left the army to teach military law."

"If his father is your father's brother, then why is his name Kirkland?"

"Uncle Josh was once one of the family's dirty little secrets. My grandfather had an extramarital affair with his secretary, and my uncle was the result of that liaison."

"Your grandmother accepted him?"

"Yes, but only after quite a few years. Once Emily and Michael were born the family had closed ranks and reconciled. Anyone named Cole or claims one drop of Cole blood is *la familia*. We're far from perfect, but the family bond is fierce and sometimes fanatical. Mess with one, and you'd better make arrangements for your funeral."

Summer froze. "It's like that?"

"Yes, Summer. It's like that."

She thought about his threat to the photographer who had attempted to take his photograph, and it was not the first time that she detected danger in her lover. She did not want to believe the man who had the face and body of an Adonis, the man who sang with so much passion that he brought one to tears was capable of such violence.

What Gabriel did not know was that she was capable of extreme violence. She'd trained to kill: with her body and a weapon. Her shield and government-issued semi-automatic weapon were concealed in a small safe in the back of a closet in her bedroom. And she wondered how Gabriel would react if he discovered he had shared his bed with a DEA agent.

Merrick Grayslake's entreaty to get out now came rushing back whenever she opened the closet and saw the small ironclad box. Lucas Shelby had planned to retire in July. What he did not know was that she planned to join him. Lucas would retire and she would leave—permanently.

"Gabriel?"

"Yes, baby."

"Aren't we going to get up and go into the house?"

His hand moved from her waist to her hips. "No. I want to stay out here tonight."

"We can't sleep on the beach."

"Why not?"

"I—"

She was never given the opportunity to reply as she found herself on her back. Gabriel loomed over her, hands catching in the waistband of her bikini bottom. Summer knew her reaction time had slowed when he eased his knee between her legs and entered her in one, sure thrusting of his hips.

They had gone swimming an hour before the sun had set, then returned to the beach to relax. Gabriel had removed his trunks in the encroaching darkness, while she had taken off the top to her bathing suit.

Raising his hips, Gabriel pulled her bikini bottom

down and off her legs. Then he began to move, slowly, in a measured back and forth motion. He did not think of the consequences of this coupling until later—much later. He, who had never slept with a woman without using a condom, risked getting Summer pregnant as he lost his mind and his heart in her fragrant embrace.

He withdrew, his mouth traveling from her lips to her throat, then lower to her breasts, where he worshiped them until she moaned and writhed, her hips establishing their own rhythm. Her gasp was magnified in the stillness of the night as he journeyed down her body, his tongue lapping up the moisture at the apex of her thighs.

The primitiveness of the act awakened a primal hunger in Summer as her body was buffeted under the sensual assault when his thumb found the swollen protuberance and massaged it in tandem with his tongue.

Gabriel increased the pressure of his thumb on the engorged nodule, swallowing his own groans when he felt his own throbbing hardness straining for release. He waited until Summer stiffened, convulsing in climax before he moved up her body and sheathed himself in her feminine heat. He rode her long, hard until he felt the floodgates open. At the last possible moment sanity reigned, and he rolled off her and the blanket, spilling his seed in the sand.

Tears leaked from under Summer's lids. Gabriel Cole possessed the power to assuage her physical need for him, but unknowingly, he also had the power to make her forget who she was and why she was teaching at Weir Memorial High School.

He had the power to make her forget everything— except the love she felt for him.

Rising to her knees, she crawled across the sand and

lay over his body. She wasn't disappointed when he curved an arm around her waist and pressed a kiss to her temple.

"I shouldn't have done that."

"There's nothing to apologize for, Gabriel."

"I hope I pulled out in time."

Summer wanted to tell Gabriel it would not have mattered if he did not pull out because she was taking oral contraceptives. As an undercover female agent she had decreased her chances of becoming pregnant by ninety-nine percent if ever she found herself in a physically compromising situation. And it would be the only time she would consider killing a man if she thought he was going to rape her.

"It's all right."

He tried making out her face in the darkness. The light from the house did not reach as far as the beach. "What if I get you pregnant?"

You can't, she wanted to tell him. "You won't."

There was a moment of silence. "What *if* it does happen?"

"Are you asking me what would I do?"

"Yes."

"I'd have it, of course."

"Would you marry me?"

She lay completely still, counting the beats of his heart. He had said it. He had mentioned the *word.* The five-letter magical word every woman dreams of hearing from the man she loves.

"I would marry you even if I wasn't carrying your child, Gabriel."

He sighed audibly. "Is that a promise, Summer?"

She nodded, the hair on his chest tickling her nose and cheek. "Yes, Gabriel, that is a promise."

They lay on the sand, listening to the lapping of gentle waves washing up on the beach, and to the other's heart.

They had made a promise to each other, a promise they intended to keep, but the only question was when would it be fulfilled.

Desiree Leighton's blue eyes squinted slightly as she stared at Summer. "Have you been to a tanning salon?"

Summer rolled her eyes at Desiree. "Hel-lo, Miss Leighton. Black women don't frequent tanning salons, thank you."

Desiree managed to look insulted. "Well, I knew one in California who did."

"Trust me when I say it, but the sister was *no* black girl."

The art teacher crossed her arms under her breasts. She even looked like a holdover from the sixties: long straight graying hair parted down the middle, small round glasses reminiscent of the ones worn by John Lennon, wooden or suede clogs, long skirts, bellbottom slacks, and turtleneck or ribbed sweaters. She always protected her vintage wardrobe by covering them with paint-splattered lab coats.

"We haven't seen the sun in a week, so you had to go away. Where did you go?"

"The Caribbean."

Desiree sat down on the edge of Gabriel's desk. "There are lots of places in the Caribbean. Where?" She had drawn out the last word.

"Jamaica."

The bright blue eyes sparkled. "Very nice. Who did you go with?"

Summer held up her hand. "I can't tell you."

"Okay, Summer. You don't have to tell me. Besides, I like it when a person's life has a little mystery."

She wanted to tell Desiree that not only was her life shrouded in mystery, but also drama. Instead, she said, "Are you busy after classes for the rest of the week?"

"Not really. Why?"

"I'm auditioning students for the spring pageant beginning this afternoon. I'm scheduled to see a total of eighty-four students for three-minute skits. That translates into a little more than four hours. I've set up to see twenty kids each day. Barring delays, I should get through them in about ninety minutes."

"What do you plan to have?"

Summer told her about her concept of profiling music through the centuries. "What I want to focus on are the songs and dances beginning with the forties through today's hip-hop."

Desiree nodded. "Sure. What time will it begin?"

"Two o'clock in the auditorium."

"I'll see you there."

"Thanks."

"There's no need to thank me, Summer. I want you to know that you've come up with a winner."

"I'm going to need some psychedelic sets for the sixties when we do *Hair* and *Jesus Christ, Superstar*."

"They're going to be dynamite. I've got some very talented art students."

"You sound like Gabriel when he talks about his music students. However, I have a feeling I'm going to come up with my own divas and heartthrobs."

"If that's the case, then it's not going to be easy selecting two students from three genres for the scholarships."

"You're right." What Summer did not tell Desiree was that Gabriel had offered to underwrite the cost of two more scholarships. Four were better than two, but six would be even better. Then, each of them could select two from their disciplines.

Summer sat in the darkened auditorium, staring up at the lit stage. One by one, students had stood in front of the microphone and sung, delivered monologues or danced to taped music they'd brought as an accompaniment. Of the first eight, only one exhibited any degree of talent.

"Not bad," whispered a familiar voice behind her seat.

She smiled, but did not turn around. "In fact, she's pretty good."

Gabriel rested his arms on the back of Summer's seat, his fingers toying with the hair on the nape of her neck. Memories of their weekend in Ocho Rios had lingered with him. It was as if he could still taste her on his tongue, while the scent of her perfume had lingered in his nostrils even after showering. Everything that was Summer Montgomery had seeped into his pores.

Summer ignored the velvet touch on her neck as she checked off a name on the list on a clipboard. "Thank you, Jody."

Jody Van Walls left the stage. Less than a minute later a short, chubby blond girl with glasses stood in front of the microphone.

"Please state your name," Summer called out for the tenth time that afternoon.

"Robyn Phillips," she said into the microphone, her voice echoing loudly. She stepped back a few inches.

The acoustics in the auditorium were perfect. "I'm sorry, Miss Montgomery, but I didn't bring my music."

"What do you plan to do, Robyn?"

"Sing."

"What song?"

" 'Respect.' "

"Can you sing a cappella?

"What, Miss Montgomery?"

"I'll play for her," Gabriel said, rising to his feet.

"Mr. Cole will accompany you, Robyn."

Summer, Desiree, and the other students waiting back stage stared through the curtains when Gabriel mounted the stage and sat down at the piano.

Summer held her breath as a spotlight shimmered on his long hair and deeply tanned face. Instead of his ubiquitous black, he had exchanged it for a camel-colored pullover sweater and dark brown corduroys. Low-heeled cordovan boots completed his outfit.

Gabriel smiled at the girl with a fringe of flaxen bangs hanging in her eyes. Tapping his right foot, he began playing. Robyn watched for his cue to begin, and when he raised his right hand she opened her mouth.

Summer and Desiree sat up straighter, unable to believe the sound coming out of the girl's mouth. If someone hadn't seen her they would've thought Aretha Franklin herself had come to Weir Memorial to perform.

"Oh, good grief!" Summer whispered. "That girl can blow."

"Tell me about it," Desiree said in agreement.

Halfway through song, Summer found herself singing background vocals while snapping her fingers. Desiree, Gabriel and the other students chorused

"R-E-S-P-E-C-T," and "sock it to me" with such enthusiasm and passion that everyone was dancing and gyrating to the rocking rhythm.

Eyes closed, face flushed, Robyn moved to a beat that would've made the Queen of Soul proud.

The song ended amid thunderous applause. Summer stood up, clapping with the others.

Gabriel, caught up in the fervor launched into "Do Right Woman, Do Right Man." Robyn took his cue and held the microphone close and belted out, "I don't want nobody always—sittin'—'round—me and *my* man."

Her classmates stomped and yelled as blond-haired, blue-eyed, bespectacled Robyn Phillips wailed the blues as if she had actually lived them. Smiling shyly, she walked off the stage and into the arms of her classmates.

Summer felt an excitement she hadn't felt since she'd left the theater. She had found her Aretha!

Sixteen

Summer lay in bed, her head resting on a mound of pillows, a cordless telephone anchored between her chin and shoulder. "I don't believe it, Gram! *You* have a boyfriend?"

"What's so wrong with me having a man friend?"

"Nothing, Gram. It's just that this is the first time I've ever heard you talk about another man other than Grandpa." She couldn't remember her grandfather, who had passed away in his sleep from an enlarged heart the year she turned three. "Is he nice?"

"Very nice, baby girl."

She smiled. Virginia Brown had always called her that. "Where did you meet him?"

"In church."

"Wonderful. At least you know he's a churchgoing man."

"Amen. You know I can't tolerate no heathen. Henry's a widower. He lost his wife last year, and you should have seen those loose hussies sashaying around him like bees to honey. He said he picked me out because I wasn't like the others."

"Is he retired?"

"Now he is. He owns a construction company that he turned over to his boys. You should see what he had them do to the house, baby girl. I have an enclosed deck on the back I can use all year round."

"That's fabulous. I can't wait to see it when I come out there for Christmas."

"I . . . I don't think you should make plans to come to St. Louis for Christmas."

Summer sat up. "Why not?"

"Henry is taking me on a cruise to Hawaii."

"Oh." The single word was loaded with disappointment.

"Of course we are going to have separate cabins. I told him I don't hold with no fornicating business. After all, I'm a good Christian woman."

Summer had to smile. "Of course you are, Gram."

"How you doing, baby girl? You taking care of yourself?"

"Yes, Gram."

She asked Summer the same two questions every time they spoke to each other. It was Virginia's way of asking if her undercover work was going well. They had made it a practice never to discuss what she did for a living on the telephone.

"Have you met a nice boy?"

Summer's expression brightened. "Yes, I have."

There came a pregnant pause. "You did?"

"Yes. He's very nice," she said, repeating what her grandmother has said about her Henry.

"What does he do?"

"He's a composer."

"I thought you said you never wanted to get involved with someone in the entertainment business."

"That was when I was in the business."

"When am I going to meet him?"

"I don't know. I was hoping to bring him home with me for Christmas."

"If you want to do that I can always cancel my cruise."

"Don't you dare do that!"

"But I want to meet your young man."

"I have several school holidays. We have a week off in February and the spring recess in April. We'll plan something at the beginning of the year."

She listened to the three letters her mother had sent to Virginia from South Africa. In all of the letters her mother had written that she was seriously thinking of retiring and returning to the States.

Summer wondered if it was too late for her and her parents to become a real family. How different, she thought, her family was from the Coles. She talked to her grandmother for another few minutes before hanging up.

She fought hard against the tears she refused to let fall when she thought of her estrangement from her parents. And now it was her grandmother. She did not blame Virginia for grasping companionship and a modicum of happiness after being widowed for thirty years. After all, she was entitled because not only had she raised her daughter, but also a granddaughter.

Throwing back the blanket, she headed for the bathroom. This was one of those times when she did not want to be alone.

Gabriel thought he was hearing things when the doorbell chimed throughout the house. His fingers stilled on the piano keys, and he listened again. It was the doorbell. Rising from the piano bench, he made his way across the living room, through the entryway, and to the front door. He opened it, and froze. Standing on the porch was the last person he had expected to see. She was wearing a dark barn jacket, jeans, sweater, and boots.

"Do you think you could put me up for the night?"

Reaching out, Gabriel pulled Summer to his chest, rocking her from side-to-side. "Of course, baby." He kissed the end of her nose. It was cold. "Come on in where it's warm." He took her overnight bag from her loose grip, pulling her into the house. He left the bag on a chair before he closed the door behind them.

Within seconds, Summer was enveloped in a soothing heat that warmed her inside and out. "I didn't want to be alone tonight."

Gabriel led her into the living room, easing her down to sit beside him on a love seat. He stared at her, seeing what she had tried to conceal: a profound sadness.

Wrapping his arms around her body, he settled her across his lap. "What's the matter, darling?"

She told him about her telephone conversation with her grandmother, and her aborted plan to return to St. Louis for the Christmas recess.

He closed his eyes, feeling her pain and alienation as surely as it was his own. Didn't she know how much he loved her? He certainly had told her enough. She wasn't alone—she had him.

"There's no way you're going to spend Christmas alone, Summer." Her head came up, meeting his gaze. "You'll share Christmas with me, and my family."

Summer shook her head. It was one thing to go to Florida as a guest in his sister's wedding, but sharing

Christmas with the Coles went beyond social correctness.

"I can't, Gabriel."

"And, why not?"

"Because I'm not family."

His eyes widened until she could see the dark brown centers in pools of gold. "But, you could be."

For a long moment, she looked back at him. "How?" The single word was a breathless whisper.

"Marry me, Summer Montgomery."

"I can't," she said quickly. If she married Gabriel it would compromise her mission—her true purpose for teaching at Weir.

His eyes darkened dangerously as a muscle twitched in his lean jaw. "Why not?"

She bit down on her lower lip. "I love you, Gabriel. I love you enough to want to spend the rest of my life with you. But . . ."

"What!" He'd spat out the word. It was the first time he'd ever offered to share his life with a woman, and she'd thrown his proposal back in his face.

Fool! He was a damn fool.

At that moment he wanted to smash things. Yell, scream at the top of his lungs. How had he become so vulnerable so quickly? Summer touched his face, and he forced himself not to pull away.

"I will marry you," she said in a quiet voice, "but not until the school year ends."

"What?" he repeated.

She offered him a sensual smile. "I accept your proposal of marriage."

He looked at her as if she had spoken a language he did not understand. "Are you saying yes?"

She curved her arms around his neck. "Yes, yes, yes!"

Gabriel stood up, cradling her to his chest. Relief and joy merged, making him lightheaded. He sat down again, dipped his head, and kissed her, sealing her promise.

"If you want to wait, then that's okay with me." He knew he would wait for an eternity if it meant having her in his life.

Her smile was dazzling. "Thank you."

"Tell me what it is you want."

"All I want is to become your wife and the mother of our children."

He shook his head. "I'm not talking about that, Summer. I need to know if you want a large wedding, or something small and very private. Do you want to marry in Florida or in St. Louis? Do you want to live here or in Missouri?"

She placed her fingertips over his lips. "Enough, sweetheart."

He pulled her hand down. "I want you to know that I'll do anything for you."

"Right now I want to go upstairs and have you hold me until I fall asleep."

He nuzzled her ear, smiling. "Your wish is my command."

At that moment she recalled Alexandra saying that the women in her family ruled, while their men served them. Is that what she had to look forward to?

Gabriel removed her jacket, boots, and socks. Next came her jeans and sweater. Clad in only her bra and panties, he carried her up the staircase and into his bedroom. Light from a table lamp in the sitting room provided enough illumination for him to make out the bed.

Holding her effortlessly with one arm, he pulled back the antique quilt and placed her on the cool, crisp sheets. Sinking down to the mattress, he lay on his side, staring at her shadowy form. Pulling her closer, he held her until her breathing deepened and she fell asleep.

He found Summer to be an enigma. Just when he thought he had figured her out, she changed before his eyes like a chameleon. She was stubborn and willful, but then she was soft and giving.

He'd attended all the auditions for the spring musical, volunteering to accompany the students who either had forgotten or did not bring music. He'd found her patient when a student had an attack of nerves or stage fright. She usually told them to wait until later or come back another day.

He saw the excitement on her face when she discovered one with natural talent. He'd watched her dance and sing along with Robyn Phillips when she had performed her incredible rendition of Aretha Franklin's hits. There was no doubt Summer would inspire her musical theater students to reach beyond themselves to become the best they could be.

She had fought him and her feelings the first time he'd invited her to Cotuit, but this time she had come without an invitation. She had come because she needed him as much as he needed her.

Summer Cole. He chuckled when he realized what the two words denoted. Mrs. Gabriel Cole. Summer Montgomery-Cole. He smiled. He liked the latter.

He slipped off the bed and went downstairs to extinguish some of the lights. Retracing his steps, he walked into the bathroom to shower and brush his teeth. When he returned to the bedroom, Summer had changed positions. Her head lay on his pillow. He managed to move her without waking her, then slipped into bed and pulled her hips against his groin.

He closed his eyes, and within minutes he had joined her in sleep.

didn't know about it, Lucas? I could've stayed in bed to nine be and been the fresher. Her hands by a jingling oughly the daughter To calm herself, she took a jenth this her find muffled crimping the was the eagle no her cough bring one her cough muffled pumbling tom

Seventeen

Summer woke early and slipped out of bed without waking Gabriel. She showered in the half-bath on the first floor. It was five-fifteen by the time she got into her car and headed back to Whitman. She had forgotten she was scheduled to meet Lucas at the diner at six-thirty. He was waiting for her when she walked in.

Smiling, she slipped into the booth opposite him. "Good morning."

He stared at her sweater and jeans. "You didn't jog this morning?"

"No."

"What do you have for me?"

"Not much."

"Give me what you have."

Summer's gaze narrowed as she studied her boss. "Are you in a hurry?"

Leaning back against the Naugahyde-covered booth, Lucas closed his eyes. "No. I'm just tired. I want to go back home and sleep."

"Why didn't you call me and cancel this meeting?"

He ran a hand over his hair. "I hadn't thought about it."

A shadow of annoyance swept over her face. "You

didn't think about it, Lucas? I could've stayed in bed this morning."

"With Gabriel Cole?"

She recoiled as if he had punched her again. "What are you doing, Lucas? Have you set someone up to watch me? Because if you have then you'd better call them off."

"Everybody watches everybody."

"That's a load of crap, and you know it. Why me?"

His face reddened. "Because you're spending more time in Gabriel Cole's bed than you have been collecting evidence for us."

She struggled to maintain calm. "I'm going to forget I heard that. I can't collect what doesn't exist. There was one incident of a girl being suspended for smoking weed in a bathroom. *One,* count it, one smelly joint," she said through clenched teeth. "Somehow that doesn't count as high-volume drug dealing."

The orange-haired waitress came over to the table and placed Lucas's order in front of him. She smiled at Summer. "Can I get you anything? We have raisin bread this morning."

Summer shook her head. "No, thank you."

Lucas picked up his fork. "Bring her a cup of decaf coffee."

"I said I don't want anything."

Lucas glared at the waitress. "Bring it, *please.*"

"Yes, sir."

Summer stared at the woman's retreating back. "I'm going to count to ten, Lucas. But if that waitress comes back before I finish counting, then you're going to be wearing that cup of coffee. One, two three, four—"

"I'm sorry, Renegade." Lucas closed his eyes for the second time. "I'm truly sorry."

"I'm getting tired of your apologies. And I want you to stay out of my personal life. I may work for the government, but I'm still entitled to have a private life. And let me tell you before your snitch does, I'm engaged." She saw him glance at her bare left hand. "Gabriel and I plan to marry next summer."

A cold smile curled his thin lips. "Ain't you a lucky son-of-a-bitch."

"Which one am I? Lucky or a bitch, Lucas?"

"Lucky. All you have to do is flutter your lashes and you've managed to land one of the wealthiest men in the country. Not bad for a little girl from St. Louie."

The cynicism of his remark grated on her, and this was the first time she could remember verbally sparring with her boss. "I stopped being a *girl* a long time ago." She gathered her handbag. "There's going to be a dance at the school on Halloween. It should be an interesting event. And in case you're interested, I'm going with Gabriel Cole." She stood up. "Leave a voice mail message on the cell phone when you want to meet again." Reaching into her handbag, she pulled out a five dollar bill, dropping it on the table. "That's for the coffee."

She walked out of the diner, smiling at the waitress balancing a cup a coffee in her right hand. "I left your tip on the table."

It wasn't until Summer was seated in her car that the violent shaking began. Miraculously, she had successfully repressed her rage. It was obvious that Lucas Shelby was either experiencing burnout or meltdown, and the result was that she had become the receptacle for his bitterness.

Covering her face with her hands, she took deep breaths to force oxygen into her lungs. The constriction in her chest eased. Glancing at her watch, she saw that it was exactly seven. Retrieving her cell phone from her handbag, she scrolled through the directory and punched a key for Gabriel's number. He answered after the second ring.

"Hello."

She smiled. She loved hearing his deep, Southern drawl. "Hello."

"Where are you, Summer?"

"I'm in Whitman. I have to pick up something at my apartment."

"You could've left me a note telling me where you were going. When I woke up and couldn't find you I thought you'd gone jogging. But when I didn't see your car I came close to losing it."

"I'm all right, darling. Let me pack a few more outfits, then I'll be back. Have breakfast waiting for me."

"What do you want?"

"Surprise me."

His sensual laugh came through the earpiece. "You may regret saying that."

"No way. I'll see you in about an hour."

"I love you, Summer."

"Love you back." Pressing a button, she ended the call.

She returned to her apartment, searched through her closet for a suit for Monday, and then filled her ubiquitous leather tote with jogging gear, sweatpants, and several changes of underwear. If she needed T-shirts she could always use Gabriel's.

Gabriel was sitting on the porch waiting for her when she drove into his driveway. The moment she felt his arms close around her she forgot everything that had occurred that morning: Lucas Shelby, and his scathing remarks, and that she was an undercover DEA agent.

"What's wrong with you, Gabriel?"

He gave Summer a sidelong glance, white teeth sparkling under his moustache. "Nothing."

He had practically thrown her into his car once he took her bags from her, leaving them on the floor in the entryway. He closed and locked the door to the house; within minutes he was speeding toward Boston.

"Nothing?" she repeated. "You're acting like a crazy man." Trees and telephone poles whizzed by as he increased his speed. "Slow down before you're pulled over."

His long fingers grazed the gearshift before he shifted into a higher gear. "You asked me to surprise you, and I'm going to grant your wish."

"What I didn't ask is for you to put our lives in jeopardy."

The low racy car took a curve so tightly it felt as if they were standing still. Gabriel's gaze was glued to the winding road in front of him. "Don't worry about us, sweetheart. We're going to live to be old and gray."

She glared at him. "You're gray now."

He shook his head. "That's cold, Summer."

A mischievous smile softened her mouth. "I call it as I see it."

"Are you saying I'm too old for you?"

"Maybe," she teased.

"Too old to do what?" When she didn't answer, he said, "I'm certainly not too old to lust after you."

"Is that all you can come up with?"

"Do me a favor, darling?"

"What, Gabriel?"

"Look over here and see if *it's* up."

It took her several minutes to discern what the *it* was, and her face burned with embarrassment. "I . . . don't believe you," she sputtered. "You've got a dirty mind."

"Yes, I do," he confirmed, deadpan. "That's because just looking at you, kissing you, and making love to you makes me *hot*—as hot as your name. So, don't blame me for harboring what you call dirty thoughts. I'm a man with what I consider a rather healthy libido. However, what we've experienced together has been rather conventional.

"Then there are a few times when I want to share the unconventional, the unexpected with you. Today is one of those days. So, sit back and relax, Summer. I'm going to take you on a ride I hope you'll remember for a long time."

She did sit back, but something wouldn't permit her to relax. All of her senses were operating on full alert when Gabriel maneuvered into a driveway leading to one of Boston's finest hotels. A valet opened the door for her, helping her out, while Gabriel came around to escort her to the entrance.

The morning and afternoon passed in a blur of activity after they were shown to a suite with views of the city and the harbor. A continental breakfast awaited them, and an hour later a member of the hotel's staff came and announced it was time for Summer's scheduled day of beauty.

A consultant at the hotel's beauty spa took down all of the information for her vital statistics before she was shown to a dressing room to disrobe. She was massaged and exfoliated, then had fallen asleep for more than an hour after her massage. She was escorted into a steam room for another half hour. A tiny woman who reminded her of Kim Cheung led her to a charming café where she dined on slivers of apples and pears, a narrow wedge of low-fat cheese, and a cup of herbal tea.

She was shampooed, trimmed, blown-out, curled and waxed to remove superfluous facial and body hair. A manicure and pedicure followed. By this time she was ready to bite into anything that hadn't moved for more than five minutes.

It was after five o'clock when she peered into a wall-to-wall mirror to see a face staring back at her she did not recognize. A makeup artist had done her face so skillfully that all she could do was stare numbly. He'd softened her eyes with a blending of shadows in hues of sable, mink, and silver fox. He'd also applied a soft dark brown powder to her waxed eyebrows. The redefined shape of her brows afforded an expression of her appearing slightly surprised. Her cheeks were flushed with a soft raspberry blush and there was only a hint of color on lips that appeared a glossy nude.

"You like?"

She smiled at the reflection of the man in the mirror. "Yes, I like."

She liked everything: her hair, face, and the feeling of total relaxation she had not felt in years. Her bangs had been trimmed and fell in soft precision over her forehead. A hairstylist had relieved her of two inches of hair, and the result was a flattering blunt-cut style that barely skimmed her shoulders.

Another woman led her into a dressing room. A

classic sheath dress in a shimmering platinum-gray
liquid satin hung from a padded hanger. Undergarments in the same pale gray and a pair of darker gray
silk covered pumps sat on a nearby table, along with a
bottle of her favorite perfume.

"Come, Madame Cole, I will help you to dress."

Summer smiled. It was the first time anyone had
called her Madame. And she wanted to tell the woman
she was not Mrs. Cole. She would not claim that name
until next summer.

Dots of perfume were applied to her wrists and
pulse points before she put on her lacy underwear. The
color reminded her of storm clouds. Sheer pale hose
followed. She stepped into the dress, staring at her reflection. Sleeveless with a square-cut neckline, its style
was similar to the dress she had worn to Alexandra and
Merrick's wedding.

"Your husband has exquisite taste in women's clothing, Madame Cole."

Summer nodded like someone in a trance. "Yes, he
does."

She removed the top off a small white box Summer
hadn't noticed before. "Now for your accessories." The
woman held up a single strand of large perfectly
matched South Sea pearls. "Please sit down, Madame."

Even without putting on the pumps, at five-eight,
Summer towered over the diminutive woman. She sat,
closing her eyes, feeling the weight of the exquisite
baubles resting on her collarbone. A pair of pearl earrings was screwed into her pierced lobes.

"Here is your purse, Madame."

Summer opened her eyes to see her holding a small
gray silk-sateen bag from a silver chain. "Thank you."

"Samples of your lip color and tiny packets with

pre-applied face powder are in the bag." Summer took the bag. "Your shoes."

Summer slipped into the pumps, smiling. They were a perfect fit. Everything she wore was a perfect fit. That explained why the consultant had requested her dress, shoe, bra, and panty size.

Rising to her feet, she smiled at the dresser. "Thank you so much."

The woman returned her smile. "Thank you, and please thank your husband for his generosity." She glanced at the clock on the wall over the door. "Come, come. He is waiting for you."

When Summer had told Gabriel to surprise her, she never thought it would end with her spending a day of being pampered at a hotel spa. Gabriel could surprise her any day and anytime he wanted.

She was escorted down a carpeted hallway and out a door that led directly into the hotel lobby. Standing only a few feet away was Gabriel, grinning. Summer closed her eyes briefly and returned his grin with a dazzling one of her own.

He wore an exquisitely tailored charcoal gray double-breasted, single-buttoned wool and silk blend suit. The stark white shirt with a spread collar made his tanned face look even darker. A dark gray silk tie was knotted in an exacting Windsor knot. Her gaze moved with agonizing slowness over the sharp crease in his trousers falling at the precise break over a pair of black wingtip shoes. As her gaze reversed itself, he crossed his arms over his chest and she noticed a pair of simple silver and onyx cuff links in the French cuffs.

Summer wasn't certain who moved first, but seconds later she found herself cradled against Gabriel's broad chest. The scent of his cologne and aftershave weakened her knees, and she clung to him like a drowning swimmer.

"I love the surprise."

Pulling back, he stared at her professionally made-up face. "You look exquisite."

She lowered her gaze, charming him with the demure gesture. "Madame Cole says, *merci.*"

His lifted his eyebrows in a questioning expression. "Is that what they've been calling you?" She nodded. "When I called the hotel to make a reservation the desk clerk must have listed us as Mr. and Mrs. Gabriel Cole."

"Does that bother you?"

"Of course not. What bothers me is that I have to wait another eight months before it becomes official."

Summer wanted to tell him that she would marry him the next day if she could. Reaching up, her ran her fingertips over his mustache. "Thank you for everything. And you're right. I'll remember this ride forever."

He kissed her forehead. "Come, sweetheart. I don't know about you, but I'm starved." Pulling her hand into the curve of his elbow, he led her toward the elevators. It was when he turned his head she noticed he had replaced his hoops with small diamond studs. Even his hair was shorter. It was still long enough to put into a ponytail, but the blunt-cut ends no longer flowed down his back. If he decided to wear it loose, it would touch his broad shoulders.

"You look fabulous, Gabriel."

He winked at her. "Why, thank you, my love."

They entered the elevator car, and Gabriel pushed the button for their floor. "I hope you don't mind that I requested room service for dinner."

"No, I don't mind." And she didn't. Not now. The

personal services had relaxed her body and her mind wherein her earlier confrontation with Lucas Shelby had been totally exorcised.

Gabriel inserted the card key in the slot to their suite, and opened the door. A large bouquet of snowy-white flowers on the table in the entryway, along with a quartet of lit candles provided an esthetic welcome for Summer.

"How beautiful!"

Gabriel cupped her elbow. "Come."

He led her into the dining area where two white-jacketed waiters stood ready to serve dinner. The table was set with china, stemware and silver. Several candles and a smaller vase filled with an assortment of white flowers served as the centerpiece.

She was seated, and the next ninety minutes passed in a blur. Summer remembered eating seafood bisque and a crab salad, but not much after her second glass of champagne. The sun had set and the lights of the city shimmered like jewels when the waiters cleared the table and surreptitiously left the suite, as she and Gabriel sat staring at each other.

"Would you like dessert?"

She shook her head, her coiffed hair moving fluidly with the gesture. "No, thank you."

He pushed a small gold box toward her. She recognized it immediately. The box contained chocolate from Godiva. "I'm allergic to chocolate."

"I didn't know you had food allergies."

"Only chocolate."

"I'm sorry, Summer."

"You had no way of knowing." She smiled. "I bet it's a truffle."

He stared at her, unblinking. "Why don't you open it and find out."

She picked up the box, untying the elastic band. Her eyes grew wide and filled with tears when she saw the contents. The box fell to the table when she covered her face with trembling fingers.

Gabriel rounded the table, going down on one knee in front of her. Reaching into the box, he removed a ring and slipped it on the third finger of her left hand.

His golden eyes sparkled like the precious jewels on Summer's delicate hand. "Will you marry me, Miss Summer Montgomery?"

Lowering her head, she pressed her forehead to his. Tears streaked her face as she struggled to bring her fragile emotions under control. All traces of Renegade had fled, leaving only Summer open and vulnerable to the man who had asked her to share his life and his future with him.

She smiled through her tears. "Yes, Mr. Gabriel Cole. I will marry you."

Light from a nearby floor lamp and the flickering candles on the table caught and fired a two-carat brilliant cut diamond ring with a pave diamond band. It was a perfect fit.

"How did you know my ring size?"

"The manager at the spa called and told me."

"I wondered why they'd asked for my ring size along with my other vital statistics." She kissed his mouth. "Even though you were quite clever and used a deceptive method, I think I'm going to keep you."

He kissed her, his tongue tracing the outline of her mouth. "You better keep me, sweetheart, because we're in this for the duration."

"When do you want to announce the news to our families?"

"Tomorrow," he whispered against her mouth. "Because tonight I think we're going to be too busy celebrating to talk to anyone."

Curving her arms around his neck, Summer closed her eyes when Gabriel stood up and carried her through the living room and into their bedroom.

She lay motionless, eyes closed, as he undressed her, and then himself. It was only when he moved over her that she opened her eyes, her legs, and her heart to let him in.

Her magical trip ended when she breathed the last sigh of her release into his mouth; she had given Gabriel all of herself, holding nothing back. He, unknowingly, had stripped away her defenses leaving her naked for a pain only he could inflict.

They slept, arms entwined, bodies joined. They woke at dawn to revive the passion that refused to burn out, and when Summer cried out her awesome climax she knew she was not the same woman who had driven from Whitman to Cotuit seeking the comforting warmth of Gabriel's love and protection.

Eighteen

Gabriel's phone rang incessantly throughout the day and evening. He had called his parents with the news that Summer had accepted his proposal of marriage, and an hour later congratulatory calls came from Florida, Mississippi, New Mexico, and Brazil.

Summer also called her grandmother, telling her that she planned to marry her very nice young man the following summer. The sound of Virginia Brown's sobbing was too much for her, and she hung up. Waiting twenty minutes, she called Gram back. This time grandmother and granddaughter were less emotional. The call ended with Virginia promising she would write her daughter and son-in-law in South Africa with the news that her baby girl was going to become a married woman. Just before she hung up she told Summer it was time her parents acted like parents and come home to reconnect with their daughter.

Summer went to sit on the porch after her call to St. Louis. A biting wind searched through the fibers of her bulky sweater, chilling her. The daytime temperature was dropping quickly. In five days it would be the end of the month and Halloween, and with the advent of November, winter would descend upon New England.

She thought about the Halloween Ball that was to be held at the high school. School officials had decided to host the dance to keep the youth off the streets and out of trouble with pranks that sometime resulted in police arrests. At least on school property, they would be monitored.

The screen door opened and closed with a soft click. Glancing up, she saw Gabriel balancing two mugs filled with a steaming liquid. He smiled at her. "One latté for the pretty lady, and a hot chocolate for her man."

He sat down beside her on the love seat, and she leaned into him, sharing his body heat. "It's getting cold."

Gabriel nodded. "This will be my first full winter here."

"Does the cold weather bother you?"

"No. If it gets too cold I'll turn up the heat or put on another blanket on the bed." He stared at her enchanting profile. "Were you cold last night?"

She smiled. "Not with you beside me. You're like a thermal blanket."

"Didn't I tell you that you make me hot?"

"Stop it, Gabriel."

He peered closely at her. "Are you blushing, baby?"

She turned her head rather than let him see her expression. "No."

The cries of circling seagulls caught their attention. Then a comfortable silence descended as they sipped their beverages.

Gabriel broke the silence. "Why don't you move in with me?"

Summer felt her heart stop, then start up again. "I can't do that."

"Why not? You could save money not paying rent."

"It's not about money." What she wanted to tell him was that she did not pay rent on her apartment. That had become the responsibility of her employer. And she had to be available to Lucas whenever he wanted a face-to-face meeting. She didn't think Gabriel would appreciate a strange man coming to see her at his home.

"Then, what is it about?" His voice was soft, non-confrontational.

"It's about tradition, Gabriel. Despite the fact I'm sleeping with you before becoming your wife, I'm still a very traditional woman. I believe in dating, falling in love, getting engaged, marrying, and having children in that order. So far, we're doing all of the right things. Moving in with you would not be the right thing. What I am willing to do is spend some weekends here with you."

He curved an arm around her shoulders, pulling her closer. "You can't blame me for asking, can you?"

She smiled up at him. "No." She regarded him for several seconds. "Have you decided what costume you're going to wear to the Halloween Ball?"

"Not really. I have so many black clothes in my wardrobe that I should come as Dracula. All I need is a pair of fangs. What about yourself?"

Summer shook her head. "I'm drawing a blank, too. I should ask Desiree for a pair of bellbottoms, some love beads and . . . wait a minute. I just got an idea. Maybe I'll come as a sixties radical: Afro, dashiki, platform shoes and a peace medallion around my neck." She made a *V* sign with her first and second finger. "Peace out, my brother."

Gabriel chuckled. "Why don't you go as Tina

Turner. After all, you did "You Better Be Good to Me" as well as or better than Tina herself."

"Then, that's it. I'll be Tina. What about you?"

"I'm leaning toward Jimi Hendrix, but I doubt if the kids will know who he was."

"I disagree," Summer argued. "Look at Robyn Phillips singing Aretha's songs. The girl's only sixteen, yet she knew the words to "Do Right Woman, Do Right Man." And where do you think she was first exposed to Aretha? It had to be at home. These kids know more than just rap and hip-hop."

"You're right. I grew up listening to my parents' music, even though I thought it was lame at the time."

"You know that everything that's old is new again. Especially with hip-hop artists sampling old songs and melodies."

Summer and Gabriel sat on the porch talking about music and performers until a frigid wind coming off the water made them retreat indoors. They went into the family room, lit a fire in the fireplace, lay on the rug and talked about what they wanted for themselves and the children they hoped to have.

A large silver ball, suspended from the ceiling in the gymnasium reflected the many colors of flashing lights. Hundreds of orange and black helium-filled balloons were cradled in a net next to the rotating ball. At exactly eleven o'clock the balloons would be released from the net, signaling the end of Weir Memorial's first annual Halloween Ball.

Summer arrived with Gabriel, having had to endure his ribald comments about her legs in a short skirt and four-inch heels. The moment she put on a frosted-blond wig she had become Tina.

Gabriel had become a reincarnation of Jimi once he donned a fringed vest, black hip-hugging leather pants, boots, colorful beads, and a tie-dyed T-shirt. Summer had styled his hair with her fingers after he had washed it. Thick waves gave his hair the body she needed to make it stand up in a modified Afro hairdo.

Faculty and staff were instructed to arrive at seven, an hour before the students, for a briefing. Dumas Gellis had met with school security to remind them that only Weir students were permitted admission, and that bags would be searched and anything alcoholic would be confiscated. Caterers would serve food and non-alcoholic drinks.

Principal Patricia Cookman, who gave Dumas Gellis the responsibility of direct oversight of her school, made a rare appearance. Most times she preferred sitting in her office behind closed doors to interacting with her faculty, staff and students.

Summer saw her as a middle-aged, nondescript woman with unflattering straight brown hair and dispassionate blue eyes. Miss Cookman had earned her reputation as an expert on curriculum. She believed students needed more than academics, which had led her to apply for and secure the cultural arts grant.

The principal's cold stare swept over her teachers and staff, the lines bracketing her mouth deepening. She would have preferred if they had not come in costume. She had agreed to hold the Halloween dance not for the adults' entertainment but the students.

"Weir is taking a big risk tonight by hosting this affair, but I'm willing to take the risk when we consider the alternatives of our children breaking the law when they do things they consider childish pranks." Her inflection with the flat A's identified her as a Midwesterner. "Turning over headstones and desecrating graves is a crime, and because my goal is to keep young adults in school and out of jail I fully support this undertaking. I thank you in advance for volunteering your time. Good night."

That said, she turned and walked out of the gymnasium. There was a pregnant silence from the assembled as they stared at one another.

"It's two months into the school year, and the old bat comes out of her cave for the first time on Halloween," mumbled a man behind Summer.

Dumas clapped his hands once. "I hope everyone remembers their assignments for monitoring the halls and checking bathrooms. I have security personnel stationed on every floor by the stairwells, so if you see something that's not correct, please alert them." He smiled. "Let's party, people."

Summer met Gabriel's gaze, then glanced away. Even though she wore his engagement ring, they had agreed to keep their liaison private. She looked for Desiree, and seeing her talking to one of the math teachers, she headed in her direction.

"Summer?"

Stopping, she turned to find Dumas bearing down on her. He had come as a pirate: eye patch, earring, pantaloons, boots and a wooden sword in a leather scabbard.

"Yes, Dumas."

"Tina Turner?"

She nodded, smiling. "Yes."

His dark eyes roamed over her body, lingering on her legs in the high heels. "I wanted to congratulate you on your engagement." He caught her left hand, examining the ring. "That must have cost someone at least a year's salary. I know he can't be one of our teachers."

"He isn't." Gabriel wasn't a teacher, but a musician. "It's beautiful."

"Thank you, Dumas." She tried pulling her hand away, but he tightened his grip. "Please let go of my hand."

"Who's the lucky man?"

"I'd rather not say. Now, I'm going to ask you once again to let go of my hand."

He leaned closer. "Or what, Summer?"

The odor of stale tobacco on his breath threatened to make her sick. Even if she had not fallen in love with Gabriel, she never would've dated Dumas because he smoked. What she could not understand was that he was coming onto her in the workplace with dozens of witnesses.

A smile trembled over her lips. "I will knee you in your groin." She had enunciated each word so he would not misconstrue her intent.

Dumas dropped her hand. His face was marked with a loathing that unnerved her. Within seconds, his expression of desire had changed to hate.

It had ended as quickly as it had begun. Nodding, he turned and walked away, leaving Summer staring at his back. She wasn't aware that Gabriel had witnessed Dumas holding her hand, and when she met his gaze his dark face was set in a vicious expression.

The students poured into the school at eight and the partying began in earnest. Music blared from the massive speakers set up by the hired DJ and his crew. Most had lined up at the food and beverage tables, getting their "eat on" before dancing.

The costumes ranged from the ridiculous to the predictable witch, nurse, nun, skeleton, soldier, and vampire. Celebrities, past and present, were well represented: Michael Jackson, Elvis, Prince, Madonna, James Brown, Marilyn Monroe, Alice Cooper, Little Richard, Bob Marley, and Kiss. It was apparent many of the students had raided their parents' attics for the vintage clothing.

The clothes may have been vintage, but the music was contemporary. Glancing at her watch, Summer headed out of the gym to monitor the second floor girls' bathrooms.

She winked at Gabriel dancing with Desiree as she wound her way through the throng eating, dancing, or standing around talking in small groups.

"Nice outfit, Miss Monty."

She smiled at a boy who had auditioned for her. "Thanks, Billy." Most of the students had shortened her name to Monty because they said Montgomery took too long to say.

She headed for the stairwell, and climbed the staircase to the second floor. Her heels made click-clacking sounds on the waxed tiles. Each floor contained four bathrooms: two for girls and two for boys. She knocked on the door of the first one, pushing open the door. Two girls stood in front of a mirror applying kohl to their eyes.

"We're vampires," they said in unison.

Summer smiled. "I know."

She rapped on a stall door, then pushed on it. It was locked. "Anyone in there?" There was no answer. "Did you see anyone go in here?" she asked the girls.

"No."

"Not me."

Sighing, she went into a neighboring stall, stood on the edge of the toilet, and peered into the locked one. It was empty. She checked the remaining stall, and it, too, was empty.

"Let's go, ladies. Do your business and leave."

They put away their makeup, then left, teetering on incredibly high heels, their wispy black dresses fluttering around them like bat wings.

Summer followed them, making her way down the hall to the next bathroom. She stopped short when she heard loud voices coming from the boy's bathroom. Moving closer to the door, she listened intently. The voices were lower, and she took a step, but stopped again when she heard someone moaning in pain.

Reacting quickly, she braced her hands on the door, pushing it open. The scene that greeted her stopped Summer in her tracks. Dumas Gellis's right hand gripped a boy's throat as he pressed him against a wall. She would never forget the fear in the kid's eyes as he pleaded with Dumas to let him go.

"I'll get it for you, Mr. Gellis. I swear I will."

Summer had seen enough. "Let him go, Dumas."

Dumas's head spun around, and when he stared at her, Summer saw the simmering rage in his gaze. "Get the hell out of here and mind your business, Miss Montgomery."

She shook her head. "I'm not leaving until you let him go."

"Please, Mr. Gellis," the boy pleaded. His face was drenched with his tears.

Summer moved closer, her hands tightening into fists. She measured how close she could get to him to land a well-aimed kick to the back of his knees. She had to remember Dumas was a former athlete who had played semi-pro football. He was tall, large *and* strong.

She blinked and before she could blink again Dumas had released the boy, who ran out the bathroom, nearly knocking her down in his haste to escape.

Summer and Dumas stared at each other in what had become a face-off. "If that kid tells his parents that you put your hands on him you know the consequences."

One corner of his mouth twisted upward. "He's not going to tell his parents a damn thing, Miss Montgomery. Do you know why?

"Why?"

"Because I believe he's been dealing drugs at Weir. I've been watching him for a long time."

"Do you have proof he's been dealing?"

"Not yet."

She shook her head. "It's not your responsibility to—"

"Don't you dare stand in my face and tell me my responsibility!" he shouted, interrupting her. The veins in his neck bulged. "This is *my* school."

Summer wanted to tell him Weir *wasn't* his school. It was Patricia Cookman's school. She was the principal.

"I want you to know that if his parents file a complaint against you for assault and I'm called as a witness, I will tell the truth."

She left the bathroom, stood in the hall, trying to understand the change in Dumas's personality. She'd found him popular with the students and staff. Whenever he walked the halls, most students gave him high-fives. Teachers found him approachable and supportive.

She wanted to believe he was having a bad day, but his display of violence directed at her and the student was unconscionable and unacceptable.

Pushing off the wall, she checked the remaining bathrooms before returning to the gymnasium.

RENEGADE

Adjusting his chin with one manicured hand, she
opened the frosted chamber to her and she turned
the right combination to the outside ... shut-u

Flinging all the way, she expected the remaining
bathrooms before returning to the gymnasium ...

Nineteen

Summer balanced a small Styrofoam plate filled with Swedish meatballs, hot wings, miniature spicy beef patties, and potato salad in one hand, while attempting to take a sip of cranberry juice in a cup from the other.

"Do you need some help with that?"

Glancing over her shoulder, she smiled at Gabriel. "Yes, thank you. Please hold my plate."

He took her plate, while she took a swallow of her drink. His gaze shifted to the middle of the gym, where students gyrated to 2Pac's "California Love."

He smiled, swaying in time with the infectious rhythm. "Dance, Miss Montgomery?"

Summer put her cup on a table. "Let's do it."

Gabriel placed her plate next to the cup, captured her hand and led her to the middle of gym. Snapping his fingers, he closed his eyes, and rolled his leather-clad hips in a movement reminiscent of riding a horse. Her fiancé was bumping and grinding as if he were a dancer in a hip-hop video. Summer turned her back to him, unable to believe his suggestive body language. She gasped when she felt his groin graze her hips.

"Show me what you got, baby," he whispered in her ear.

Accepting his challenge, she raised her right hand, spread her legs, and wiggled her hips, then dropped her hips until they were inches from the floor before she wiggled her hips again without moving her feet. A loud roar erupted from the students as they formed a circle to watch two teachers who quickly had become favorites challenge each other in a dance-off.

Summer strutted in her heels, her hips moving as if they had taken on a life of their own as she smiled seductively over her shoulder at her colleague and lover. Executing a quick spin on her toes, she faced him, spread her arms, and thrust her chest at him.

Gabriel's right arm snaked around her waist, pulling her flush against his body, right leg anchored between her knees, and dipped her low enough for the untamed wig to sweep the floor.

The boys howled, pumping their fists in the air and giving one another high-fives.

"Don't let him do that to you, Miss Monty," a girl screamed over the blaring music.

Smiling, Summer pushed Gabriel back. Within seconds she became Tina Turner as the DJ segued into "Proud Mary." Half a dozen girls joined in, becoming Ikettes as they spun around, then executed high kicks.

The dancing became infectious as other teachers and staff joined the students in what had become a montage of music that overlapped generations.

The fever-pitched dance music continued non-stop for the next half hour, until it finally slowed once a ballad by Sade came through the speakers. A collective sigh of relief went up by everyone.

Summer walked off the dance floor, her skin moist from the unaccustomed exertion. It had been years since she'd danced that much. She was breathing heav-

ily, her heart racing; she was so wrapped in a silken co-
coon of euphoria that she did not want to acknowledge
that she wasn't in the best physical shape she could be.

She missed lifting weights, pounding the heavy bag,
and sparring with a partner trained in marital arts. What
she did do was jog for endurance and go for marksman-
ship qualifying training at least four times each year.

What she refused to acknowledge was that she
missed being on stage. Whenever she performed in
front of an audience she wasn't Summer, but the role
she had assumed.

She had come to Weir Memorial as Summer Montgomery, drama teacher, and that was who she was and
wanted to be again. She wanted to work with young
people to help them recognize their talents.

Although some of the students who had auditioned
for lead parts for the spring musical would not get the
roles of their choice, they still had talent and ambi-
tion—enough to come on stage to become the subject
of ridicule and rejection.

She had selected her principal singers and dancers,
but none of the eighty-four who had auditioned would
be rejected outright. She would utilize them either in
the chorus or in crowd scenes. Desiree had offered to
take several and train them to change sets, help with
costume changes, lighting, and sound.

Summer went over to the table where a waiter
poured drinks, asking for water. Smiling, he screwed
the top off a bottle of water and handed it to her. "Nice
performance."

"Thanks." She took a deep swallow, enjoying its ici-
ness bathing her parched throat.

"I'm impressed, Summer."

She forced herself not to glare at Dumas. The image

of him holding that boy by the throat against a wall was still too fresh in her mind for her to be civil to the assistant principal.

Cutting her eyes at him, she said, "You should be." Turning on her heel, she strutted away, feeling the heat of his eyes boring into her back.

She had met a lot of men she did not like because of how they'd earned their money, but this was the first time she had met one who did not sell or traffic in drugs that made her want to cause him pain—intense pain.

To her, children were gifts to love, protect, nurture, and inspire, not beat, threaten or intimidate. If Dumas suspected the boy was dealing, then he should have alerted the authorities responsible for authenticating his suspicions.

Dumas followed Summer as she walked out of the gym. She may have been an artist-in-residence, but she was still a part of the faculty, and that meant she answered to him.

The first time he saw her he couldn't believe how much she looked like his ex-wife: tall, slender, with a drop-dead gorgeous, in-your-face body. Even her coloring and hair was similar to Beverly's. The only difference was that Summer looked young, too young for thirty-three, while Beverly looked like a woman—a woman under whose spell he had fallen the first time he saw her waiting for him after a college football game.

And when he'd looked at the ring on Summer's hand, in that instant she had become Beverly. It was a ring his ex-wife would've been willing to sell one of her ovaries to flaunt.

He had been at the top of his game when he met

Beverly, and a lot of women were throwing their panties at him. He deflected all of the others, and caught Beverly's.

They dated each other exclusively for a year, became engaged, and married a week following his being drafted by the NFL. He'd sat on the bench the first season, but life threw him a vicious curve when two weeks before the start of the next season he hurt his knee when he tripped over a toy his wife had neglected to pick up after playing with their young son. He underwent arthroscopic surgery to repair a shattered kneecap. He'd gained sixty pounds while convalescing, which compromised his recovery. He missed a second season, and his contract wasn't renewed, neither was he picked up by any other team.

Having a wife, and now two children to support, Dumas signed with a Canadian semi-pro team, earning just enough money to keep his head above water. It was when Beverly came to him, saying she wanted out of the marriage and that she was taking his sons that Dumas thought about taking her out, then himself. She said she'd married him because she thought he would get product endorsements that would permit them to live in a mansion, drive luxury cars and wear expensive jewelry. The Gellises were living in a three-bedroom split-level and traveled around in a minivan in a country where winter temperatures were comparable to those in the Arctic.

He'd called his minister, who counseled him about losing his soul. His thoughts of murder-suicide were quickly dashed, and he granted Beverly her divorce. After meeting with their respective lawyers, she told him she would take him back if he ever had enough money to give her want she wanted.

And he wanted his ex-wife. He wanted to see his sons every day, not just during school holidays and summer months. What he wanted was his family back. He was close, so very close to achieving his greatest wish.

Dumas Gellis knew he had two things going for him: intelligence and patience. He had found a way to amass a small fortune without declaring any of it. He had fooled them all: the police, IRS, and the DEA.

But all of that had been jeopardized because Summer Montgomery had come into the boys' bathroom. He couldn't believe his eyes when he saw her staring at him with his hand around Omar Knight's throat.

Quickening his pace, he caught up with her. He touched her arm. "Wait, Summer. Please." He dropped his hand.

She stopped, but did not turn around. "What do you want?"

"Look, can we go somewhere and talk?"

She closed her eyes. "No, Dumas. Not tonight."

"When?"

"Monday. I'll come to your office after classes."

He smiled, his gaze admiring her straight back, the womanly flare of her hips in the short skirt, and the perfection of her incredibly long legs in the heels. Hell, Tina Turner had nothing on Summer Montgomery in the legs department.

"Thank you." He continued to stare at her until he heard approaching footsteps. Shifting, he saw Gabriel Cole. Affecting a smile, he said, "Hey."

Gabriel slowed, placing one booted foot in front of the other in what had become a swaggering stroll. He lifted his chin in acknowledgment. "Hey, Dumas. I just came to ask Summer if she needed a ride home."

Summer turned around for the first time since Dumas

had stopped her. Her features were deceptively composed. "Thanks for asking. And yes, I'll take that ride."

Gabriel smiled, but the warmth never reached his eyes. "I'll you see you later." He inclined his head. "Dumas."

Summer watched Gabriel walk, then without glancing at Dumas, she followed him.

The return trip to Cotuit was accomplished in complete silence. There was no conversation, no music—nothing to break the swollen silence.

Gabriel pressed a button on the visor of the car, and the garage door slid up silently. He maneuvered into the space, shut off the engine, and came around to open the passenger side door for Summer. He felt the delicate bones in her hand as his larger, stronger one closed on hers. She was so fragile, delicate. All he had to do was increase the pressure and the bones would break.

Holding her hand called to mind what he had observed when Dumas had held the hand of the woman whom he now thought of as *his*. What he had wanted to do was launch himself across the gym and tackle Dumas before he had a chance to react. A jealous rage had threatened to turn him into a wild man wherein he would cause another human being serious physical harm.

Tucking her hand in the curve of his elbow, he led her along the path to the front door. He had to let go of her hand when he unlocked the front door. A wave of heat greeted him as he stepped into the entryway, pulling Summer in with him. He closed the door, pressed her back against it, his hands anchored on either side of her head.

Light from a lamp on the table in the space permitted him to see her questioning expression. "What's up with you and Dumas?"

Summer did not blink, as she said, "Nothing. Why?"

Gabriel moved closer. "Every time I looked I saw him hovering over you."

Her expression softened as a smile played at the corners of her mouth. "Jealous, baby?"

His expression was impassive. "Yes."

She leaned forward and her breasts touched his chest. "There's no need for that, sweetheart. Who was it I was shaking my booty for tonight?"

A grin overtook his features until his whole face spread into a smile. "How did you do that little step where you stand still and your booty bounces?"

"Step back and I'll show you."

He complied, and Summer took off her coat, placing it on a chair. Showing him her back, she leaned down and grasped her ankles while keeping her knees straight. She did not see Gabriel's shocked expression as she gave him an up close and personal view of her buttocks moving as if they had taken on a life of their own. She completed her routine when she dropped down then sprang up, peering at him over her shoulder.

"That's called 'dropping it like it's hot.'"

The blood roared in Gabriel's head, as he stared at Summer mouthing words. The only thing he registered was *hot*.

He did not give her time to react when he looped an arm around her waist, lifting her high off her feet. Her legs flailed as he took long strides through the living room and to the staircase, taking the stairs two at a time.

Summer knew they had crossed the threshold of their prior coming together when they fell on the bed, tearing at each other's clothes. She heard her heels hit the floor with a dull thud, following by the sound of Gabriel's boots joining them. He ripped off her Tina Turner wig, throwing it across the room. She laughed because it looked like a small furry creature running to escape a larger predator.

Naked, mouths open, and breathing heavily, they literally tried to devour the other. Her shock was magnified when Gabriel lifted her off the bed and carried her into the adjoining bathroom.

He opened the door to the shower stall, pulling her in with him. Closing the door, he turned on the water, adjusting the temperature until it was a softly falling warm spray. The water beat down on their heads and bodies as they clung together. They danced together for the second time that night, this dance of desire, wild and unrestrained.

Gabriel strummed her body like he did a guitar. He tasted the nectar of her sweet mouth the way he licked a reed to moisten it before he inserted it in a mouthpiece for a sax or clarinet.

Cradling her breasts, he moved down her body, ignoring her plea for him to stop. He would stop, but only when he got his fill—for now.

Still holding her breasts, he went to his knees and drank the honey flowing between her thighs. He felt the bite of her nails against his scalp, heard her hoarse gasps as she sucked much needed air into her lungs.

Her moans turned into a keening that snapped the last fragile thread on his control. He kissed the wet curls between her legs as he retraced his upward journey. The look on her face would be imprinted on his brain forever. Eyes closed, lower lip trembling in desire, Summer was in the throes of a passion every man wanted to glimpse just once in a lifetime from the woman he loved.

Cradling her face between his hands, he licked at her mouth, leaving teasing kisses at the corners. She licked him back, and each time their tongues met, she moaned her pleasure.

"Drop it like it's hot for me, baby," he crooned against her swollen mouth.

Her body went pliant as she turned in his embrace and bent forward. Holding her waist with one hand, Gabriel guided his hardness into her feminine heat. A growl escaped his constricted throat when he felt her squeeze him once, twice, three times. He lost count after that as her hips moved against his thighs in a motion that was old as time itself.

He felt the convulsions shaking her womb squeeze him, and lowering his head, he slid down to the floor of the stall, bringing her with him.

The liquid fire in her body incinerated his, and he pressed his head to the tiled wall and waited for the flames to burn out. They sat, water beating down on their fevered bodies, joined in a passion that flooded them with lingering joy that went beyond words.

Water spiked Summer's lashes as she rested the back of her head on Gabriel's shoulder. His hands were clasped over her belly, adding to the heat that did not come from the water pouring over their bodies.

She shivered when his tongue touched her ear. A knowing smile curved her mouth. Closing her eyes, she whispered, "I love you, Gabriel."

There was a moment of silence before he said, "I know."

Twenty

Dumas stood up when Summer was shown into his office by his secretary. "Thank you, Jackie. Please close the door after you." He walked around his desk, pulling out a chair at a small round table. "Please sit down, Miss Montgomery." She sat, and he took a chair opposite her.

She looked different today—much different than she had at the Halloween Ball. A black slim suede skirt, white turtleneck sweater, leather waistlength jacket and black riding boots pulled her winning outfit together. Her hair, with a fringe of bangs falling over her forehead, was pulled off her face with a black velvet ribbon.

How staid she looked now when only a few days ago she had strutted and wiggled her hips like a dancer in a video. He'd watched her, like most of the boys and men, with his tongue hanging out.

Summer observed Dumas through her lashes, seeing what he did not want her to see: fear. He was afraid she was going to tell someone that she saw him choking a student. She did not know the student's name, and could not make inquiries without calling attention to herself. However, she had called Lucas on her cell phone early Saturday morning during her jog, promising she would get a name for him.

She had gotten up early, leaving Gabriel asleep in bed, and completed her three-mile run. He was up and had showered by the time she returned. They'd spent the morning avoiding each other like cautious strangers. Their wanton coupling in the shower had frightened her because she was not aware that she was capable of such grand passion.

They shared a walk along the beach later that afternoon, holding hands and talking about everything and anyone but themselves. She retired for bed first, waiting for Gabriel to join her. She fell asleep, and when she woke early Sunday morning he was beside her, his arm thrown over her hip. When she attempted to leave the bed, he implored her to stay. She did stay, moving closer to his warmth. Within minutes they both had gone back to sleep.

She crossed one leg over her knee, resting her hands on the arms of the chair. "What did you want to talk about?"

Dumas did not drop his gaze. "You and me."

She blinked once. "What about you and me?"

"Your insubordination, Miss Montgomery."

"Wrong choice of words, Mr. Gellis."

"I don't want to argue with you, Miss Montgomery."

"Then don't, Mr. Gellis," she retorted.

He ran a large hand over his face in a weary gesture. It was apparent he couldn't intimidate Summer. He breathed deeply, successfully curbing his rising temper.

"What happened between me and Omar Knight was unfortunate, and I regret losing my temper. I've apologized to him, reassuring him it will never happen again. And I promise you, Miss Montgomery, that it will never happen again with Omar or any other student here at Weir.

"You weren't here when we lost two of our best and brightest students to drug overdose. Meanwhile, another lies comatose as we speak, brain-dead because of someone selling death in my school. I can still see the faces of these kids, laughing and enjoying what they didn't know would become a very short life. So, when I heard rumors that Omar was dealing on school property I . . ." His words trailed off as he buried his face in his hands. When he lowered his hands, moisture glistened in his dark eyes.

Summer's expression did not waver as she waited for Dumas to continue. Despite his impassionate monologue, she did not believe him. Unlike Patricia Cookman, who was childless, he was the father of two sons. Would he have wanted his sons' teacher to put his boys in a chokehold? No, she mused, answering her own question.

"I was thinking of my own sons," he said, his voice hoarse and filled with emotion.

"Would you want someone to choke them if they were suspected of doing something wrong? People have been known to riot and burn down cities because of what they perceive as police brutality. What you did to Omar bordered on brutality."

"And I said I was sorry."

"Don't say it to me, but to the boy's parents."

"Omar said he didn't tell his parents."

Why? Is it because you threatened him with retaliation? She longed to speak her thoughts aloud, but held her tongue.

"The only thing I can say is that you're lucky Omar is

not my son. First of all, I'd raise him to trust me enough to tell me anything—good or bad. And if he'd told me that you'd choked him, then you never would've been given the opportunity to say you're sorry."

A sheen of perspiration formed on Dumas's shaved head. "Are you threatening me, Miss Montgomery?"

She gave him a chilling smile. "Of course not, Mr. Gellis."

Dumas returned her smile. "That's reassuring to know."

Summer uncrossed her legs. "Are we finished here? I still have a few things to do before I leave for the day."

He gave her a long stare before his gaze dropped to her left hand. "Yes, we're finished."

She rose to her feet, nodded, then walked out of the office, closing the door softly behind her. She had lied to Dumas. She had threatened him, because if Omar had been her son she doubted whether Gabriel would've been able to restrain her.

Every time she and Gabriel made love she thought about his seed growing inside of her. She wanted a baby. But, that could not become a reality until next year.

It was as if her life had been placed on hold until June twenty-fourth. It would be the twenty-fourth if no days were lost due to snow accumulation, otherwise it would be June thirtieth.

A smile curved her mouth as she made her way to her office. She had a name! She would call Lucas and give him Omar Knight's name.

Gabriel and Summer changed positions at a rest stop in Maryland. Adjusting the seat to accommodate her shorter legs, she settled in behind the wheel. Gabriel had driven non-stop from Massachusetts to Delaware, stopping only to refuel the Porsche. They'd planned to celebrate the Thanksgiving holiday weekend with Tyler and Dana Cole in Hillsboro, Mississippi, however, fogged-in conditions had closed Boston's Logan Airport for more than twenty-four hours, which precluded any aircraft from landing or taking off. The only option was to drive to Georgetown. Once there they would connect with Merrick, Alexandra, Michael Kirkland and his family, and fly out of Washington-Dulles.

Summer stared at Gabriel. "Why don't you try and get some sleep."

"You'll be okay?"

Summer cut her eyes at him. "Of course I'll be okay. Just go to sleep."

Reclining in his seat and crossing his arms over his chest, he closed his eyes. He did not relax until she shifted into gear and pulled out of the rest stop and into the flow of interstate traffic. A knowing smile curved the corners of his mouth. She handled his car better than he did.

Summer shifted, signaled and changed lanes as if skating on glass. She occasionally glanced at the navigational screen displaying the interstate and local roads. Gabriel, with the push of several buttons, had electronically calculated the route from Massachusetts to Washington, D.C.

She drove past familiar buildings, sites and neighborhoods: Walter Reed Army Medical Center, Rock Creek Park, the campus of Howard University, and Georgetown University and Hospital. Seeing them brought back memories of the first time she had come to Quantico as a recruit trainee. So much had happened in five years; it was as if she had lived two lifetimes in those five years. But her dangerous masquerade would end in seven months, whether or not she identified the dealer or dealers at Weir.

Turning into the cul-de-sac where Michael and Jolene Kirkland lived, she reached over and shook Gabriel. "We're here. Which house?"

Gabriel came awake immediately. He raised his seat, blinking. "It's the one with the red pipe fence."

Summer stared in awe at the structure, which looked like a Frank Lloyd Wright Japanese-inspired design. "It's beautiful." She maneuvered into a driveway that curved around to the back of the house. Soft lighting was illuminated as she passed motion detectors.

A side door opened, and Michael Kirkland stepped out, pointing to his right. "Pull it in over there." The door to a garage opened silently and she maneuvered next to a black SUV with West Virginia plates.

"Alex and Merrick are here," Gabriel said, opening his door. "I'll get the luggage."

"Leave the luggage here," Michael said as he approached them. "The car service just called, and they'll be here in an hour."

Summer smiled at him as he extended his arms. "Hey, cousin. Welcome to the family."

She went into his embrace, her arms going under his shoulders. "Thank you."

Pulling back, he stared at her. "Do you really want to marry this moody SOB?"

Summer laughed. "I wouldn't have him any other way."

Gabriel chuckled. "I guess that told you, *primo.*"

Michael laughed loudly. "That's what I like. A woman who takes up for her man."

"Hush, Michael," came a woman's voice from the doorway. "You're going to wake up the children."

Michael lifted his eyebrows. "The boss speaks."

"I heard that, Michael Kirkland."

"I meant for you to hear it, Jolene Kirkland."

Gabriel shook his head as he placed his luggage and Summer's near several others lined alongside the door. "You're talking that smickedy smack because you're standing out here, *primo*. If I were you, I wouldn't go back in the house tonight."

Jolene Kirkland stepped out of the house, hands folded on her hips. "Why are you hanging out here, Michael? Don't you realize Gabriel and Summer have been driving more than half the night?" Walking over to Summer, she wound her arm through hers and kissed her cheek. "Come inside and relax a bit before we have to leave. Alex and I also want to see your ring," she added sotto voce. "Have you eaten?"

"Gabriel and I had a quick bite in the car when we stopped to refuel."

"Even though we're not scheduled to take-off until after midnight, we'll eat during the flight." She led her into the kitchen. "Let me see your ring." Summer extended her left hand. Overhead light reflected off the flawless center stone. "I'm afraid of you," Jolene gasped. "It's beautiful."

Summer smiled. "Thank you."

Jolene shook her head. "Don't thank me, girlfriend. Thank your man."

"Believe me, I did."

Snapping her fingers, Jolene said, "Hel-lo."

Jolene Walker-Kirkland led Summer through the chef's kitchen and into a room that resembled a Japanese teahouse. Octagonal in shape, the walls were made entirely of screened-in windows. A low lacquered table, surrounded by large black and pale green floor cushions, was set up in the middle of the room. A woven rug made of straw covered the gleaming oak floor, while low tables overflowed with delicate bonsai plants. Towering stalks of bamboo in glazed containers grew in wild abandonment. Gurgling water from a large indoor corner pool created a soothing mood. Flickering candles and soft lighting invited one to come and stay a while.

"Your house is beautiful."

Jolene smiled. "Thank you. We expanded it a couple of years ago. Unfortunately, I can't give you a tour now, but why don't you and Gabriel come down whenever you guys have a school recess."

"I'll talk to him about it."

"It can't be Christmas, because everyone goes to Florida, so consider it for February."

Summer did not want to tell Jolene that she would probably go to St. Louis in February. It had been too long since she'd seen her Gram.

Merrick, who sat next to Alexandra, stood up. Closing the distance between them, he hugged Summer, his smile warm and genuine. "Congratulations," he said, kissing her cheek.

She kissed him back. "Thank you."

"Now that you're family, I'll make certain to keep an eye on you," he whispered close to her ear.

She pulled back, staring into the silver-gray eyes. "Keep out of it," she mouthed.

"Can't," he mouthed back.

Pulling away from Merrick, Summer sat down next to Alexandra. The two women shared a hug. Summer thought there was something about Alexandra that looked different. Her hair was professional coiffed, but there was something about her face. It was fuller.

Alexandra reached for Summer's left hand. "Whoa! Jolene, take a look at this."

"I saw it. It's breathtaking."

Jolene sat on Summer's left. No one would've taken her for the mother of two young children. Her hips were still slim, stomach incredibly flat in a pair of fitted jeans. Like Alexandra, her curly hair was cut short, and at first glance she could be taken for a fashion model.

"Who picked this out?" Alexandra asked, smiling at Summer, who stared at the circle of diamonds in an eternity band on the hand of her soon-to-be sister-in-law.

"Gabriel."

"All by himself?" Alexandra asked.

"Yes."

Jolene and Alexandra stared at each other. "No!" they chorused in unison.

"My brother never buys jewelry," Alexandra argued softly.

"But he wears earrings," Summer said in defense of her fiancé.

"He wears *my* earrings," Alexandra said, laughingly. "I buy them and he takes them from me. He only wears a watch because it was a gift from Dad after he'd won the Oscar."

Gabriel walked in with Michael, and Summer noticed similarities in the first cousins. Both were tall, broad shouldered, dark-haired with hard slim bodies.

"Who helped you pick out Summer's ring?" Alexandra asked her brother.

He managed to look insulted. "No one."

"You are the most bling-bling challenged one in the

family," she countered. Alexandra squinted at Gabriel. "Hey, you're wearing my earrings. I was wondering where my studs were."

Gabriel touched the diamonds earrings in his lobes. He had put them in the day he'd proposed to Summer, and hadn't gotten around to taking them out. "These aren't yours, brat. I bought these the day I bought Summer's ring. And if I can remember correctly, yours were larger."

Alexandra stared at Merrick. "If Gabe doesn't have my earrings, then where are they? I need them for our daughter."

"Daughter?"

"You know you're having a girl?"

Michael and Gabriel spoke at the same time.

Summer stared at Alexandra. That's what was different about her. She was pregnant.

"I had a sonogram yesterday, and the baby looks like a girl."

"How are you going to handle having a daughter, Merrick?" Gabriel teased.

"Easily. I'll sit at the end of the driveway and pop the little knuckleheads before they can get to the front door."

"Now you sound like Michael with Teresa," Jolene said.

"Can we go back to the ring, Brother Love. Who helped you pick it out?"

Gabriel gave his sister a lingering look. "Why can't you believe I picked it out? I may not be into shopping, but when I do buy something I think I have pretty good taste. What do you think, Summer?"

"I agree. You selected me, didn't you?"

Everyone laughed, while Jolene and Alexandra exchanged high-fives.

The three couples talked and joked until the doorbell rang. The driver had arrived to take them to the airport. Summer went upstairs with Jolene to get the Kirkland children. Two-year-old Teresa and one-year-old Joshua Michael were in their cribs, sleeping. Both were dressed in pajamas. They wrapped the children in blankets and carried them downstairs.

Merrick took Teresa, while Gabriel carried Joshua Michael out to the awaiting van. Michael and Jolene lingered to extinguish lights and activate their security system. The children did not wake up even when belted into child safety seats. Summer sat next to Alexandra, Merrick with Gabriel, and Jolene with Michael, flanking their children.

The driver backed out the driveway, and within minutes cruised through the quiet Georgetown neighborhood to the airport. Despite the lateness of the hour, pre-holiday traffic was heavy.

They arrived at the airport and were processed quickly. It was one-forty when the ColeDiz jet lifted-off and after two when two flight attendants served the passengers entrées of marinated grilled chicken, salmon, sesame ahi tuna, and shell steak with sides of garlic sautéed spinach, butternut squash risotto, and a mixed green salad. The men opted for wine, while Summer, Jolene and Alexandra drank mineral water; the Kirkland children slept undisturbed.

It was the third time Summer had flown on the private jet, and she had come to appreciate its luxurious interior. The aircraft had a forty foot cabin that was configured for eleven to thirteen passengers with sofas that folded out into beds, a full gallery, and rest rooms. One of the two flat-screens showed a movie featuring the antics of Jim Carrey.

As the plane flew over West Virginia and into Kentucky everyone claimed a bed. Summer lay next to Gabriel, listening to his soft snores. The lights in the cabin dimmed as sleep claimed everyone but the flight attendants, pilot and copilot.

Twenty-one

Tyler and Dana were up waiting for their guests, welcoming everyone with hugs and kisses.

Tyler Cole held Summer's hands. "I knew you would become family the moment I saw you." He flashed the trademark Cole dimpled smile.

If Summer could attribute the word beautiful to a man, it would be Dr. Tyler Cole. His close-cropped hair was a shimmering black and liberally feathered with gray. He was right; he wasn't as gray as Gabriel. His smooth deeply tanned olive coloring and high cheekbones made him look exotic. Sweeping black silky eyebrows curved over a pair of large glossy dark eyes. A thin nose and full sensual mouth completed his startling, arresting face. And there was a marked resemblance between Tyler and Gabriel, indicating they were related by blood.

"I want to thank you for thinking of me as family." He leaned down, squinting. "Not think—*are*."

"Yes, sir," she drawled, charming Tyler with what had become an authentic Southern drawl.

Dana Cole took Joshua Michael from Jolene. Petite, golden-eyed, with sun-streaked brown hair, she claimed a delicate beauty that was refreshing.

"We are going to have to work out sleeping arrangements. Chris and Emily and Salem and Sara have claimed two of the three guest suites. That leaves one, which I've decided to give to Merrick and Alex, since they are still honeymooning."

Merrick looped an arm around his wife's waist. "Come, Alex. You need your sleep."

Dana looked at her husband. "Tyler, please go with them."

Tyler winked at her. "Yes, ma'am."

Dana bit back a smile. "I have given the children two of the four bedrooms. All of the boys in one room, and the girls in the other."

"You're real brave," Jolene said. "You know Teresa and Esperanza get along like oil and water."

"That's because Esperanza wants to boss Teresa, and because your daughter is Little Miss Independent, she's not having it."

Jolene threw up a hand. "I'm not going to play referee this weekend."

"I'll monitor the girls," Summer volunteered.

"You've got to be a glutton for punishment," Jolene said, shaking her head. "I prefer the boys any day, any time."

Dana nodded in agreement. "Now, that leaves one bedroom, other than Tyler's and mine. Michael and Jolene can you bear not sleeping together this weekend."

"Yes," replied Jolene.

"No," Michael said.

Dana, Gabriel and Summer laughed.

"Sorry, Michael, but you're about to be overruled. You, Tyler and Gabriel will take my bedroom, while Jolene, Summer, and I will take the other."

Michael affected a pout. "I was never much for sleepovers, especially with dudes."

Gabriel pulled Michael close and kissed his cheek. "Come on, *primo,* you're a *man!* You can go without your woman for a few days."

Michael's light green eyes burned into Gabriel. "Can you?"

"No," he said sniffling, "but I'm going to try."

Dana chuckled at Michael and Gabriel's antics. "Let's get Teresa and Joshua Michael bedded down, then we'll see how much sleep we can get before the kiddie center opens for business."

Summer followed Dana up the winding staircase to the second floor, admiring the meticulously chosen furnishings in the Southern-style Greek Revival mansion and feeling as if she had stepped back in time.

Dana directed her to a large bedroom with twin beds. A sitting area claimed a third one—a daybed. She went into the adjoining bath to shower and brush her teeth. Neither Jolene or Dana had returned by the time she'd slipped between cool, scented sheets.

The house was filled to capacity. Sleeping arrangements would have been even more chaotic if Arianna, Silah and Marguerite Kadir, and Eden and Clayborne Spencer had joined them. The Kadirs had decided to remain in Florida, and Eden and Clay were with their parents at their Mexican retreat.

Summer refused to think of a time when she and Gabriel would offer to host a Thanksgiving celebration. Where would they put everybody?

Gabriel told her that the younger generation of Coles, Delgados, Lassiters, Kirklands, and now Grayslakes had established the tradition of meeting for Thanksgiving. Christmas, however, was always celebrated in West Palm Beach at the Cole family estate. He said the festivities began Christmas Eve and culminated New Year's Eve, and because Summer would not return to St. Louis this year, she would experience her first Christmas with Gabriel's family even though she officially was not a Cole.

Summer walked into the kitchen Thanksgiving morning, finding Dana and Tyler sitting in a breakfast area, sharing a cup of coffee. Dana saw her first and flashed a friendly smile, her amber eyes crinkling.

"Pay up, Tyler."

Shifting on his chair, Tyler saw Summer and stood up. Reaching into the pocket of his jeans, he pulled out a bill and dropped it on the table. "How did you know?"

"It's easy. Our east coast relatives are an hour ahead of us, and the New Mexican ones are an hour behind. It's not quantum physics, doctor."

Summer smiled and greeted her hosts. Both were casually dressed in jeans, T-shirts and running shoes. "Good morning."

"Good morning." Tyler pulled out a chair at the table. "Please sit down. What would you like? Coffee or tea?"

"Coffee. I'd prefer decaf if you have it."

"Decaf coffee coming up."

Summer turned her attention to Dana. "I see you won." She pointed to the dollar on the table.

"I always win. Tyler and I were wagering who would get up first. He said Emily. Whenever she and Michael used to spend the summers with Sara and Chris in Las Cruces, they would get up and find Emily in the family room watching television. I said it would either be you or Jolene because you're joggers."

Tyler returned to the table. The kitchen was filled

with the distinctive aroma of brewing coffee. "First you said it would be Jolene or Gabe."

Dana rolled her eyes at her husband. "I'd never say Gabriel. Remember, he's a musician, and they're notorious for sleeping days and partying nights."

"Gabe has redeemed himself. He's now a teacher," Tyler argued.

"I have to agree with Dana," Summer said, giving her a wink. "I'm always up before Gabriel."

Tyler gave Summer a long, penetrating stare. "So, now he's getting *some?* "

"Tyler!" Dana gasped.

He stared at his wife. "What?"

"You shouldn't get into the woman's business like that."

Tyler waved his hand. "Hell, Summer's family. And with family nothing's sacred. And it's not like Gabe openly denied he was on a sex diet. When he told us in Boca Raton that he and Summer were just friends we simply offered him a little manly advice."

Dana cut her eyes at Tyler again. "The only advice you need to give, Dr. Tyler Simmons Cole, is to the women who lay up on your examining table and open their legs for you to check out their kitty cats." She snapped her fingers, rolling her head on her neck. "Me-*ow!* "

Tyler threw back his head and roared, while Summer doubled over laughing, holding her stomach. They were still laughing when Merrick and Alexandra walked into the kitchen, holding hands.

Summer bonded easily with Gabriel's family because of the smaller gathering. She had come to recognize and identify all of the children: five boys and five girls, ranging in age from nine months for Dana and Tyler's Astra to eight-year-old Isaiah Lassiter.

She had kept her promise to entertain the children as she laughed with them when viewing the annual Tournament of Roses parade; she cheered as loud as they did when Santa Claus appeared on the screen, signaling the end of the parade. After lunch she played a heated competitive game of Candy Land with Isaiah Lassiter, his twin sisters, Nona and Eve, Alejandro, and Esperanza Delgado.

Once she settled everyone down for a storytelling session, Martin Cole II and Teresa Kirkland challenged each other for a coveted place on her lap. Before she'd finished the second story all were asleep on a blanket on the solarium's carpeted floor. Tiny Astra Cole was asleep on her knees, sucking her thumb. Summer decided to take advantage of the inactivity to retreat to the kitchen for a glass of water.

She walked into the kitchen, finding it buzzing with activity as Emily basted an enormous turkey, her sister-in-law, Sara crimped the edges of several pies, and Dana and Alexandra chopped the ingredients for potato salad.

As Dana stared at Summer, her eyebrows rose in amazement. "I see you haven't pulled your hair out."

Resting her hands on her hips, she said smugly, "They're all asleep. Albeit on the solarium floor, but still asleep."

Raven-haired, green-eyed Emily Delgado crossed her chest. "What have we done to reap such blessings? Summer has to have special powers to keep ten children from holding the first annual WWE Kiddie Smack Down."

"They're not that bad, Emily," Alexandra said.

Emily glared at her cousin. "Wait until you have

more than one, and all you'll hear is 'he took my toy,' 'she's bothering me,' or 'that's not fair, Mommy.' What you will come to appreciate is afternoon naps and bedtime. Chris talked about trying for another girl and I can't repeat what I told him. He was very serious when he said threatening a judge is a felony."

Summer smiled at Emily as she took a pitcher of water from the refrigerator and filled a glass. "I thought men wanted sons to carry on their name."

"That's true. Chris loves Alejandro and Mateo, but Esperanza has him wrapped around her little finger."

"I agree," said Dana. "Even though Martin is Tyler's biological son and his grandfather's namesake, he's already begun spoiling Astra shamelessly. I'm not certain whether it has anything to do with her being alone in the world after her fifteen-year-old mother died giving birth to her, or if it's because she's a girl. He says every man needs a daughter to soften him a bit."

The women continued their conversation about children while Summer retreated to the solarium to look in on her charges. She sat on a love seat, picked up the book of fairy tales and began reading. After a while she put it down. Why hadn't she realized how frightening and violent the stories were: ogres, witches and their spells, giants, and wolves, and wily foxes trying to eat cookies? She shuddered at the same time a loud roar went up from a room at the other end of the hallway. She smiled. The men had gathered in Tyler's library to watch the countless televised Thanksgiving Day football games.

Tyler sat at one end of the table, his dark gaze lingering on those who had traveled hundreds of miles to celebrate a very special gathering in his home. It was to become the first time he would preside over a Thanksgiving celebration as heir apparent to the Cole dynasty. As the only son of Martin Diaz-Cole, the current reigning patriarch, Tyler was expected to relocate to West Palm Beach, Florida, to guide and protect the next generation.

He loved his wife, and children, his work as medical director at the Hillsboro Women's Health Clinic, and he enjoyed the comforts of his home. And like his father, Tyler felt that his life was perfect. Pushing to his feet, he raised a goblet of water. All eyes were on him, even those at the two smaller tables crowded with the children of the Cole legacy's third generation.

"I'd like to offer a special thanks," he began in a soft drawling voice, "for all who are gathered together under this roof. We have much to be thankful for this year. Dana and I now have a daughter and Alexandra and Merrick are expecting their first child, whom I hope I will be given the privilege to help bring into this world." Tyler had delivered most of the ten children sitting at the kiddie tables.

"This year we welcome Merrick Grayslake and Summer Montgomery as our newest family members, and hopefully next year this time we will be able to toast Gabriel and Summer as they await the birth of their son or daughter." He extended his glass in Gabriel's direction. "Here's to not shooting any dummy sperm."

The entire table erupted in laughter, while Summer's face burned with humiliation. The children laughed hysterically even though they did not have a clue why.

Gabriel stopped laughing long enough to say, "I'm going to pay you back for that remark once I get your tired behind on the basketball court tomorrow. Then

I'll see what you have to say about another kind of shooting."

Gabriel held the family record of the most consecutive three-pointers on a regulation basketball court: sixteen. Tyler had constructed his home to include an in-ground pool, tennis, and basketball court.

Tyler's dimpled smile faded quickly with the challenge, and he sat down while everyone laughed even harder.

Twenty-two

*We've found nothing on Omar Knight which would
lead us to believe he's dealing.* It had taken Lucas eight
weeks to come up with nothing—*nada*—on a student
Dumas Gellis suspected was dealing drugs at Weir.

Summer had replayed Lucas Shelby's statement in
her head over and over as she sat in the auditorium that
was quickly filling up with students, faculty, staff and
family members for Weir's Holiday Concert.

When she'd told Lucas about Dumas's over-the-top
physical confrontation with Omar, Lucas had merely
shrugged it off, saying the assistant principal was
overzealous like many of his agents.

Lucas's assessment of Dumas bothered her, because
whenever he directed a bust he always cautioned those
on his team about going above the law. What she had
wanted to do was remind him of the time he'd punched
her in the face during the Robertson bust.

Focusing on the activity on the stage, she stared at
the students warming up their instruments. The girls
were dressed in black skirts and white blouses, the
boys in white shirts and black slacks.

She and Gabriel hadn't seen much of each other
since their return from Mississippi, except on weekends, because of his rehearsal schedules. Most days

found him lingering behind after the dismissal bell to
practice with his students for the concert. Not sharing
dinner with him during the week permitted her more
time to write the skits for her spring concert. She had
just completed one for the Big Band era. She had
given herself a December thirty-first deadline to complete the production.

Tomorrow would become the last day of classes
until January second. The entire school system was
scheduled to close for the winter recess, and on Sunday she and Gabriel were scheduled to fly to Florida
for a weeklong celebration with the Coles. She looked
forward to reuniting with her new family with an excitement that was somewhat frightening. It would
become the first time in a very, very long time that she
would feel a part of a real family.

After Thanksgiving, she had embarked on a shopping
spree with a vengeance that surprised even her. Never
one to brave the stores and malls during the Christmas
shopping season, she had made the rounds of toy stores,
shops that sold clothing for the newborn through pre-
teen, prowled the children's section of bookstores, and
purchased gift certificates for Gabriel's sisters, brother,
and many cousins. She had bought a magnificent Waterford vase for her future mother and father-in-law.
She'd mailed a gift certificate to her grandmother for her
to redeem at her favorite apparel shop for a new wardrobe for her upcoming cruise.

She spent hours wrapping gifts with festive paper,
ribbon, and name tags before she packed them in large
cartons to be shipped to Martin and Parris Cole's residence in West Palm Beach, Florida. The gifts, which
would be placed under a massive tree, would be
opened Christmas Eve at the stroke of midnight.

The only gift she hadn't shipped to Florida was Gabriel's. She had purchased a status bracelet with alternating links in platinum and yellow eighteen-karat gold. It was what she'd called an impulse buy. She saw it and put down the plastic before she could question herself as to the price tag.

The stage's spotlights dimmed and Gabriel walked onto the stage, hair flowing to his shoulders and dressed in his ubiquitous black. Summer's breath caught in her chest at the same time a loud roar went up from the students sitting in the audience. Gabriel had become one of their favorite teachers. They claimed he was *"cool"* because he understood and respected their music.

He was cool to the students while Summer thought he looked "hot" strutting on stage in a black cashmere jacket with a shawl collar, a mock turtle cashmere sweater, flannel slacks, and a pair of low-heeled boots. His salt-and-pepper wavy hair grazed his shoulders whenever he moved his head.

Observing him from a distance made her aware of the little things in the man to whom she'd committed her future that she hadn't noticed before. Gabriel Cole did not walk, but swaggered, methodically placing one foot in front of the other as his shoulders rocked from side-to-side. He had a way of raising his chin slightly in what she thought of as a haughty or challenging gesture. And whenever he smiled it usually wasn't spontaneous, but slow in coming like a drop of heated wax sliding down a lit candle.

Holding a baton loosely between the fingers of his right hand, he snapped it once on the music stand, and in one measured motion violins and viola went from thighs to chins, cellos positioned between knees, bows touched the strings of bass violins, and the mouth-

pieces to clarinets, oboes, flutes, trumpets, saxophones, trombones, French horns hovered next to
waiting lips. Gabriel's hand went up in a graceful arc
and the familiar strains to "O Come All Ye Faithful"
swelled in the auditorium. Halfway through the classic
carol Summer knew the concert should not have taken
place without choral accompaniment.

The song ended with applause, then a hush fell over
the assembly as Gabriel picked up an acoustical guitar
laying across a chair and sat down near two flutists and
played the beautifully haunting notes of "Joy to the
World" as cellos, violins, flutes and French horns provided a quiet background.

"Joy to the World" segued into a jazzier version of
"What Child Is This" as a sax player and percussionist
had everyone nodding their heads in time with the tune
also known as "Greensleeves."

The pace and tone changed when a student placed a
microphone in front of Gabriel and adjusted the
height. The sound of tinkling bells, crisp plucking of
the guitar strings, and his passionate voice singing
"River" sent chills up and down Summer's spine.

She stared at him, stunned by the passion in his face
as he closed his eyes and sang from his heart.
Gabriel's singing Joni Mitchell's "River" was as moving as the version she had Kenny Lattimore sing.

He accompanied the orchestra, they watching him
carefully when he set the rhythm with either his hand
or head. Forty-five minutes and six carols later the first
half of the program ended with a standing ovation and
whistling. Gabriel stood, bowed, then motioned for his
students to stand. On cue, they stood and bowed their
heads as one. Seconds later the curtain closed, and the
lights brightened.

Summer sat, grinning from ear to ear. Gabriel was
right—his students were extremely talented. When she
had asked him what he was working on with his students, he refused to tell her, saying she would have to
wait until the night of the concert. Well, she had waited,
and there was no doubt the wait was more than worth it.

The lights dimmed again, the curtain opened, and
this time there was no guitar. He tapped the stand with
his baton, and there were gasps of recognition when
the students began the allegro non troppo from
Beethoven's Symphony no. 9 in D minor.

Summer's eyes glittered with excitement. The first
time she'd appeared as a principal singer in a production at the school of dramatic arts in St. Louis had been
to sing soprano for Beethoven's Ninth. Singing the part
wasn't as challenging as learning to sing it in German.

She found herself on her feet, cheering with the others when the overture ended and the final curtain came
down. Tears pricked the backs of her eyes as she struggled not to cry.

Gabriel was magnificent!

His students were magnificent!

She loved him so much that she felt lightheaded
with the soaring passion sweeping her up in a mael-
strom of desire that threatened to stop her from
breathing.

Pushing her way through the throng, she made it
back to her office and waited for Gabriel. It was almost forty-five minutes later when he walked in, his
eyes shimmering with excitement. Closing the door
behind him, he turned and smiled at her.

"How did you like my kids?"

She quelled the urge to go to him and kiss him with

all of the passion and desire heating her blood. "They were fabulous. You were fabulous."

He nodded. "Thank you, Summer." His expression changed, becoming almost somber. "Will you come home with me tonight?"

Summer felt the repressed energy radiating from him, recognizing it immediately. It was the joy, the thrill of knowing you had given the best performance you could. It was as if you'd bared your soul for everyone to see, and they had made the sacrifice worthwhile.

"Yes." The single word was a whisper. "Let me go home first and pick up something to wear tomorrow." Her bags for her weeklong stay in Florida were already at his house.

He nodded. "I'll pick you up in half an hour."

Reaching for her coat and handbag, she brushed past him, their bodies barely touching, walked out of the office and then made her way out of the school to the parking lot.

Summer shivered as she huddled against Gabriel as they made their way to the front door. "It feels like snow."

"Let it snow," he sang at the top of his lungs. He dropped his arms and unlocked the door. Heat swept over their chilled faces, welcoming them in.

Summer left her bag on the chair in the entryway, hung up her coat on a nearby coat tree, and followed Gabriel through the living room and into the kitchen.

He made his way into the half-bath. "How about a latté?"

She crowded into the bathroom with him. "Yes, thank you." Pushing her hands under the running vater, she smiled up at Gabriel as he washed her hands, kissed her fingers, then dried them.

"Why don't you go upstairs and get into bed and I'll bring you your latté."

She kissed his cheek, inhaling the faint scent of his woodsy aftershave on his skin. "Okay."

She climbed the staircase, removing the cardigan to reveal a pale yellow twin set. A lamp on a table in the sitting area spilled soft golden light onto the bedroom. Undressing and leaving her clothes on a padded bench at the foot of the king-sized bed, she went into the bathroom and removed her makeup and brushed her teeth.

She was in bed, wearing one of Gabriel's T-shirts when he walked in with their lattés. He handed her hers before he placed his cup on the table on his side of the bed. Leaning over, he kissed her hard on the mouth.

"Don't run away, I'll be right back."

"Where am I going in this weather, wearing this?" She pulled up the T-shirt.

"Don't," he groaned, staring at the outline of her firm breasts rising and falling sensuously over a waist small enough for him to span with both hands.

Summer giggled softly and watched him as he disappeared into the bathroom. The latté was too hot, so she waited for it to cool. She lay with her back against the pillows when Gabriel reemerged from the bathroom, naked.

Her admiring gaze was trained on him as he moved closer. Even though he had confessed to loving her, even though she wore his ring, she found it difficult to believe she had fallen in love with someone who had truly become her soul mate. His relatives thought of him as moody, while she thought of him as reflective. They hadn't understood his tuning out everything around him whenever he heard, as he had explained to her, music in his head. And she was secure enough to know that his periods of silence had nothing to do with her inability to engage him in conversation.

Gabriel slipped into the bed beside Summer, reaching for her. "Is it too cold in here?"

"No," she murmured, her face pressed to his hairy chest. She placed tiny kisses over his shoulders and throat, and moved lower over his flat belly.

She rested her cheek on his belly, and he reached down and rested a hand on her head.

They hadn't made love last week because she'd had her period. He had asked her about contraception, because twice they had made love without his protecting her, and she'd confessed to being on the Pill. And although they'd talked about waiting to start a family until after they married, the urge for fathering a child had overwhelmed him with its intensity after seeing Summer with his young cousins. She was a natural with children, and several of the children had become tearful when they realized Summer was leaving to go back home to a place where they wouldn't see her for a long, long time.

He was godfather to Michael and Jolene's son, Joshua Michael, and holding the infant in his arms while the priest had anointed the child with oil and water had left Gabriel shaking with emotion. Michael and Jolene Kirkland had offered him the responsibility of caring for their son if anything were to happen to them, and that was when he realized there was the remote possibility that he might have to take care of someone other than himself.

His initial reluctance to become responsible for a child had changed because he wanted Summer to have his baby; he had teased Tyler about making babies, while harboring his own fear that perhaps he would not be able to father a child.

Everyone teased Emily, although they knew she loved her children, because she complained about their sibling rivalry, while Sara and Salem Lassiter's children did not compete or challenge each other the way hers did. Gabriel had been the one to tell her that she was rearing her children like his parents did—as free spirits, wherein the Lassiter household was more structured and subdued. He'd teased her, saying she should look to have a musician or artist in any one of the three. His explanation seemed to belie some of Emily's apprehension as she kissed him and thanked him for his observation, but tapped him on his shoulder once he reminded her that the DNA of the late Alejandro Delgado-Quintero and Joshua Kirkland has been passed along to her children.

The Delgado children's grandfathers were men who were unique in their own way. The elder Delgado and Kirkland's destinies were entwined when Alejandro identified prominent Mexican drug traffickers for a major U.S.-Mexican drug sweep orchestrated by retired U.S. Colonel Joshua Kirkland, former associate coordinating chief of the Defense Intelligence Agency.

It was after his conversation with his cousin that he wondered how would he raise his own children—the way his parents had or more like Sara and Salem Lassiter?

"Summer?"

"Hmmm."

He smiled. Her voice echoed the heavy satisfaction making it difficult for him to move. "I'd like for you to consider something."

"What?"

"I want us to consider trying for a baby now."

Her head came up, and she stared at him as if he were a stranger instead of someone with whom she had pledged her future. "A baby?"

Sitting up, he reached down, anchored his hands under her arms and pulled her up to lie flush on his body. "Yes, a baby."

Her brow furrowed slightly. "Are you telling me to come off the Pill?"

He shook his head. "No, darling. I'd never tell you to do anything that has to do with your body. I'm *asking*, Summer."

Her frown deepened. "What happened to us waiting until after we marry?"

"I've changed my mind."

Summer registered the depth and quiet emphasis in his words. He'd changed his mind. He wanted a baby *now*. She also wanted a baby *now*, but the reality was that she did not want to carry a baby while still undercover.

Moving up, she pressed her mouth to Gabriel's, feeling his breath feather over her lips. "Why now, Gabriel? I don't want to be a bride walking down the aisle with a belly."

"You won't be the first pregnant Cole bride." He chuckled when he heard her slight gasp. "My mother was at least three months along with me when she married my father. Alexandra was pregnant when she married Merrick. Regina waited until after she'd delivered Clay to marry Aaron. The one to take the rag off the brush was Uncle Martin. Regina was nine before he found out he had a daughter."

"Who *wasn't* pregnant?"

"Emily, Sara, and Arianna."

"What about Jolene?"

"I forgot about her. She, too, had a little bun in the oven when she married Michael."

Summer wanted to tell Gabriel that there was nothing she wanted more than to become his wife and the mother of his children, except for a little obstacle. She was playing a dangerous masquerade, one that she did not know how it would play out.

She and Merrick had argued during the return flight from Mississippi, both managing to keep their voices low and expressions impassive while she told him to back off. He had stubbornly refused saying that he would use his own methods to make certain nothing happened to his unborn daughter's aunt.

"I can't, Gabriel." He stared at her so long that Summer felt as if his shimmering gold eyes were going to burn her face with their intensity. He was angry while she was resolute in her decision.

Without warning, she kissed him, her tongue pushing into his mouth. At first he resisted, then he parted his lips. She teased, tantalized until his hands moved down and cradled her hips. Within seconds, the T-shirt she wore slipped off the bed and onto the carpeted floor. She slid down his body, her mouth and tongue charting a determined path.

"No!" Gabriel bellowed when he felt her take him into her mouth. He collapsed to the mound of pillows on his side of the bed, breathing heavily through his open mouth as her hot mouth and tongue worked their magic.

He forgot his annoyance at her stubbornness to marry before the school year ended; he forgot about her reluctance to get pregnant, and once his flesh swelled between her teeth he even forgot his own name.

The women rule and the men serve.

She had come to fully understand the family motto because she had found herself an equal with Gabriel out of the bed, while she had assumed control in bed. And she was not above using her body in the most skillful way possible to get him to agree to anything she wanted. And *this* moment she was in control and ruling with the absolute power of a despot.

"No, Sum-m-er!" He'd groaned her name out in three syllables instead of two. She was driving him crazy. Her hot mouth was doing things to him that threatened to strip him bare where he'd become more malleable than soft clay.

Tears of pleasure—pure and explosive—pricked the backs of his eyelids as he convulsed violently. His control shattered as a growl escaped his constricted throat and somewhere where sanity and insanity merged he found the strength to extract Summer's mouth from his swollen flesh.

He picked her up like a small child, pressed her back to the mattress, lifted her legs over his shoulders and entered her like a heat-seeking missile striking its target.

This coupling, this joining was so passionate, intense, that Gabriel was certain he had experienced *le petit mort* for the first time as he and Summer climaxed simultaneously. He was dying, drowning in the pure and explosive pleasure of the woman writhing sensuously under him.

Head lowered, chest rising and falling heavily, he stared at the satisfied smile on her lush mouth. "I'll wait," he gasped.

Summer opened her eyes, and her smile widened. *I know you will,* she mused.

Twenty-three

Gabriel's refrain of "let it snow" had become a reality. And it did snow—for three days and two nights without stopping. The northeast had been hit with the storm of the new century with thirty-eight inches of snow, with drifts up to six feet.

Summer sat in the sitting room, staring at the thin television screen cradled on its own stand, unable to believe the flickering images. The snow had crippled the nation's capitol. Blowing snow and drifts stretched from portions of West Virginia and up the east coast to portions of Maine.

This would become the first Christmas that the second generation of Coles, Kirklands, and Grayslakes would not celebrate Christmas and New Year's in West Palm Beach, Florida. Merrick and Alexandra who were spending the weekend with Michael and Jolene, were now stranded in Georgetown.

The sound of popping embers and the smell of burning firewood filled the bedroom and several downstairs rooms as Gabriel lit fires in the fireplaces.

Gabriel sat across from her now, his sock-covered feet tucked under him in a yoga position. He bobbed his head in unison to the music coming through the headset in his ears while he scribbled notes on a staff-lined paper.

Another image flashed across the screen, and Summer went completely still. "Gabriel, look!" She stared when he did not answer, and she jumped up and pulled the wire on the headset. His head came up quickly. "Come look at this!"

Shifting positions, Gabriel stood next to Summer as they listened to the news commentator's voice reporting that the Boston police had found the frozen body of a young boy who had been identified as Omar Knight. His parents had reported that he and several other boys had gone out to shovel snow for several of their elderly neighbors. The boys had returned to their homes later that evening, but Omar had not come home.

Summer did not realize she was crying until the images on the television blurred. She couldn't believe it. The frightened young boy whom Dumas had trapped against a bathroom wall was gone. She heard Gabriel mumbled an expletive, redirecting her attention to the news anchor's voice.

"Police officials report that the boy, who was reported missing four days ago by his family, appears to have suffered a broken neck. An autopsy will determine the exact cause of death. Omar Knight, who is a junior at Weir Memorial High School, is reported to be well liked and a good student." The picture shifted to an image of Omar's mother sobbing in her husband's arms.

"Turn it off, Gabriel. Now!" Summer shouted when he appeared transfixed by the report. He picked up the remote, pressed a button, and the screen went blank.

"Why?" she sobbed against Gabriel's sweatshirt-covered chest. His arms tightened around her body.

"He was so young, so innocent. Why would anyone hurt him? Why? Why?" she sobbed over and over.

Closing his eyes, Gabriel rested his chin on the top of Summer's head. "We don't have any of the answers, baby."

"They lost their baby, Gabriel. They had him for a very short time, then he was taken from them."

Gabriel felt his self-control tested as he held the woman he loved in his arms to his heart. He knew Summer was reliving her own brother's death. The grief-stricken faces of the Knights had become the Montgomerys all over again.

He held her until her sobbing subsided, then he picked her up and carried her to the bed. They lay together in the quiet silence that had become so much a part of who they had become.

Gabriel felt Summer slip out of bed early Christmas morning, but made no attempt to stop her. In that instant he cursed Nature, which demonstrated her power with delivering three feet of snow to the east coast. If the storm, which had developed in the Ohio Valley, had blown out to sea instead of turning north, he and Summer would be in Florida where the news of Omar Knight's death would not have reached them until their return. He knew he was selfish and unrealistic, but he wanted to shelter Summer from the pain of reliving the loss of her brother.

Summer squinted through the lenses of her sunglasses as she jogged along the road. It had been plowed, the snow pushed to one side like a wall of pristine white crystals. Because of its proximity to the ocean, the Cape did not have the monstrous accumulations that had occurred in-land.

She punched the programmed number for Lucas Shelby. It rang several times, then she heard his voice mail message. "Renegade. Call me." Pressing a button, she ended the call.

Three minutes later, the cell phone rang, she answering before it rang again. "Yes?"

"I guess you heard about that poor kid."

"His name was Omar, Lucas, not that poor kid."

"I'm sorry, Renegade."

"What do you know?"

"We've made inquiries, and the police said that the M.E. found traces of narcotics in his stomach."

She frowned. It was apparent the DEA had uncovered information that had not been released to the press. "Did they identify the substance?"

"Preliminary tests are leaning toward MDMA."

"Ecstasy? I thought you told me he was clean."

"We didn't find any evidence of him selling, but that did not mean he wasn't abusing. We have to identify who was supplying him with the tablets."

"School is closed for the week, but once it reopens there's going to be a lot of grief counseling sessions for Weir's student body. Remember, this is the third peer they've lost in three years."

"Do whatever it is you have to do, Renegade. If you feel you need to lean on somebody, then do it. I want Omar Knight to be the last drug statistic at Weir."

She slowed her pace, breathing heavily in the frigid air. "I hear you."

"Renegade?"

"Yes, Lucas?"

"Merry Christmas."

She smiled. "Merry Christmas to you, too."

Summer hung up and reversed direction. Her boss had verbally given her the go ahead to become more aggressive in her search for Weir's drug dealer.

Gabriel was waiting on the porch upon her return. She surveyed his tall figure as he stood up. It had become a habit for him to wait for her to come back from jogging. She had invited him to join her, but he said he preferred walking to jogging. Wherein she jogged three miles, he would walk the three miles. What he did do was push-ups and sit-ups to keep his body toned.

Despite the frigid temperature, he wore a pair of jeans, T-shirt, and socks. The wind swept his unbound hair around his face. Their gazes met and fused as she mounted the stairs leading up to the porch.

Removing her gloves, she placed her palms against his cold cheeks. "What are doing out here half-dressed?"

He stared at her through his lashes. "Waiting for you."

She kissed his cold mouth. "The next time you wait for me, put more clothes on."

"Why? I'm not cold."

"It's fifteen degrees, Gabriel. That's not cold?"

A hint of a smile played at the corners of his mouth. "No."

"You're kidding?"

"No. I'm always hot around you. There are not too many men who live in Massachusetts that can say they have summer every day of the year." Reaching into the back pocket of his jeans, he pulled out a silver-foil wrapped narrow flat package. "Merry Christmas."

She took the gift, smiling. "Thank you, darling. Let me get yours and we'll open them together."

They went into the house and into the family room where a fire blazed behind a decorative wrought-iron screen. Summer removed several books lining a built-in bookcase and took out the gift she had hidden there.

"Now I'll have to a find another hiding place," she teased Gabriel, handing him his gift. They shared a smile. It was apparent they had given each other jewelry because the shape of the boxes were the same.

Summer peeled off the paper, gasping loudly when she raised the top on a blue velvet case cradling a bracelet with bezel-set diamonds lining a graceful scroll of vines and flowers and reminiscent of estate jewelry.

"It's absolutely exquisite."

Gabriel lifted an eyebrow. "I hope you like it."

She held out her right arm. "I love it. I love you."

Gabriel put the bracelet on her wrist, smiling when she kissed him. He wanted to tell her that he loved her, more than anything and anyone in his life. The item was perfect for her delicate wrist.

The bracelet was much heavier than it appeared, and Summer knew it had to be platinum. So much for her lover not knowing how to choose bling-bling.

Gabriel opened his gift, the lines around his eyes deepening when he stared at the sophisticated links. "I suppose we were thinking along the same lines." It was an ideal match for the stainless steel and gold Rolex watch his father had given him after he'd earned an Oscar for his *Reflections in a Mirror* movie soundtrack.

He held out his right arm. "Please put it on." The

deep yellow gold was a warm contrast against his brown wrist. Smiling, Gabriel nodded. "Very nice, Summer. You have exquisite taste."

"I know," she said without a hint of modesty. "I chose you, didn't I?"

Reaching for her, Gabriel pulled her to sit on his lap. "Wrong, baby. I was the one who chased you."

She affected an attractive moue. "Now you're the one talking smickedy smack. If I hadn't wanted you to catch me, then you still would be staring with your tongue hanging out."

He winked at her. "My tongue only hangs out when you drop it like it's hot for me."

Looping her arms around his strong neck, she pulled his head down. The light from a table lamp reflected off the precious stones circling her wrist. "I'll see if I can't accommodate you later."

He kissed the end of her nose. "I can't wait."

It was later that night when Gabriel and Summer celebrated their first Christmas together—their own special way—that Summer decided she did not want to wait for June to marry or have a child. She wanted it now. But more than that she wanted to rid herself of the dangerous masquerade.

As she lay in Gabriel's embrace, savoring the aftermath of their passionate coupling, she redefined her role as Renegade because she no longer had six months to identify Weir's drug dealer. She had given herself three months.

If she had brought down Richard Robertson who was indicted for money laundering conspiracy in only thirteen months, if she focused, really focused, then there was no reason why she couldn't stop the drug dealing at Weir.

And she knew Lucas was right when he accused her of spending more time in Gabriel Cole's bed than she did collecting evidence. But all of that would change with the second day of January.

She would give Lucas Shelby what he wanted, Gabriel Cole what he wanted, and in turn she would get what she wanted most.

Twenty-four

School psychologists, social workers, and grief counselors were available for the six hundred students at Weir Memorial High School once classes resumed January second. Summer felt the pain and loss of Omar Knight as acutely as she had when she lost her younger brother. The scene of the students at Charles's school had become an instant replay when tears flowed down the faces of both boys and girls who'd wept openly, unashamedly at the loss of one of their own.

Patricia Cookman had canceled classes for the day as the students gathered in the auditorium and gymnasium for impromptu memorial services.

The Knights had opted for a private funeral, which left many students feeling deprived because they had wanted to see their friend for the last time. The elder Knights' decision had left many feeling angry and alienated.

Summer had sat in the back of the auditorium, staring at Dumas Gellis. Something silent, unknown, communicated to her that he had something to do with Omar's death.

Without warning, he turned and stared at her. A hint of a smile touched his mobile mouth, and her gaze narrowed. The SOB was playing a cat and mouse game with her! He knew she knew and he was sitting there like a pompous Cheshire cat cheesing at her.

Anger radiated from her. *I'm going to get you, Dumas. One of these days it's going to be just you and me.*

Dumas Gellis had become all of the other men she had taken down and *out!* Names, places, and faces merged into one as she closed her eyes. When she opened her eyes the seat where Dumas had sat was empty.

Early February, Summer began setting up rehearsal schedules for her spring concert, rescheduled for mid-April and a week before the beginning of spring recess. She had divided the students who would participate in each skit by centuries, then, once she reached the twentieth century, by decades.

Meanwhile, Gabriel had begun introducing the musical selections to his students, while Desiree had designed various set decorations with her art students. However, she was reminded of Omar Knight every day whenever she saw his smiling photograph behind a case in the main floor hall, along with the two other students who had died, and the one still comatose from their drug overdoses.

There were a total of nine photographs of students who had lost their lives in traffic fatalities, swimming accidents, and a house fire. The banner in the case announced: GONE, BUT NEVER FORGOTTEN.

The elderly were living longer, and the young were dying at an alarming faster rate. Whether it was drive-bys, or drunk driving, raves, or binge drinking, it appeared that today's young adults were on a fast track to an early grave.

Dumas Gellis walked into the auditorium, taking a seat in the last row. His penetrating gaze was fixed on Summer as she demonstrated the samba for a group of students sitting on the stage floor. Her voice, though soft, carried easily to the back. His gaze narrowed when he saw Gabriel Cole sitting on a chair off to the side, a conga wedged between his knees.

"It's a quick shuffle with African roots," she said, her bare feet skimming the smooth wood floor as her hips swayed sensuously. "And when a woman is being exceptionally flirtatious, she can lift her skirt and snap it back and forth in a fanning motion." The students giggled as she peered at them seductively over her shoulder. "The samba and the tango are dances of desire."

"Are we going to do the tango, Miss Monty?" asked a girl who was a serious dance student.

"Yes."

"Show us the steps."

Summer smiled. "I need a partner. Can I get a volunteer?" None of the eight students stood up. "Come on, don't be shy."

"Why don't you dance with Mr. Cole? You two dance good together," said another girl.

Summer affected what she hoped was an intimidating stare. "Don't even go there, Ivette." What she had tried to do was live down her less than dignified dance exhibition at the Halloween Ball, but the students refused to let her forget it.

Slapping their palms on the floor, they chanted in unison, "Mr. Cole. Mr. Cole."

Gabriel put aside the conga, and rose to his feet to their unrestrained cheering and applauding, while Summer put on a pair of ballet slippers. "I've danced this once, so don't snap on me if I make a mistake." He walked over to Summer and held out his arms. She moved into his embrace.

She smiled sweetly up at him. "You're going to pay for that maneuver, Mr. Cole." She had threatened through clenched teeth.

"How?" he whispered against her ear.

"Concentrate, Mr. Cole," she chastised loud enough for everyone to hear her.

Gabriel executed a smooth step, Summer easily following his strong lead. He spun her around, she keeping her balance as she danced on her toes. They moved across the stage as one. The quick spins and his lifting her leg as they leaned into one another had every eye watching the moves that had become a tangible dance of desire.

Dumas did not move, not even to blink, as the woman on stage held his rapt attention. It wasn't Summer Montgomery dancing with Gabriel Cole, but his Beverly, his beautiful Beverly who had deserved more than he had given her. She was his angel—his queen—and queens lived in castles not prefab split-levels.

He had saved enough money to give Beverly what she wanted, but she'd called him last night to inform him that she had gotten engaged. It was Valentine's Day and she had accepted another man's proposal to marry.

Everything he had worked for, risked, had fallen apart with her, *I'm getting married, Gellis.* Beverly had refused to call him Dumas.

He had planned to wait until the end of June, and then he would leave Weir Memorial High School and everything it represented. Besides, it was time for Patricia Cookman to run her own school. At first he had been flattered by the extra responsibility, but after his first year as assistant principal he'd recognized that Patricia wasn't a hands-on administrator. That's when he decided to make Weir *his* school.

It was under his helm that test scores improved, school-based violence was almost non-existent, and he had gotten the full support of parents when he sought to institute a school uniform policy. He'd run his school in a modified boot camp fashion with degrees of detention meted out accordingly.

The basketball team was third best in the state last year, and had continued their winning tradition with the new school year. They were currently 6-0. Yes, he was very good for Weir, but after eight years, two as an administrator, it didn't mean spit because he had lost his wife for the second time. Lost her to another man.

He'd congratulated her, wishing her much happiness, then hung up and cursed her. He'd used words he did not even know he knew. There was no way he was going to permit another man to play "daddy" to his sons. They already had a daddy—Dumas Gellis!

He stood up and walked out of the auditorium. He had seen enough!

Summer had not known Dumas was sitting in the back of the auditorium until she saw him leave. It was then that she decided if the mountain did not come to her, then she would have to go to the mountain.

It was late, after five, but she knew Dumas was still at the school because his car was in its assigned parking space. She went through the outer office where his secretary usually sat and stared at the door bearing his nameplate. The light was on.

Peering into the office, she saw him sitting at his desk, his back to the door. "Dumas." He swiveled at the sound of her voice. To say he was surprised to see her was putting it mildly. He popped up like a jack-in-the box.

"Summer, please come in."

She moved slowly, feigning reticence. "I hope I'm not disturbing you."

"Of course not." He rounded his desk, pulling out a chair for her at the round table. "Please sit down."

She sat, forcing a smile she did not feel. She wanted this over so she could get on with her life. She wanted to take Dumas down, because it meant saving other young lives. And she intended to do it by seducing the assistant principal.

Lowering her head, she stared at her hands clasped tightly in her lap. Sighing heavily, she glanced up, her eyes filled with tears. Hard pressed not to laugh, Summer continued in the role which she had chosen to play—a spurned lover.

Dumas saw the tears shimmering in her dark eyes, and he half-rose from his chair before he could restrain himself. "What's the matter?"

Covering her mouth with her hand, Summer let the tears flow. "I . . . I came to you, because I needed someone to talk to." Her hands were trembling.

Dumas got up and pulled tissues from a box on his desk, handing several to her and resisting the urge to pull her into his arms. "It's okay, Summer."

She made a big show of blotting her eyes and blowing her nose. Blinking back more tears, she covered her face with her hands. That's when he finalized reg istered what she had wanted him to see: her bare left hand.

Pulling his lower lip between his teeth, Dumas bit down hard enough to draw blood. The brilliant glitter of diamonds that always reminded him that Summer Montgomery was promised to another man was missing. Could he hope that she had broken her engagement?

He laid a hand on her shoulder. "Perhaps we can go somewhere and talk."

Summer sniffled again, shaking her head. "It's all right, Dumas. I'm sorry I bothered you."

"Nonsense. You'd never be a bother. Now, you know I've always made myself available for my teachers."

Bracing her hands on the arms of the chair, she rose to her feet. "I've changed my mind. I . . . I . . . can't talk about it now."

"It's your boyfriend, isn't it?"

Her eyes widened as she gave him a genuine look of surprise. "How did you know?"

He smiled. "That headlight you usually wear on your left hand is missing."

Spreading her fingers, she stared at her hand as if it didn't belong to the rest of her body. "I gave it back."

"What!" The word exploded from Dumas.

She stood up straighter. "I gave it back to him. We were supposed to go down to St. Thomas next week for February recess, and out of the blue he told me he couldn't get off from his job. We argued, because he'd put in for vacation time and was approved months ago. But when I pressured him, he finally told me that he wanted to take another woman with him.

"That dirty, low-down, stinking bastard told me he wanted to take her so that he could have one last fling before we tie the knot." Bitterness had spilled over into her voice. "Never had I wanted to murder anyone as I did at that moment. Imagine him telling me that crap on Valentine's Day."

Dumas couldn't believe his luck. Was it a coincidence that he had lost his wife on the same day that Summer had lost her boyfriend? He did not have time to analyze the events in his life when he curved an arm around her waist.

"Look, why don't we go somewhere and have something to eat? I'm sure you're going to feel better even if you have a cup of coffee?"

Summer smiled up at him through spiked lashes. "Maybe you're right, Dumas."

"I know I'm right. Let me get my coat and I'll be with you directly."

She waited for him to get the trench coat from the hook on the back of the door, then walked out of the school with him to the parking lot.

He stood next to her car. "Where do you want to go?"

"I know a diner where the food is quite good." She gave him the name of the diner where she occasionally met Lucas.

"Okay. You pull out first, and I'll follow you."

Dumas waited until she had gotten into her car, and started it up before he returned to his at the far end of the parking lot. He followed her as she drove slowly through the side streets.

He had to admire Summer, because she was a strong woman and most of all a professional. When he had observed her with her students in the auditorium there was nothing in her voice or body language that communicated the emotion she had exhibited in his office. They would make a wonderful couple.

She was waiting for him when he maneuvered into the diner's parking lot. He held her hand as he escorted her into the restaurant. He continued to hold her hand until they were shown to their booths.

Summer removed her coat, noting the direction of Dumas's gaze as it settled on the middle of her chest. It was the tightest sweater in her entire wardrobe. The jacket she had worn over it was still hanging on the coat tree in her office.

She stared directly at him. "I think I need more than a cup of coffee right about now."

Dumas reached over and covered one of her hands with his. "Why don't you order a cocktail?"

She shook her head, and her ponytail fell over her right shoulder. "I can't."

"If you're afraid of being carded, I'll buy it for you."

Summer leaned back against her seat and smiled. "Thank you for the compliment, but I don't look *that* young."

He tightened his hold on her fingers. "Yes, you do. In fact, you look as young as some of our students."

Her smile faded. "Please let go of my hand, Dumas." The moment the command had left her lips she remembered another time when she'd told him the same thing. "Right now I can't stand for *any* man to touch me," she apologized softly. "I feel so used, so deceived."

He withdrew his hand, nodding. "I understand."

The waitress came and placed menus on the table. As she turned to walk away, Summer saw Lucas Shelby coming toward her. He didn't notice her until he was several feet away. Then, he walked past as if she did not exist, and sat down at a booth behind her. She saw the flicker of recognition in his gaze, but she also saw something she had never seen before: fear.

A sixth sense told her that he knew the man with whom she was sharing a booth. She lowered her head, then stared up at Dumas through her lashes.

"Look, Dumas, I'm sorry I'm being flaky tonight, but I really don't have much of an appetite." Reaching for her coat, she slipped her arms into the sleeves. "I'm going home."

She slid out of the booth, and Dumas was right behind her. She quickened her pace and he caught up with her in the parking lot. His hand stopped her when she pressed the remote device to her car.

"Let me follow you home. I want to make certain you get there safe. Right now you're an emotional mess, Summer."

She nodded, biting down on her lower lip. "Okay."

Dumas followed her as she drove, this time even slower than before. Searching in her handbag, she pulled out her cell phone. It took some skill, but she steered with one hand while she scrolled through the directory and punched in Lucas's number.

"Yes?"

"Renegade."

"What the hell do you think you're doing?"

"So you do know him?"

"Of course I know him. He's our dealer."

"How long have you known!" she screamed.

"We found out after the Knight kid was murdered."

"And you didn't tell me?"

"We wanted to wait, Renegade. He's only one . . ."

"One, Lucas?" she interrupted. "You're willing to sacrifice more kids because you want to reel in bigger fish. Forget it!"

"I'm warning you to let him go."

"It's too late for you and your warnings. I will not be

responsible for another death. Not another kid will die under my watch!"

"Renegade . . ." His line went dead when Summer disconnected the call.

Summer tossed the cell phone onto the passenger side seat. Lucas knew. He had set her up. He knew all along who was dealing at Weir. Well, it was going to end tonight. She would take down Dumas Gellis or die in the attempt.

She pulled into the parking lot at the housing complex where she had resided since last August. There was no way she could call it home, because she now thought of the house in Cotuit as home.

The headlights from Dumas's car temporarily blinded her as he maneuvered into the parking area. He'd rolled down his window. "Visitor parking is against the fence." Nodding, he drove over to where a sign identified the space for VISITOR PARKING. Summer was waiting for Dumas when he alighted. "I can at least offer you a cup of coffee for what I've put you through tonight. Would you like to come up?"

He stared at her for a full thirty seconds, contemplating her offer. "Yes, I would."

"Follow me."

Twenty-five

Summer felt his presence before she glanced up. Standing at the top of staircase outside her apartment was Gabriel Cole. His expression was one of shock and cold fury.

"What are you doing here?" Her hushed voice quivered.

"I was waiting for you."

She tried to capture his gaze, but he was glaring over her shoulder at Dumas. "I'm sorry, Gabriel, but this is not a good time for us to get together."

He frowned at her. "I can see that."

"Can we meet tomorrow?"

Gabriel looked at Summer as if she had taken leave of her senses. He couldn't believe she had invited another man to her home—a man she knew was interested in her. His gaze lingered on her left hand. The ring was missing. What the hell kind of game was she playing?

He recalled the times when she said she couldn't see him—had she been seeing Dumas, too? Was that why she had been so reluctant to marry, because she couldn't make up her mind as to which man she wanted?

"I'll let you know tomorrow. Have fun," he added as he headed down the staircase.

Summer felt a momentary wave of panic as she watched the man she loved descend the staircase. Panic rioted through her but within seconds she brought her fragile emotions under control. She had a job to do. Gabriel Cole would come later.

"Please come in, Dumas."

He followed Summer into her apartment, a triumphant grin on his face as she turned and closed the door.

Dumas moved into a small, but neatly furnished living/dining area. He was disappointed, thinking, *she deserves better than this.* Removing his coat, he placed it on one of two facing love seats.

Summer saw Dumas cataloguing her apartment. "It's not much, but it's ideal for crashing."

"You deserve better." He'd spoken his thoughts aloud.

Taking off her coat, she folded it over her arm. "I thought I was going to get better. The guy I'd planned to marry is loaded."

"Is that why you agreed to marry him? Because he's loaded?"

The corners of her mouth turned down in a frown. "Of course not. I love him."

"You love, Summer? After what he's done to you?"

"It's not that easy to fall out of love when it took me a long time to fall in love."

"Do you think you'll ever go back to him?"

There was a moment of silence before she said, "No, Dumas. I don't deal with emotional pain very well." Her expression brightened suddenly. "Let me change into something a little more comfortable."

Turning on her heel, she retreated to her bedroom, cursing Gabriel. Damn him for showing up at her apartment unannounced. He had never done that before. He'd never come before calling her first, and she wondered what could've been so important that he had to wait for her to come home.

Closing the door to her bedroom, she slipped out of her sweater and slacks and into jeans and a sweatshirt. When she opened the closet to get a pair of running shoes, she saw the safe. Kneeling, she turned the knob, feeling the tumblers click with each revolution. She opened it and removed the automatic from its holster. She then picked up her shield, tucking it into her back pocket. The feel of the automatic was cold and heavy in her palm. It was fully loaded with a clip holding sixteen high velocity bullets.

She registered a familiar sound. Within seconds she had released the safety and concealed the gun in her waistband behind her back.

"What are you doing in here?" She stood up, facing Dumas. He had opened the door and come into the bedroom. His suit jacket and tie were missing, and he had unbuttoned his shirt to the waist. He stood in the doorway with a silly grin on his face.

"You know why I'm here, Summer, so don't look so surprised."

She pulled her shoulders back. "No, I don't."

"You want me."

His cockiness made her smile. "Yes, I do want you, Dumas. But not for sex."

His face fell. "What?"

"I want to pay you back for what you did to Omar. You think you're man because you can intimidate kids. Well, you are not! You are pus, a sick piece of—"

She never finished her statement when Dumas charged at her, head lowered. He came at her like his intent was to sack the Sunday afternoon quarterback. Summer anticipated his move and stepped aside like a matador, reaching for the handgun and bringing the butt down on the back of his neck. He went down, but did not stay down. His hand snaked out around her ankle, pulling her off her feet.

She fell, the gun sliding across the floor. Using her free leg, she kicked him hard against the side of his head. He howled in pain as she scrambled to her feet. Bouncing on her toes, she kicked him again. He went down and came up again. This time she gave him a roundhouse kick, snapping his head back. Blood spurted from his nose and mouth.

Dumas glared up at the woman bouncing on her toes like a boxer. He lowered his head and collapsed face-down to the floor.

Summer watched for movement from Dumas, and finding none, she went to retrieve the gun. She didn't see him, but she felt his hot breath on the back of her neck seconds before his fingers closed around her throat. The blood roared in her head as she clawed at the fingers cutting off precious oxygen to her brain.

He's going to strangle me to death like he did Omar Knight!

Objects spun in front of her eyes as she felt herself losing consciousness. She had always thought she going to die from a bullet, not by strangulation.

She felt her lungs exploding from lack of oxygen as her arms hung limply at her side. She couldn't die—not like this. There were so many things she wanted to do: marry, have babies, and lots of grandbabies. She and Gabriel would start their own traditions, and when she closed her eyes on this world she would sleep in peace knowing she had finally gotten everything she wanted and deserved.

Blackness descended slowly, then miraculously she was freed. The sound of Dumas's heavy breathing echoed in her ear. "No, Summer. I'm not going to kill you yet. I'm going to take what you've been teasing me with ever since you came to *my* school."

Closing her eyes, she drew in deep breaths. The roaring in her ears stopped. When she opened her eyes she spied the gun on the floor less than ten feet away. If she could get to it she would do what she'd promised herself she would do if any man attempted to rape her: kill him.

The possibility of reaching the gun was dashed when Dumas jerked her up by the back of her sweatshirt. *Don't fight him.* The three words played in her head as she was hauled and thrown viciously onto the bed.

Summer knew she would only be able to subdue Dumas if she had the advantage of surprise. Not only was he larger, but very strong. She lay on her bed, staring at him as he removed his belt. Blood flowed from his nose and into his mouth.

Holding the belt, Dumas wrapped the buckle around his fist. He raised his arm, but before he could bring it down he doubled over. Summer had kicked him in the groin. He fell to his knees, moaning like a wounded animal. Moving slowly, he reached for her, but she was gone.

He had taken direct hits from men his size and larger on the gridiron, but that pain paled in comparison to the one between his legs. Growling, he launched himself across the bed and looked into the barrel of the powerful handgun pointed directly at him. Summer lay on her back, staring up at him.

"Let's make this easy, Dumas." Her voice, though soft, was lethal. "Don't move," she warned, "or I'm going to blow your head off." She saw his gaze shift to something behind her, but she still did not glance away.

"Summer."

Her eyes widened when she recognized the voice behind her. Gabriel had come back. "Yes, Gabriel." She would not take her gaze off Dumas.

"What's going on here?"

She smiled. "Nothing much, that is if Weir's assistant principal doesn't get funky where I'd be forced to dispatch him to another time and place. I want you to get the phone and dial nine one-one. Tell the operator that Special Agent Montgomery from the Drug Enforcement Administration needs assistance."

Gabriel couldn't believe the drama being played out in front of him. He'd left Summer's apartment enraged. He had walked several blocks before realizing he had left his car in her Visitor's lot. It was when he returned that he knew he couldn't walk away, couldn't give her up without knowing why.

He had to know why she was so reluctant to marry him.

Why she wanted a long engagement.

Why she wouldn't move in with him.

Why they had kept their liaison secret from those at Weir.

Didn't she know he loved her? He wanted the world to know he loved her. He wanted answers to his questions, but he also wasn't going to hand his woman over to another man without a fight.

And it was love and determination that had forced him to climb the staircase to Summer's apartment for the second time that night. The elderly woman who lived on the first floor recognized him when he was ready to ring the bell, and had let him in. He had knocked on her apartment door, but when Summer did not answer, he'd tried the knob, and found the door unlocked.

"Are you going to be all right, baby?"

"Yes, darling. Please go and make that call."

"DEA?" Dumas whispered as blood trickled down his chin. Bright red drops fell to the stark white sheet. It was full minute later that he registered the endearments. "He's the one."

She smiled. "Yes, Dumas. He's the *one.*"

He managed a lopsided smile. "Well, I'll be damned."

"You are," she snapped angrily. "Selling drugs in a school will get you an extended membership to prison. Coupled with murdering a sixteen-year-old should give you lifetime privileges."

Dumas wagged his head side-to-side. "No, Summer, you're wrong. I'm not going out like that. I'm not going down like a punk."

"You're going down because you are a punk."

Before the last word was out, Dumas lunged. The explosion was deafening as the odor of cordite filled the room.

Dumas fell back, the force of the bullet propelling him off the bed. He lay on his back, staring up at the ceiling until blessed darkness descended on him.

Gabriel stood in the corner of the bedroom, arms crossed over his chest as uniform and plainclothes law enforcement personnel crowded into the small room.

He'd been asked to leave, but Summer had insisted he stay.

He'd spent the past forty minutes staring at the woman he loved, telling himself he did not know her. They had shared a bed, their bodies, but he still hadn't known she was living a double life. The man everyone had addressed as Special Agent Shelby kept referring to Summer as Renegade. And it wasn't until she'd looped a chain around her neck with a badge identifying her as a Special Agent that everything she'd said about wearing masks, she not being able to live in his world or he in hers came rushing back.

Emergency medical personnel had stabilized Dumas from a gunshot wound to his shoulder. His injuries also included a broken nose, jaw, and missing teeth.

Dumas Gellis had met a tiger—and lost!

Summer closed her eyes. She was tired—no, exhausted. She had endured Lucas Shelby's wrath because there was no more fight in her. All she wanted was for everyone to leave so she could wash away Dumas's blood.

She wanted to go to Gabriel and tell him everything. Then she wanted to go to the house in Cotuit and stay.

Reaching down, she removed the gun from the holster strapped to her thigh before she removed the chain from her neck. "Take them, Lucas. I'm out."

He stared at her outstretched hands. "No, Renegade."

Her dark gaze met his. "I am out *now*. I'll come into the division office and officially resign in a few days. I can't take it anymore. I have to leave now, or I'll wake up and decide to eat my gun. I wouldn't do it by slicing my wrists, I'd do it Renegade style by blowing off the back of my head.

"I have a man waiting over there that loves me as much as I love him. And I'm not going to do anything to jeopardize that love. I intend to marry him as soon I can and have his baby. I'm going to stay home with my babies, and tell them every day of their lives that I love them. Renegade is dead, Lucas. She died tonight. But there is one thing I need to know."

He took the gun and shield. "What is it, Rene— Summer?" He had caught himself.

"Who fingered Dumas?"

"The Boston division got a call from someone in Langley, informing them about someone named Dumas Gellis having several offshore accounts in the Caymans. There was no way the man could've amassed that much money playing ball or teaching. We were in the process of securing warrants for several others in his network when I saw you in the diner with Gellis. What I didn't want was for you to spook Gellis where he would warn them."

She smiled for the first time in over an hour. Lucas did not have to tell her who at Langley had contacted the DEA, because she knew it was Merrick Grayslake. He had kept his promise to "keep an eye on her."

"Gellis was too busy trying to get me into bed to worry about calling anyone."

Lucas shook his head. "I guess he didn't know."

"He knows now." She sobered. "I know it's time for me to get out because I had considered shooting Dumas in the head rather than his shoulder. I didn't want to kill him, but execute him."

Lucas nodded. "Yeah, Summer. It is time you got

out." Leaning over, he kissed her cheek. "Good-bye and good luck."

She touched his arm. "Will you come to my wedding?"

"Of course."

"I'll see you in a couple of days. Now, can you get these people out of here so I can clean up? I'll move all of my personal items by the weekend. I'll be on the Cape if you need me. I know I don't have to give you the address."

"You're right. Enjoy your new life."

"I intend to do just that."

Lucas gathered all of his men, and together they filed out of the apartment, leaving Summer and Gabriel staring at each other.

She smiled at him. "Now you know."

He pushed off the wall, closing the distance between them. "Yes, Summer, now I know."

Tears filled her eyes. "What now?"

He pulled her to his chest. "We're going to get you cleaned up, then we're going pack your clothes. After that, I'm taking you home. Then we're going to call my folks and your grandmother to let them know we're getting married next week. We'll spend the February recess in Puerto Rico or Ocho Rios, or anywhere you want before we come back and fulfill our commitment to the grant. After I write the music for that movie soundtrack, then we can make plans for what we want to do with the rest of our lives."

She smiled up at him. "I like the sound of that."

"I thought you would," Gabriel crooned as he lowered his head to kiss her. The kiss was soft, healing, and filled with a love that promised forever.

Epilogue

A year later . . .

Martin Cole, Joshua Kirkland, Matthew Sterling, and David Cole sat in a circle in the library at the Cole estate in West Palm Beach. Tall, solidly built, silver-haired with faces lined with experience and character they toasted one another.

Martin's dark eyes sparkled like polished onyx. "I'd say we haven't done too badly with our kids." He smiled at his brother, David. "I know we've been teasing you for years about your children not giving you grandchildren, but I must say that Gabe and Alex have done you proud. I think you hold the record for two grandbabies in one year." Merrick and Alexandra had welcomed a daughter, Victoria Grayslake, while Gabriel and Summer celebrated their son's birth on Christmas Day. He wasn't expected until the beginning of January, so they decided to name him Emmanuel David Cole.

David flashed a smug smile. "Now that Ana has found a boyfriend we don't have to threaten to break either his neck or kneecaps, I think Serena and I can look forward to another wedding and a few more grandchildren. And because I have the twins, there is the possibility there may be more twins in the future."

Matthew Sterling's gold-green eyes narrowed. "Hey,

you're not the only one with twins. Remember Sara gave me twin granddaughters. I have twin sisters, so if Sara and Salem decide to have one more—maybe, just maybe I will have more grandchildren than Joshua."

Joshua Kirkland's impassive expression did not change. His light-green eyes surveyed his two brothers and his lifelong friend whom he had come to think of as a brother. Retired horse breeder Matthew Sterling had come to the aid of the Coles more times than they could count, but he had finally joined the family when his stepson married Joshua's daughter.

"You're not going to ever catch up with me," Joshua stated in a deep, quiet voice. "Chris and Emily have three, and now with Michael and Jolene on their third you can't possibly catch up. They told Vanessa and me that they'll stop at six."

Matt whistled softly. "Damn."

"Who we don't want to catch up with is our sisters," Martin said, laughing.

"Oh, hell no," David sputtered. "Nancy and Josephine had nine children between them before we even thought about making babies."

Martin raised his glass again. Attractive lines fanned out around his eyes. At eighty-three, he still was a man who could walk into a room and turn heads.

"To our family. And to the legacy we have created because we were never afraid to risk everything for love."

The four men tossed back their drinks, stood up and hugged one another. Tears shimmed as they took turns kissing each other on both cheeks.

Gabriel walked into the library, coming to a complete stop when he saw his father and uncles, offering hugs and kisses. He stepped back at the same time his father glanced up and saw him.

David smiled at his son, winking. Gabriel returned the smile, then turned and walked away.

It was apparent the older warriors were bonding and celebrating again. It was something they did more often now. If was if they knew the circle would be broken one day, but Gabriel hoped it wouldn't happen for a long time.

He walked down a wide hallway to the dining room where he would find his wife and infant son. He had stayed on at Weir, teaching music and encouraging the students to become the best they could be.

He loved teaching, but his greatest joy was when he arrived home to find Summer waiting on the porch for him. It was a tradition they had established—one he hoped would continue for an eternity.

Walking into the dining room, he saw Summer holding Emmanuel to her breasts. His son had fallen asleep. Moving closer, he took the tiny infant from her.

"Come, let's put him to bed, then I want to show you something."

Summer gave him a questioning look. "Where are we going?"

"I walk you to join me for a walk in the garden."

"And do what, Gabriel?" He gave her a lecherous grin. "No!"

"Come on, baby."

Summer stared at him, then smiled. Tyler had just given her medical clearance to begin sharing her body with her husband again. "I'll do it, but I'm not going all the way."

"All the way? What the hell do you mean by not going all the way?"

"Put the baby to bed and join me in the garden, and I'll show you."

Serena Morris came up behind Gabriel, tapping his shoulder. "Please give me my grandson and do what your wife says."

Gabriel stared at his mother. "You heard?"

Serena smiled into a pair of eyes so much like her own. "Yes, I heard. Now, give me the baby."

Gabriel placed Emmanuel into Serena's outstretched arms. Leaning down, he kissed her. "I love you."

"I love you, too."

She watched his tall retreating figure as he followed his wife. She and David had done well. Their children had done well, and she was willing to bet their grandchildren would do very well.

Cradling Emmanuel to her chest, she headed for the staircase and into the room where many a Cole baby had slept. She lowered him to a crib, staring at the little boy who was all Cole.

Serena sat down on a rocker near the crib. Closing her eyes, she smiled and thought of the time when she saw David Cole for the first time, not knowing the joy his love would bring.

The love in her son's eyes when he looked at Summer was similar to the one still burning in her husband's dark gaze.

The Cole men were really something else, she thought. They offered a woman their protection, passion and a love that promised forever. Yes, she mused, Summer was very lucky because she knew what was in store for the young woman. She had reunited with her parents, but she also had a new family who had claimed her because she was now a Cole.

And being a Cole was all that mattered to the generations of men and women who dared to risk everything for love.

Dear Reader:

When HIDEAWAY debuted May 1995 I had no idea what I'd originally conceived as one novel would evolve into a multigenerational series of ten.

The legacy hasn't ended with RENEGADE because the love shared by Martin and Parris, Matt and Eve, Joshua and Vanessa, David and Serena, Aaron and Regina, Salem and Sara, Christopher and Emily, Michael and Jolene, Tyler and Dana, and Gabriel and Summer will continue forever.

I would like to thank everyone for their letters, e-mail, and telephone calls telling me how they've come to enjoy the characters who dare risk everything for love.

I extend to all the love of the wondrous gift God has given me to have shared this experience with you.

Peace,

Rochelle Alers
Post Office Box 690
Freeport, New York 11520-0690
roclers@aol.com
www.rochellealers.com